Just a few reviews...

A pure delight. Want some good old-fashioned reading fun? Then this series of three is for you. -- *Richard Morris, Pacific Northwest Book Sellers book review*

...a 3-D jigsaw puzzle of clues... *(Western World newspaper)*

I have been enjoying your books... *Joseph Stephen Vizzard, author Eye for an Eye*

The books arrived, have about 50 pgs. to go on number 3. Where's number 4??? – *Gina O. Portland*

#3 is fun but I may have to go get my arteries router rooter, too much pizza, they do love to eat. – *BB, Portland*

"Have been impatiently waiting for book #3!! Glad to hear it is on Kindle, will have to get on Amazon and get it ordered!!!! You are great Art!!!" – *Elsie, Oregon)*

Mike loved the (Drago Holiday Pack) gift! Can't wait to read the books after him. Many, many thanks!! – *Teresa R (Coquille, Oregon*

My mother just loves them (Drago mysteries). – *BH, Oregon*

I just started Drago 3! Love your books!!!!!" – *TM, Portland, OR*

I love the Drago series, each story is exciting and full of surprises. This is a great book to purchase for yourself or as a gift; it's hard to put down and leaves you looking forward to future books featuring Nick Drago and his mystery solving friends. – *Tracy A., California*

Just wanted to let you know that I enjoyed your books, I even figured out the user name and password.

However Drago and his buddy sure do eat a lot. Looking forward to book 3. – *Diane M., Michigan*

Great read!... Started reading and quickly got to the point I couldn't put it down... -- *ST, Oregon*

Darn you, Drago. You made me late for work! – *MJ, Oregon*

Great read capturing my attention from page 1. – *CGM, Oregon*

Great books, next?? – *FG, Oregon*

For a free autographed Drago Bookmark, email your address and name to <u>Arts@cnwmr.com</u>

To have your copy of Drago autographed, mail it to PO Box 744, Bandon, Oregon 97411

Include your mailing address. We'll pay return postage.

DEDICATION

Caspar, the 18-pound companion who sits on my lap while I write.

Blue, the new addition that enjoys pushing pencils off of my desk and editing paragraphs that degrade her species.

 (Blue editing Drago #4)

Lillie, who provides insights into the world of wild animals on my office deck.

Brothers and Sisters Coos Bay Harley Owners Group.

And of course Cookie, who always makes life brighter.

DRAGO #4

PROLOGUE

Conspiracy International Associates Group, a play on the letters CIA, was formed in the mid-1960s. It's a loosely knit assembly of scientists, politicians, professors, military strategists, newspaper reporters and editors, retired intelligence officers, "thinkers" and others who attempt to find the truth in international and national events by posing theories and arguments both for and against those events.

The foundation was the assassination of John F. Kennedy and the multiple theories of how and who. It has delved into everything from the International Monetary Fund to the flying saucer events in Roswell, New Mexico.

The CIA Group is both real and serious. Some of the dissertations and evaluations are literally hundreds of pages long. Each is peer reviewed and graded on logic, accuracy, standards of probability and other critical measurements.

Membership is by invitation only and no member (except a three-person board of directors) knows the others. Each is given a code number that indicates field of expertise, areas of interest and level of membership (ranging from one to 20).

All communication is by snail mail which leaves no digital data trace.

As a lowly (Level 3) member of the CIA Group, I can read the treatises and provide comments, but that's about it. In two more years, I'll be able to submit outlines of conspiracies that might be of interest to the Group. I don't know who my invitation came from and at my level cannot suggest new members. Nor am I privy to the actual number of current members, although I suspect it is more than 200 in at least 10 countries.

If this sounds farfetched, I don't blame you for doubting the existence of the CIA Group. I can only tell you that it does, in fact, exist and has spent all of its 47 years keeping a very low profile. It has no web site or blog or Internet communications between members. Email, in fact, is forbidden as is writing on anything other than plain white paper. No letterhead allowed.

I bring this up because Drago #4 is drawn from some of those treatises. While much of the story is true and most of the intelligence knowledge is real, this book remains a piece of fiction. To receive permission from the CIA Group to present some of the information, it had to be wrapped in the exploits of Nick Drago and Sallie Rand, which I gladly did.

I hope you enjoy this bit of curtain lifting into the thoughts of the CIA Group.

Truth is stranger than fiction... because fiction is obliged to stick to possibilities; truth is not.

– Mark Twain

Post Script: DRAGO #3 (This is not a spoiler)

"Good mornin' Nick."

I cringed at the greeting, as I always do, looked up to see Karl, a local reporter for the *Western World* newspaper and a freelancer for the *Oregonian* standing next to the table. I pointed to the empty chair across from me. The chair Sal would usually occupy.

Karl sat.

"Got a minute?"

"We're at the Minute Café, Karl. Sure."

I leaned back in my chair, pushed my empty plates to the center of the table and waited. Karl's brow was furled.

"I'm on the horns of a dilemma."

"Horns of a dilemma."

"Yeah, horns of a dilemma."

"And this dilemma is?"

"I know who killed the Captain and crew of the Pismo Bay."

"The ghost paddle wheeler."

"Yeah."

"Wow, Karl. That's great."

"Not so great."

"And thus the dilemma?"

"Yeah. Do I report it?"

"Why wouldn't you?"

"The family is still in Coos Bay. Been here for over a hundred years. Big time boosters of the city. Lots of money spent on charities and helping kids and putting ex-cons to work in their businesses."

I gave my head the Bandon scratch – two fingers at the front of the hairline. "Tell me how the crew was killed first."

"Okay. It's 1894. The ferry business between Bandon and Coquille is thriving. This businessman in Coos Bay wants to cash in on what is seen as a pretty lucrative enterprise so he builds the largest and most modern paddle wheeler possible."

"So far, I know this stuff. Remember?"

"Yeah, I know you do, but I got to put it all into context for my own satisfaction and to show the horns of the dilemma."

"Go on."

The owner of the Pismo Bay wanted to cash in on the ferry business from Coquille to Bandon. Builds this first-class ferry boat. Steals lots of business from the existing paddler wheelers. Gets push back from the local paddle wheeler owners. He doesn't worry about it because he's getting more than his share of the business and making money hand over fist."

Karl pauses, waved for a coffee.

"Then the county announces it's going to build a road from Coquille to Bandon. A good road. That sets the Coos Bay businessman to thinking."

"Long story short," I interrupt, "he decides to collect the insurance on his paddle wheeler by, what, sinking it?"

"Yeah, but he's got a problem. The captain and crew get wind of the plan. Captain Solomon is big, mean and honest. Refuses to just scuttle the Pismo Bay. Argument ensues. Captain storms out of the meeting and back onto the paddle wheeler."

"Two days later, the Pismo Bay disappears. The captain and crew disappear. And for a hundred years no one knows what happened to them, until you come along."

"Who killed them, Karl?"

"That's my dilemma. The businessman hired some sailors off of one of the British opium boats that used to stop in Coos Bay on their way to China. Told the sailors he wanted the captain and crew as well as the boat to disappear."

"And these sailors killed Captain Solomon and his men."

"In their sleep. Then took the boat to that cove and sank it."

"And you found this out, how?"

"The question about the killers bothered me. A lot. I figured the killers had to be out-of-towners, otherwise someone would have said something to someone and the story would have come out. Even if it were rumors. So I started looking into cargo records, library historical documents, bills of lading, shipping schedules and the like. Saw that there were a few British ships in Coos Bay at the time the Pismo Bay disappeared. Checked with families of the sailors, when I could find them, to see if they had any historical info like letters.

"I hit the jackpot with an English sailor named Gadsfield. The family has a virtual museum of everything the family has done going back to the middle 1400s. Erik Gadsfield was a piece of work. Jail time, knife fights, bar brawler, suspected of killing his girlfriend's secret boyfriend, joined the British fleet to avoid prosecution for a number of crimes including assault.

"In 1894 he wrote a letter to his sister that he was involved in something horrendous, his word, in a port in the Northwest Territory of America. Said he was paid 'a hundred quid sterling to assist a local businessman with a problem.'

"Cross referenced the letter's date with the shipping, arrival and departure logs and found he was here at the time of the murders."

"So where's the dilemma?"

"If I tell you the name of the businessman can I trust you won't tell anyone else?"

"Nope. But I won't."

Karl took a napkin from the dispenser on the table and scribbled on it. Pushing it toward me, he stared directly into my eyes. Waiting to see my reaction.

I glanced at the name, felt my heart skip a beat. "Are

you sure?"

"Absolutely."

"His kin and descendants have almost singlehandedly brought thousands of jobs over the decades to the county. For God's sake, his name's on schools and hospitals and roads all over the county."

Karl nodded.

"You're right. It is a dilemma."

"What do I do?"

I thought about it for a minute, pulled a long swallow of cold coffee, "What's your gut tell you?"

"Gut says report it. After all, it's a piece of history and an important piece. Bad guy's family capitalizes on the blood money made by killing four honest men."

"And your heart?"

"Hold back. Don't print it. The repercussions would be pretty severe. The family could become viewed as pariah. There's no statute of limitations on murder and while the ancestor is dead, the legacy – especially the wealth – left behind would be legally problematic."

"Without a doubt, it would taint everything the family has done for Coos County. But, Karl, you've already reached out to the victim's families and given them the story of where their ancestors are buried."

"The ones I could find, yeah. But they don't know how or why or who killed them."

"Does it matter now? It's been a hundred years."

Karl gave that a second. "Not sure."

"It's a prize winning story, Karl."

The reporter's face flushed. "I know. Career maker if written right."

"Not sure I can help you, Karl. I know what I would do, but I'm not you."

"What would you do, Nick?"

"No, not gonna tell you. This is your dilemma, the horns you're on, not me."

Downing his mug of coffee in a single swallow, Karl pulled out his wallet.

I waved him off. "I got it."

"Well, thanks anyway Nick. This isn't something I can talk to my editor about. She'd insist it run."

"Or she may decide the family is just too powerful to mess with."

Karl smiled, the furrows disappeared. "All the more reason she'd want to run it."

The reporter stood, waved and left the restaurant.

I ordered another round of eggs, bacon and wheat toast. Horns of a dilemma make me hungry.

CHAPTER ONE

Mort Brodsky sat in the worn metal chair, the Russian guard hovering over the small man. The vibrating tip of the Iron Customs pen touched his bare skin. Brodsky didn't flinch. This was not his first time under the tattoo needle.

"Here?" the Russian asked.

"Yes."

"Is 15th?"

Mort bobbed his head and noted that over the past 20-plus years, the Russian's English had improved dramatically. He smiled to himself.

"Yuri, you've been tattooing me for more than a decade. We have grown old together. I will miss you when I am gone."

"You go nowhere, Mort. We all go nowhere."

"Some of us have."

"Da. The journey has been long in distance, longer in time. We have lost many. But all roads eventually come to an end. I sense our end is near."

"A philosopher now? You're a *mench*."

"Yiddish word I like." The Russian smiled as he repeated the word. "Da, Mort. You and me. *Mench*. Good friends." The needle sketched Brodsky's skin. "Is simple design, this one."

The needle buzzed, the black ink mingling with a bit of blood. The small Jew closed his eyes, putting his thoughts into the next days and week. His road was indeed coming to an end. And perhaps the road for the others, if his plan succeeded.

And if the person who stumbles on his plan – 15 years in the making – could decipher the tattoos.

It would take a puzzle-master.

CHAPTER TWO

Cookie. Gone.

Sal. Gone.

Forte. Gone.

Line, Richard Line. Gone.

Tatiana. Gone

Artemus. Gone.

The kids. Spread to the four winds. Gone.

Willow Weep, the name given to our piece of Oregon Territory just north of Bandon by my oldest daughter some decades ago, quiet. Damn quiet.

Bored near to death, I'd done all the usual things around the Weep. Cut the back off of a 1990 Ford Festiva with the lame idea of turning it into a pickup truck. Okay, that's not a "usual" thing for most folks, but not so odd for me.

Cleaned the Harley with Q-Tips.

Installed a wood stove in the Bunk House workshop so it wasn't so blasted cold in the winter. That meant cutting down a couple of small snags and splitting firewood.

Toyed around with the Lionel trains layout, building a couple of working industries.

Listened to a lot of Dwight Yoakum through an antique
MP3 player with big honkin' Coby headset clamped to my
ears that I'm sure was making me deaf.

Waxed the Harley.

Tightened up the side exhaust on the Crown Vic.

Re-waxed the Harley.

Made bacon-grease sandwiches for Lilly the raccoon.

Sat on the porch and cut my fingernails. Three times in
a week.

Squirted WD-40 into the raucous front-bathroom
ceiling fan.

Scraped the paint off an old window then put it back in
the workshop after I figured there was no place to install it.

Swept the pine needles off of the roof onto the
driveway. Blew the pine needles off of the gravel driveway
into the garden. Blew the pine needles out of the garden
into the woods.

Washed the '55 Ford.

Re-re-waxed the Harley.

Even attended a Tupperware Party at Cookie's friend
Mary Ann's house. Don't snigger. Those snappy-shutty
bowls make great containers for nuts and bolts.

Watched the second hand revolve around the face of the
kitchen clock.

Took a nap.

So much for the second week of May. Now what?

I dropped the mail on the front table with the other eight pounds of unattended letters, bills, flyers, magazines and catalogues. A tingle of guilt made me sweep up the pile and move it to the dining room table.

Three stacks: Toss, Read, Cookie.

Radio Shack brochure. Read.

Electricity bill. Cookie.

Renovation catalog. Toss.

And so it went for the next half hour. The "toss" pile clearly the tallest, I gathered it up and dropped the five pounds of paper into the waste basket; the "Cookie" pile went on her desk in the kitchen. She wasn't around and eventually I'd have to deal with the bills, but that was more boring than Mary Ann's Tupperware party.

Putting the "read" pile on the side table next to my chair, I popped the top on a *Dos Equis*, ripped open a bag of Doritos and settled into the leather. Smith, my 18 pound gray cat, eyed my lap.

"Not now, pal."

He snorted and hobbled out of the room to find Wesson, his 18 pound son, for some ear licking.

A large manila envelope about half-way down the "Read" pile intrigued me. Addressed to "Mr. Nicholas Drago" – a first name few used – and without a return address, only the initials DBC in the upper left hand corner. Written in black thick-tip Sharpie.

Slid a thumb under the flap and ripped. Reached in and came up with a pack of 3x5 cards and a letter, obviously run out on a computer printer.

"Dear Nicholas:

As you may have read, the Federal and Washington State authorities have arrested Clarence G. Oates claiming he is D. B. Cooper, the famous skyjacker. They are wrong. I know this because I am the real D. B. Cooper."

Aloud, shaking my head, I muttered, "Oh, geez, here we go. It's wacko time in the woods."

A pull from the *Dos Equis.*

"You may well disbelieve my claim, but that doesn't make it any less true.

"I've enclosed eight cards with individual clues that will prove to you I am who I claim. It is imperative you decipher these clues and insist the authorities release Mr. Oates immediately. He and his family are innocent victims.

"Please hurry, Nicholas, before a serious injustice takes place.

"Warmest regards, D. B. Cooper."

Another long pull from the *Dos Equis.* I climbed from the lounger and went to the kitchen, opening a drawer and bringing two boxes back to the living room. I put each card carefully into a sandwich bag. The envelope and letter individually went into large Ziploc bags. No reason to add any more of my fingerprints to the clues.

Laying the sandwich bags on the coffee table in two rows of four, I read each.

■A song-writing invisible rabbit.

■You can't find me. But I am there.

■Not one of the three, but one of the three.

- Vestus virum facit.
- Magician David Copperfield.
- Sergeant Joe Friday has one.
- Not a mountain. Not a saint.
- An apropos child's board game.

Putting them into a mental mix master to juggle the clues around, some made sense. Others didn't. Combined, it was tough to see a quick solution. But there was an inkling of a thread. It would require a bit of research on the skyjacking, though.

That would require a pizza and another beer. Maybe two.

The kitchen sink was clean as a whistle. Dishwasher empty. Neither gets much use when take-out and frozen Hungry Man dinners rule the day. And years as a bouncer in a Eugene sports bar meant a Hefty Bag full of plastic utensils. I didn't say it was a high class sports bar.

The thermostat was dialed to exactly 71 degrees. My comfort zone for roaming the place in a t-shirt and jeans. Since the side of the house was blown to smithereens and rebuilt, and bullet holes were already in the drywall, it made sense to add some blow-in insulation.

The May drizzle streaked the new front window – another addition since the second Battle at Willow Weep.

The oven buzzed. The DiGiorgnos bubbled. The beer bottle top clinked in the trash can. All was right with the world.

Well, not really. There was no one around to share the

mood.

Sighing, I slid the pizza and beer onto the dining room table, fell into a chair, listened to the sound of silence and stared at the laptop's screen. Plugging "D. B. Cooper" into Google, a long list of references popped up. MSNBC, ABC, Wikipedia and a raft of others had bits and pieces about the hijacker. Most were simple news stories without much detail. Even Wikipedia didn't delve much into the case.

But one caught my eye: *www.TruTV.com*. A multi-part dissection of the crime, its impact on flight safety, and most importantly the sequence of the skyjacking including a long section on the horribly unsuccessful search and boundless theories about how D. B. Cooper was able to get away with the crime. If he did.

I printed out the various versions, read all of them between bites of pizza and swigs of beer, underlining passages and giving an occasional snort of derision at the total folly of the investigation into the skyjacking.

On my lap, a notepad. I'm a puzzle lover. Putting odd facts together to find an answer is not only a hobby, but an almost manic obsession. Just ask Sal, my long-time friend, neighbor, fellow Harley rider and the big man who frequently occupies the passenger seat in my Crown Vic.

We've been called on to solve an occasional crime that Chief Forte, Bandon's head cop, didn't have the manpower or funds to deal with. Lately, those crimes have turned from simple local issues to international tar pits. Don't ask me how that happens, it just does. And we've had to use Sal's long-time government connections to dig our way out.

Sal's got a backlog of favors due him from somewhere in Washington D.C. He won't tell me why. My guess is he served with the Central Intelligence Agency for the dozen years he'd been "out of touch" before moving back to Bandon. He swears he never was nor would he ever be CIA.

Far as I know, Sal's never lied to me. He just doesn't tell me everything.

Solving puzzles, especially ones with lots of innuendo, suppositions and conflicting analysis, takes a critical eye for facts. And only the facts. The stuff that was proven, that isn't a guess. The core information everyone agrees is true.

As far as D. B. Cooper's hijacking of a Northwest Orient airliner is concerned, the facts weren't as long as the narratives that surrounded the only unsolved skyjacking in U.S. history.

D B Cooper FACTS ONLY

1971. Thanksgiving Eve.

Boeing 727-100

Flight 305

Cooper dressed in dark suit, white shirt, tie and hat (fedora)

Paid $20 for ticket from Portland to Seattle, one way

37 passengers and five crew

Hijack note saying he had a bomb

Briefcase with two red cylinders and wire

Demanded $200,000

Wanted two parachutes and two backup chutes

Ordered plane to circle until chutes and money delivered

Demanded $20 bills – weighed 21 pounds

All bills started with "L" series and dated 1969

FBI microfilmed all 10,000 bills

Cooper refused military chutes with automatic opening

Plane landed at 5:39 p.m.

Passengers and one attendant disembarked through rear stairs

Cooper ordered altitude of 10,000 feet, flaps at 15 degrees and speed of 150 knots

Agreed to refuel in Reno on way to Mexico

Cooper agreed to alter his route to avoid the Cascade Range, Mt. Rainier (14,411), Mount St. Helens (9,677 feet) and Mount Adams (12,276 feet)

Flew west of the high peaks (Vector-23)

Cabin left depressurized

Took off at 7:46 p.m.

No peepholes in cabin door

Aft stairs UNLOCKED at 8 p.m.

At 8:24 Aft stairs deployed plane genuflected

Captain ID'd the location: Lewis River, 25 miles north of Portland

Air temperature 7 degrees below zero

Plane actually traveling at 170 knots 195 mph

Plane touched down in Reno at 10:15

Passenger cabin was empty

Missing: Hat, overcoat and briefcase, cash and one set of

chutes

   Nylon cords of one parachute missing

   In the cabin: Cooper's tie, tie tac, Raleigh cigarette butts, spare chutes.

   66 fingerprints left behind. FBI says they led nowhere.

In all, 35 facts most everyone would agree were true. Everything else is supposition and guesswork. The FBI might consider those educated guesses or an analysis of events, but no one, for example, can say with any certainty that Cooper actually jumped wearing his street shoes or tied the bag of money to his chest with the nylon cords of the second parachute. These were mere assumptions.

And, I thought, just not right.

CHAPTER THREE

Mort reviewed his plan as he pulled on the suit. He had spent nearly seven years accumulating the necessary materials to make it and another three years revising the design.

He knelt beside the cot he had been assigned 20-plus years ago and said Kaddish, a Jewish prayer of mourning, first in Hebrew then English. Mort always joked that God probably spoke Hebrew, but just in case he didn't, English would work.

Yehei shmëh rabba mevarakh lealam ulalmey almaya, "May His great name be blessed forever, and to all eternity."

As he recited the lines, his eyes glistened, lids closed and a tear slid down his leathery cheek.

"*Amen.*"

Standing, Mort glanced around the room. Over the decades he had accumulated very little. Other captives hung photos and mementos of friendships made over the years, but Mort had only the barest of necessities or needs. Over the decades he had carefully penned all of the prayers he could remember from the days of his youth and the hours upon hours spent in the Synagogue, putting them into a small notebook he once had to hide from his jailers but now could carry in a pocket without retribution.

He wrapped the prayer book in cheap pulp paper – the only kind he had access to in this place. In his precise handwriting he wrote, "For Abraham," gently touched the package to his lips and placed it on the desk top.

The sun was sliding below the horizon. It would be dark soon.

Mort began the long process preparing his body to slip into the suit.

By midnight, he was done.

Peeking out of his door to make sure no one was in the hallway, Mort carefully edged down the musty, humid corridor.

Once outside, he tugged the hood over his head and fumbled with the roll of Gorilla tape.

"Strange name," he thought to himself. A new invention, he assumed. Hard to pilfer from the storeroom, but worth it. He had tested its abilities and found them far superior to his original notion of using duct tape.

Wrapping the Gorilla tape a dozen times around his neck, joining the hood to the body suit, until the roll was empty.

Mort's breathing was already becoming labored. As it should.

Even though he said it aloud, no one heard his final word.

"*Shalom.*"

CHAPTER FOUR

Bright sky, but overcast. It was unusually warm for May. Something north of 65 degrees, but not by much. A rainy winter left the air tasting of mildew and moldy leaves. Not my favorite time of year. But spring was burning off those smells, replacing them with sweet hints of Cookie's new flowers, magnolia blooms and wild roses.

The toy shed felt damp, but that was probably just me since a dehumidifier runs 24/7 to keep the assortment of motorcycles, hot rods and Lionel trains from corroding. The Harley Fat Boy's battery tender eye glowed green.

Harley-Davidsons are a unique breed of motorcycle. Not only because of what the name seems to imply to the general public, but the almost religious fervor long-time Motor Company customers seem to lavish on the brand. Kids who can't peddle a tricycle covet a Harley t-shirt. And how many times have you seen 10,000 *Kawasaki* bikes in one place at one time except on the boat bringing them from Japan?

Think Sturgis or Bike Week or Marlon Brando or John Stamos' flick *Born to Ride* or Lorenzo Lamas in *Renegade* or even the comedy *Wild Hogs*. Harley gets top billing.

Ozzie, my red metallic 100th Anniversary Fat Boy –

everything I own seems to have a name – blipped to life with the first press of the starter button. The V-Twin quickly settled into a nice throaty rumble that Harley once thought it could patent.

Pushing back out of its spot between the V-Rod and Cookie's Trike, snicking into first, I rolled out of the Toy Shed, clicked the automatic door shut behind me and eased onto our gravel road. Still didn't know where I was going. Would figure that out when I got to Highway 101.

The ride north smelled of wood smoke, like a just-sharpened pencil. Folks were taking advantage of the dry weather to burn the piles of brush that accumulate in rural Oregon from cutting back crowded paths and bushes that never stop growing. That was always Cookie's job. Guess I'd have to face the chore soon.

D. B. Cooper ran through my mind. Folk hero. Super star to skydivers worldwide. Mystery man. What makes a guy want to hijack a plane and jump out of it at 10,000 feet, 190 miles per hour in below zero weather?

My dad would have called him a "fruitcake."

I may be alone, but I love fruitcake. Cherries, pineapple, pecans, raisins and cake batter. Especially the pineapple.

Why not get away to Hawaii? They have pineapple there. Pineapple's good.

What was his name? The guy in the Hawaiian shirt who played a ukulele? Godfrey. Arthur Godfrey. My grandmother used to watch him.

He was a pilot. Saw a flying saucer once, so he claimed.

Read that in a book about Area 51.

The wind pressed against my chest and face and arms. Quick glance down; doing 70. The road was dry and clear with only an occasional motorhome or travel trailer heading south. Beams of reflected chrome, newly added 80-spoke wire wheels, played on the black asphalt.

Maybe that's where Sal had worked. Area 51. CIA. Super-secret. "The Ranch." Workers flown in each morning from Las Vegas, flown out at night. All on a government airliner.

Home of the SR-71 spy plane. Could fly at 90,000 feet, Mach 3. Three flavors. One to spy. One to deliver A and H bombs and a two-seater for combat. It was supposed to be the RS-71, Recon and Strike, but no one wanted to correct President Johnson when he accidentally reversed the letters in a speech so the name was officially changed.

Wonder if an old U-2, America's first high-altitude spy plane, would ever sell on e-Bay?

That would be a kick, flying a U-2.

The Harley had settled into a nice even one-ness where everything felt in harmony. Zen, if I knew what that really meant. Ride, exhaust note, engine vibration, road feel. Nice.

There were seven Harleys backed into parking spaces at Tony's Road House Pub when I hit the Coos Bay city limits. A one-time donut place, a few guys got together and turned it into a biker bar. It's one of those places Harley riders like to hang.

Pulling in next to a blue Electra-Glide Ultra, I tugged

off my helmet, hung it on the handlebars and pushed my way into the pub.

An antique Wurlitzer juke box, lights bubbling, playing Golden Oldies. *"My Boyfriend's Back"* the current vinyl spinning behind the yellow-tinted glass. Beer in long necks littered the mixed vintage four-tops around a half-dozen pool tables. The smell of leather and peanuts and 12-percent-fat beef burgers fried on a super-hot grille rode the air current out as I walked in. It was barely 3 in the afternoon so the crowd was small. In a couple of hours the place would be wall to wall and the parking lot crammed with baggers, choppers, cruisers and crotch rockets.

The backdrop of Tony's is typical of such establishments. Well-worn stools at a long wooden bar. Motor Company posters tacked to wood walls and Harley memorabilia nailed or hanging from wires helter skelter in no particular order.

More cows had lost their hides to Harley riders than to any other group of humans. Everyone wore leather. Motorcycle boots, chaps, jackets, vests. More than the typical bar's share of gray hair wrapped in bandanas bearing the U.S. flag, tribal or old-West patterns. Body types tilted toward the "Why settle for a six pack when you can have the whole keg." The women tended toward top heavy and cute in a hard sorta way.

The smell of fresh beer, snap of pool balls, a tinge of Marlboro smoke (illegal inside, but no one ever called the cigarette police) and the laughing chatter of folks having a good time.

Greetings back and forth as I made way to the dollar
taco table and raised a hand for a *Dos Equis* to Tony who
stood in his usual spot behind the bar. Dumping ground
beef into a crispy taco shell, I scanned the room. Country
(one-time model, tall and thick), Bubba (baby face and big)
and Casper (who people thought was Sal's twin brother)
were deep in some discussion about Casper's Great
Pumpkin orange Harley puking another gear, this time
third. Ray stood over the pool table, eyeing a bank shot.

Todd stood at the end of the bar, beard finally growing
back after his first shave in decades (a bet); Marc, ex-
military cop, spinning tall tales about his days in Germany
to Ken who spun tales back.

Doctor Jon rotated from conversation to conversation,
easily the friendliest of the group, smiling as he always
seemed to be. He and Ray's wife Dudi casually talking
some sort of medical shop.

Other women were clustered in groups. Amanda and
Mylene near the juke box, the former dancing in place to a
rock tune from the '80s; Tupperware Queen Mary Ann (the
Roadhouse owner's wife), Robbyn and Ginger at a stand-
up table with Ginger doing most of the talking, the three
sharing a platter of double-fried potatoes.

Three tacos on a paper plate, I made way to the bar
where my beer was waiting, bottle sweating.

"How's business, Tony?"

"Which one," a grin, twinkling eyes.

"Either. Both."

Tony not only owned part of the bar, but had a metal

fabrication business in town. "Stainless steel prices are stable, aluminum is going through the roof, sheet steel is killing me. But we've got work and that's the name of the game."

Inhaling the first taco, special salsa dripping onto the paper plate, I groaned. "This is making my day."

Tony smacked me on the arm and moved down the bar to pull another Bud for Todd.

Cell phone buzzed in my pocket. A text message from Cookie.

"You must do it," was all it said.

I don't respond well to the word "must." I've always worn a motorcycle helmet – well, on occasion not – because it's a logical and practical safety precaution. But when the government said I "must" wear one, my hackles went haywire. Personal choice is one of my core tenants. *Convince* me something is a good idea, fine. *Tell* me it's a good idea and the chances are pretty good you just got put on my Nazi list.

I typed a response, *"Ain't gonna happen,"* hit the off button on the phone and slipped it into my shirt pocket.

This ongoing spat began at the end of an anniversary dinner at Edgewaters, one of the better restaurants in Old Town. Anna, perhaps the best waitress in Bandon, started us off with a bottle of Riesling for Cookie, a beer for me. A pair of well-aged steaks cooked just right with all the side dishes and a shared chocolate thing for dessert, all while overlooking the Coquille River lighthouse with a spectacular sunset blooming on the horizon. We idly chattered about the kids, an idea for an upcoming trip, Cookie's return to the Cubs as a color announcer on WGN and the prospects for a World Series returning to Chicago.

Two hours and that mellow gut feeling telling me the world was swell. A long way from logging and bouncing drunks from Eugene bars or scratching for survival money with odd jobs.

And then she mentioned "the procedure."

It made me pucker.

From an acorn mighty Oaks grow.

By the time we returned to Willow Weep, neither of us was in any mood to talk. Electric silence.

"...and he's gonna be trouble..." from the Wurlitzer.

Over the next half hour I rustled through the room, boots crunching peanut shells, picking up on conversations, exchanging old jokes that somehow always seemed to be funny no matter how many times you heard them, filling each other in on political points of view and generally feelin' the love of being part of a group with a common interest and who would watch each other's back if need be.

And the "need be" came in the form of a near-dozen German bikes.

The sound of heavily muffled motorcycle exhaust pulling up to the building. Not Harleys.

Mike, standing next to the window, announced in his smoker's gravel of a voice, "BMW riders."

"Must be lost," Casper joked, bringing sniggers from the group.

The door opened and one-by-one 10 guys rolled into
the room. All of them prototypical BMW riders. Narrow
hipped, more runners than kick boxers. Younger than us
and on average a bit taller. Lots lighter.

Mike, as expected, was first to break the ice. "Sorry,
guys, but we're all out of Chardonnay."

That resulted in guffaws and hoots.

One of the BMW riders smirked, "With all of the farm
implements parked out front, I thought I was at an
International Harvester dealership." That got chuckles from
the Bavarian crew.

I knew where this was headed. Winked at Country and
saw Casper whisper something to Doctor Jon who moved
around the group and slipped out the front door.

The Beemer riders edged their way to the bar, crowding
those of us who were already riding the brass foot rail.

To Tony, "You got something other than Budweiser?"

Never one to let an opening get by him, "For you? How
about a Bud... Light."

BMW #1's eyes went dark. "Cute. Hef."

"How many?"

"All of us."

"Ten Hefs comin' up."

Tony toed open the under-bar fridge, pulled out the
long-necks, popping the top on each as he slid them across
the bar.

A thin guy with a black bristle moustache, dressed in
the full Gor-Tex BMW gear put his elbows on the bar.

"Gimme a glass."

Tony grinned, "Extra quarter. Gotta pay for the soap and water to wash it."

"Whatever." Turning to another BMW rider standing next to him, "Hey, did you know that 98 percent of all Harleys are still on the road?"

"Didn't know that, Jimmy."

"The other two percent made it home." Black moustache giggled at his own joke.

I saw Casper roll his eyes. Todd closed his eyes, lowered his head, fists clenching and unclenching.

Jimmy wouldn't let it go. "The question of the day: If Harley-Davidson built an airplane would you fly in it?" More laughter from the BMW riders. Even I thought that was a funny line.

Picking up on the banter, a wiry little guy no bigger than 5-foot-4 said, "How many Harley owners does it take to change a tire?"

"Don't know, Jason. How many?"

Todd turned a beet red. Short fuse. Not a good thing on a big guy. "I wouldn't answer that if I was you," he growled.

Jason, the midget, shot back, "Why not?"

"'Cause there just isn't any answer that won't get your ass kicked."

Jason ignored him. That's not smart. Looking straight at Todd, "A dozen," he started, "because…"

Todd has to struggle hard to check his temper. He

closed the three-step gap between himself and the midget in a single stride, grabbed the little guy by the neck and crotch, hoisted him over his head and body slammed the Beemer rider to the pine floor.

The rest is history.

BMW Rider #1 grabbed the Hef bottle and swung it in my direction. I caught it in my left hand. Stepped inside his reach. Twisted the bottle from his grip and pitched it over the bar. Swept my right leg under him and BMW #1 went down on his ass.

Pointing a finger at him, an inch from his nose, "Don't you ever swing a beer bottle at me again. It's just not nice." I leaned over plowed a left into his temple. His jaw went slack. Even I could see the stars I knew he was seeing.

Two down.

Someone tried to level Casper with a chair. That's like moving an aircraft carrier with a row boat. The chair's splintered legs, seat and back spiraling across the room, clattering to the floor. With a forearm against the BMW rider's neck, Casper pushed his attacker to the wall. Bubba moved in, planted two quick elbows to the BMW rider's gut leaving him gasping for air and sliding to the pines. The two Harley riders high five'd and turned to see what other mayhem could be caused.

That's three.

Seeing Ray, one of the BMW riders grabbed his pool cue and tried to pry it out of his hands. Ray, who looks a lot like Charlie Manson, gives up his pool cue for no man. Pulled it back, swung the blunt end into the Beemer's gut, clubbed him with the other end sending him to the floor. Out colder than a Michelob on ice. Ray turned, relined up his triple combination shot as if nothing happened.

That made four.

Robbyn charged another of the BMW riders, grabbing him around the middle, pushing him backwards. Dudi grabbed his hair, yanking it hard to the left while Ginger stuck out a leg, sending the guy to the pines. Mary Ann, blonde hair perfectly combed and never mussed, planted a boot between his legs.

Harley women. You gotta love 'em.

That made five.

Sweeping the room, I saw Mike at the taco table watching and grinning, a beef taco in one hand, his camera-phone in the other snapping pictures. No shortage of material for Facebook.

Chuk, chuk.

Nothing gets attention quicker than a shotgun being racked. Tony stood behind the bar, Remington 12 gauge held cross body, barrel aimed toward the ceiling. The Harley guys knew what came next. We clamped hands over ears.

In the ceiling, Tony had nailed a three-quarter-inch thick plywood square and painted a bull's eye on it.

The blast shook the building. The salt load hit the target in a heated rush. The BMW riders who were still conscious sent up a chorus of "holy shit" and "Jesus Christ" and moans of pain. Their ears would be ringing for days.

That was also the signal for Doctor Jon to return to the

bar. He did, carrying a medical bag, and began the task of bandaging knuckles and checking for pulses.

"Nick! Get that guy's wallet," Tony said, pointing at BMW Rider #1.

Pulling it from his back pocket, I tossed it onto the bar. Tony flipped it open, removed a Visa card and slipped it into his plaid-shirt pocket.

Doctor Jon gave Tony thumbs up. Everyone was still alive. The bandaging would take a few minutes.

"Okay, you BMW riders, get your asses out of my place. Except him," pointing at BMW Rider #1 who was still sleeping in a puddle of Hef.

Those who could walk dragged those who couldn't out the front door.

Tony slid the shotgun back under the bar, grabbed an order slip and began writing. "Three chairs, $140, one table, $65, ten beers, $40, one Pilsner glass, 25 cents, one shotgun shell, $2.70." He punched the amounts into the cash register, ran the Visa card and handed it and the receipt to me.

Lifting Rider #1 to a sitting position, I took his hand and scribbled on the "signature" line and shoved the card back into his wallet.

Tony leaned over the bar. "Did you add a tip?"

CHAPTER FIVE

The Whitetip shark nudged the package, rubbing its smooth flank against the silvery bundle. Swimming ahead of the current, the 13-foot long female used her dorsal fin to make an abrupt turn to re-approach the mass.

Having just given birth, she hungered for a meal, but her usual feeding grounds in the deep-water Pacific had fewer tuna, dolphin or marlin than at any time in her 16 years. And she couldn't pick up the scent of her typical prey. The silver bundle didn't seem worth the effort being spiny and lacking the odor of her usual food. But eat she must.

Carefully moving toward the package, her jaws spread, the rows of serrated teeth bared. Her first snap would use a tiny fraction of its enormous power, capable of ripping a four-foot chunk from a mature tuna. Instead, with caution, she closed her teeth around the extreme tip of the bundle and was greeted with a palate-searing pain. Quickly releasing the package, she spun and moved rapidly away, leaving behind deep in the silver bundle one of her broad, triangular upper teeth.

By 5 o'clock, the BMW riders had limped on down the road, probably stopping at a local Coos Bay motel to lick their wounds. The after-work crowd began showing up at the Roadhouse. Ted bemoaning the fact he had missed all the fun. George, the club's big-weapons-for-little-problems go-to guy, struggling to decide if he wanted a Bud or a Hef.

"What's new, George?" I asked, elbows on the bar, beer bottle sweating into a puddle on the plank top.

"Not much. Thinkin' about getting a new bike, but probably will put that off for a year or so."

Nodding, "I've been thinking about it, too, but I hate to get rid of the Fat Boy." Long pull from the bottle. "What do you know about D. B. Cooper?"

George settled on a Bud, waited for Tony to pop the top and slide it across the bar. "Crazy guy, that's for sure. Think that McCoy guy was him, though."

Richard F. McCoy, Jr., a Vietnam vet, was a skydiver who flew helicopters. He was caught after hijacking a plane to Los Angeles, demanding a half-mil in small bills.

"Found a boatload of money at his house in Utah, I think," George said. "Even found an eyewitness who said McCoy bought a burger or a milk shake then paid a kid to drive him home. Seems pretty open and shut to me."

And when McCoy escaped from the medium-security prison after being convicted, the FBI went in guns blazing and killed him at which point the Special Agent in Charge said, in effect, "When McCoy died, so did D. B. Cooper."

I tumbled that around for a second, having read a

similar account in the TruTV.com transcript. But it still didn't make much sense. How could anyone say the handwriting in the skyjacking note in Flight 305 was the same as McCoy's when the note was taken by D. B. Cooper and only seen by the flight attendant?

As for the boatload of money, McCoy had nearly a half-million bucks, his take from Flight 855 skyjacking, but that was it. None of the bills matched those given to the Flight 305 hijacker. Where was the $200,000 from the Cooper job? If McCoy had been D. B. Cooper, he should have had closer to $700,000 stashed somewhere. How was he able to get rid of the $200,000 in 20-dollar bills taken from Flight 305? The FBI speculated he just lost it in the jump.

"Don't buy it, George." Another long draught of *Dos Equis*. "Let me show you something and get your take."

I pulled copies of the clues from my hip pocket and put the eight 3x5s on the bar top.

"What do you make of these? They're supposedly from the real D.B. Cooper."

George stared long and hard at the clues.

- A song-writing invisible rabbit.
- You can't find me. But I am there.
- Not one of the three, but one of the three.
- Vestus virum facit.
- Magician David Copperfield.
- Sergeant Joe Friday has one.

- Not a mountain. Not a saint.

- An apropos child's board game.

"Well, the last one is *Chutes and Ladders*, I'd guess," George said.

"My notion, too. But it could be Monopoly since there's a lot of money involved." I scribbled both onto the 3x5 card.

"How about 'Clue?'" I hadn't seen Tony standing nearby and listening.

"Or 'Where's Waldo?'" Casper had roamed over when the name D. B. Cooper came up.

"Or 'Guess Who?'" chimed in Ted. "That was always a favorite of mine."

"I used to love Old Maid." Mary Ann, the inveterate game fanatic in the group, added.

I didn't give any of them much credence, but out of politeness, added all of them to the card.

- An apropos child's board game.

Chutes and Ladders

Monopoly

Where's Waldo

Guess Who

Old Maid

Clue

It didn't take long for tables to be pushed together, pitchers of beer and 25-cent Pilsner glasses to be assembled as the 3x5 cards passed around. I sat at the head of the table and watched the interplay of these Harley riders.

"This one's easy," Ted said, holding the "Not a mountain, not a saint" card. "It's Mount Saint Helens!"

"You dope," Casper chided, "It specifically says it's not a mountain and not a saint."

"Helen, then," Ted countered.

"Helen of Troy," Ginger nearly shouted.

"How about Helen the Barbarian," someone said.

"Who the hell is Helen the Barbarian?" another asked.

"A female wrestler in the '80s. Don't you watch sports?"

"Wrestling isn't a sport, you dope," Casper responded.

"Is so," Mike said.

"Since when?"

"Since it was in the original Olympics."

I had to cut it off. "Enough. Write it on the card."

Ted scrawled "Helen the Barbarian" and "Helen of Troy" on the 3x5.

"What's vestus virum facit mean?" someone asked.

"The clothes make the man," Casper again.

"Write it down," I said.

"And Joe Friday was a cop so he had a gun."

"And a badge."

"And a partner, what's his name? Uh, the little guy who

played the colonel on M.A.S.H."

"The only invisible rabbit was Harvey," Mary Ann interrupted.

"Yeah, but he didn't write songs," someone countered.

"So what? He was invisible. Maybe it was a talent we didn't know about?"

That caused beer-soaked laughter around the table.

"Write it down," I said.

"This one sounds like God," Bubba said, sliding the "Not one of three, but one of the three" card to the center of the table.

Ted reached for the card, glanced at it. "Yeah, it's God."

"Add it," I said.

"Maybe it's the devil? Like in 'the devil made me do it?'" Tony laughed.

"Or one of Little Bo Peep's sheep," another voice from the wilderness of one-too-many beers. "A sheep that was part of the herd, but a black sheep so it wasn't part of the herd. Get it?"

"You smokin' again?" Robbyn asked.

"You may be onto something," Bubba broke in. "The black sheep is a sheep and part of the herd, but not really an accepted part of the herd. Maybe D. B. Cooper was the black sheep of his family." To me, "All you gotta do is find someone who is an outcast in his own family?"

"Like everyone around this table?" Dudi joked.

That resulted in a raucous round of hoots and hollers.

The clues kept on comin' for another hour spiced with tacos, beer, laughs and good friends.

Having collected the cards with the various scribbles and scratches on them, I rode home in the cold and dark. The banter and input from the group would have to be put into some semblance of order later. For now, it was enough that a set of different eyes looked at the clues. Usually Sal's and Cookie's job. That, in turn, would give me added fodder for determining where to go next.

D. B. Cooper was most likely dead. McCoy was as good a suspect as anyone, but not someone who exactly fit the profile or circumstances. I'd have to look at the facts again, and, of course, the cards.

But if the letter *did* come from the real D. B. Cooper, and if, in fact, the clues were truly a path to the real skyjacker, maybe a call to Artemus – the Homeland Security guy who got Sal and me involved in the stolen cars and Red Ball mystery a year ago – would give me access to more of the internal FBI info on the case.

It would be worth a try. But for now, I was craving some clam strips.

CHAPTER SIX

Four p.m.

My early morning phone call to Artemus at Homeland Security went unanswered. Left a message, but never got a call back. That was effectively the only thing on my agenda related to D. B. Cooper, so I ate half a pizza, watched the tail end of a Giants baseball game and dozed on the couch.

In all my years of living in Oregon, one of the great pleasures has been days like this with nothing to do. Well, actually, *lots* to do, but not doing them. The winter-to-spring weather erupts in either cold sunshine or warm rain, the latter my choice if I had a choice. But without Cookie around, Willow Weep suffered the silence of her in the kitchen making homemade soup or trying out new recipes or washing the glass fronts on the cabinets with her headset tuned to the Major League Baseball network and holding one-sided arguments with the talking sports guys.

And then there was the lack of Sal thumping around the living room, trying to suck me into some inane conversation about cars or motorcycles or economics or politics or if the moon landing was real or not. Going silent when I'd counter his argument so he could churn it around like cream-to-butter before nodding his bearded head in agreement or puffing out his cheeks and professing that I'm so totally incorrect it would make voodoo look positively mainstream.

Where the heck was he?

When the military officer came to the house and whispered some super-duper classified something in his ear, all he said to me was "Watch my goldfish." Sal doesn't have goldfish so I knew something major was in the hopper. That was months ago and nary a word since. Much like the 12 years he'd been gone from Bandon and no one knew where he was or what trouble he'd gotten into.

Sal is brilliant. The New York Times' most difficult crossword puzzle? Give him 10 minutes and he'd toss the paper to the floor in disgust at the simplicity of the clues. At a quarter-inch under 6-feet tall and a pound shy of 300, the grizzly beard and ability to have his eyes go blank convince people he's nothing more than a hick country boy with the IQ of a broken pencil.

Watched him once listening to a physicist attempt to explain fusion to a crowd of matrons who were clearly lost in the dialog. Sal, in only a way Sal can do it, stepped in and provided an explanation that was simple, clear and left the women that much smarter. The physicist watched the big man in stunned amazement as if he, too, had just learned about fusion.

I often find myself attempting to decipher a puzzle with "What would Sal do?"

Getting up from the couch, I shuffled around the desk top to find the pack of 3x5s with the D. B. Cooper clues,

pulled them out from under my raggedy cowboy hat. I
broke open another set of clean 3x5s from the drawer and
sat at the dining room table.

Struggling to decipher some of the hen scratches made
by the Harley group, I finally had a new stack.

I am not one of the three, but one of the three.
God
Religious reference
Out of the loop, in the loop
Three letters one of which is the letter "I"
Pilot, co-pilot, navigator
Three-in-one oil
Three wheel motorcycle
Trident
Little Bo Peep sheep
Black sheep of the family
Pitch fork
Kitchen fork
BBQ fork
WWII 97th division

The last had to be written by Ted so I Googled the
division and came up with the Trident patch used by the
97th.

An appropos child's board game
Chutes and ladders
Monopoly
> Where's Waldo
> Guess Who
> Old Maid

You can't find me. But I am there.
Hide and seek
Ghost
Peep hole
Hidden

Vestus virum facit
Clothes make the man (Latin)
What I'm wearing
What others are wearing
Uniform

Magician David Copperfield
Cute *(that had to be Mary Ann)*
Sleight of hand

Card tricks
Poker
Black Jack
Pick a card, any card
Four stacks, four aces on top
Something seems it's not there but is
Rabbit in a hat
Blood to water
Wine to blood
Joe Friday has one
Gun
Partner
Badge
Distinctive voice
Acting ability
Monotone voice
Not a mountain. Not a saint.
Helen of Troy
Helen the Barbarian
Helen Keller
Helen Reddy
Helen Hunt

A song writing invisible rabbit
Harvey

Gathering up the cards, extracting a cold *Dos Equis*

from the fridge, a bag of Doritos, and a fist full of red vine
licorice, I made way to the picnic table on the deck. It was
close to 5 p.m. when I put the cards on the redwood planks
and began shuffling them around, searching for the
beginning and end of the puzzle. Find the opening gambit
and figure out the end of the story and the rest will fall into
place.

To do that requires getting into the head of the puzzle's
designer. If this were really D. B. Cooper, no matter how
hard the attempt to hide a pattern, it would be impossible
because the mind likes to think in linear logic. D. B. may
have mixed up the cards before sliding them into the
envelope, but somewhere in this pile of paper fiber there
was A-to-B-to-C. There always is.

The human mind can't really devise a set of random
numbers. Statistically and mentally it's impossible. Using a
particular number results in that one being put aside for the
next making the second number no longer random.
Magicians rely on this human inability as do cops and
priests and a boss or wife. Lies eventually fall apart
because of this quirk of *homo sapiens* nature.

So within the cards there had to be a pattern. D. B.
wrote the clues with the solution already in mind. By
putting them in the proper sequence, I could bust the puzzle
and determine if the sender was actually Cooper or a
hoaxer.

The beer went down easy, the sun was slipping behind
the tall shore pine and the salty tortilla chips disappeared as
I put one card then another at the top of the row.

An appropos child's board game
Magician David Copperfield
I am not one of the three, but one of the three.
Not a mountain. Not a saint.
You can't find me. But I am there.
Vestus virum facit
Joe Friday has one
A song writing invisible rabbit

My gut told me the child's board game had to lead the pack. It was the broadest clue in terms of scope no matter what the game was. This had to be the framework, the border in which the other clues were contained. The rest were components of the hijacking.

The tug on my pant leg came as no surprise. Lilly, the runt raccoon that adopted me some years ago, looked up, her hands resting on my shoe. I pulled a red vine from the stack I'd brought and offered it up which she gladly took and ate slowly as if savoring the flavor. Lilly has a sweet tooth. Cookies, Hershey kisses, cinnamon-sugar bagels, name it and she's there.

People think raccoons wash their food before they eat it. Actually, they're washing their hands because that's where the nerves are telling them if something is edible or not. Getting the dirt off of their paws heightens that ability. Don't ask me how I know that. Read it somewhere.

My cell phone buzzed.

"Drago."

"Hi, coach. Do you have some time to help me out?"

"Sure Billy. Over the phone or in town?"

"At Lloyd's if you got half an hour or so."

"On the way."

Billy was filling in for Bandon PD's Chief Forte ever since he was hospitalized for PTSD after the Vector Partners blow up a few months ago. Sal had pulled some government strings to get the Chief into a secret hospital for "psychological reconstruction." I had no idea what that meant, but it took Forte out of the game and left my former first baseman from the days of coaching the high school team in charge. Young but sharp, Billy loved being a cop but really wanted out of the administrative clutter and back on the street.

Shuffling the cards back into a stack, dropping a couple of red vines for Lilly and collecting the beer bottle and Dorito bag, I pushed through the slider and dropped it all on the counter, reached in the drawer for my Taurus Magnum, checked the wheel to make sure it was loaded, and clipped the holster on my belt.

At 6-foot-5 and 230 pounds, I'm big enough to intimidate without a gun strapped to my hip, but the Magnum adds a little persuasion, if needed.

The Crown Vic burst to life, the side exhaust rattling the house windows, and I backed out to the gravel road and nosed toward Highway 101. Aiming the hood-flames toward town, I crossed the Coquille River bridge at a sedate 65. The water was high and calm with a few boats a bit up river.

Everytime I crossed the Coquille, the ghost paddle wheeler and the men who died on it crawled their way back into my thoughts. And the dilemma Karl, the reporter, faced. If I were him, I'd probably hold off reporting the story. It had been a secret for a hundred years, and what good would its telling serve?

That was my thinking today. Yesterday I'd been mentally in favor of broadcasting the story far and wide. The dead sailors deserved to have their day in the light.

The Crown Vic rumbled into Bandon, under the Welcome to Old Town arch. I parked in front of WinterRiver Books and walked back up the street to Lloyd's. Billy's BPD Tahoe was parked in front.

Walking into the bar-half of the building, Billy was standing near the cash register, hands on hips. Two guys I recognized were seated on stools looking glum. All the lights were on. Having been a bouncer once upon a time I learned to hate bright lights in a bar, club or lounge. It reveals all the pimples. Dirty carpet, scratched tables, poorly painted walls, smoke stained fixtures, smudges of grease everywhere and upholstery that in the dark looks inviting but under harsh lighting makes you wonder what diseases are lurking in the vinyl seams.

"Hey, Billy, what's up?"

The skinnier of the two, Lacey Porlan, tried to smile but the two missing canine teeth turned him into Rocky the Squirrel. "Hi, Nick."

"Lacey. What trouble you'd get into this time?"

We'd been classmates at Bandon High School years back. He was always the guy tossed from class for smart remarks or purposely scrapping his fingernail on a chalkboard or firing spitballs at another kid.

"Nuthin', Nick. Honest."

The second bar stool was being smothered by Jack Porlan, Lacey's older and uglier brother. At nearly 400 pounds, the seat was testament to the strength of native Redwood trees. I know it was old growth Redwood because our high school shop class made these stools some 25 years ago as a project.

"And you, Jack?"

"It was Lacey that done it, Nick."

I looked at Billy. "Done what?"

He cocked his head for me to follow and pointed at the two Porlan brothers. "Stay."

On the outside of the building in the cedar siding, Billy removed a makeshift "Closed" sign hanging on a nail. Under it, a common and too often used cuss word had been burned into the wood.

"Cute."

"Well, the owner covered it with this sign. It's right here on the main sidewalk of Old Town and doesn't reflect well, you know?"

"Tourists have sensitivities, for sure." I ran a finger over the small near-black circles spelling the epitaph scorched into the wood. "Even spelled it wrong," I laughed.

"I know, the 'c' is missing. But still…"

"Cigarette burns."

"That's what I figured. My problem is we know one of the two did it, but we don't know which. They both smoke. I'm not interested in making a big deal out of this, but I want the one who did it to get out the old sandpaper and fix it. Neither will fess up, though."

"Don't you love small towns?"

Billy smiled, "Yeah. Is there a way to figure out which one is dumber than a stump?"

"If I recall, both failed English and spelling in high school so this isn't a surprise," fingering the space where the "c" should be.

I glanced around the sidewalk. In the gutter, seven cigarette butts, two crushed under a heel; of the others, just filter tips remained with a bit of paper attached, but no tobacco. Toeing the filter tips, I picked one up, winked at Billy and walked back into Lloyd's.

The Porlan brothers were still sitting where we left them. Sour faced. Sending dagger-eyes to each other.

"Lay your hands on the bar top, boys."

"What for, Nick?"

"Jack, just do it okay?"

The two men put their hands flat on the bar. I checked the fingernails of each man.

"Bill, have Lacey get the sandpaper and fix the damage."

Bill looked at me like I was an alien. "Really?"

"Really."

Jack picked up his chin and gave his brother a hard stare. "Told you not to do that."

"Up yours, Jack." To me, "How'd you know it was me?"

I tossed the cigarette butt on the bar top. "What do you see?"

"A cigarette butt. So what?"

Bill chimed, "That's all I see, too, Nick."

"Filter tip and cigarette paper, but no tobacco in the paper."

Billy looked closely. "Okay."

"Now look at Lacey's right-hand ring finger."

Jack bent his head down close to his brother's hand.

"Not you, Jack. I want Bill to look at it."

Billy squinted at the fingers and shrugged.

"See the black smudge on his ring-finger finger nail?"

"Sure do, coach."

"Comes from holding a nearly burned down cigarette in your thumb and forefinger and flicking the hot ash from the butt with your ring finger. The crushed butts in the street were down to the filter tip. The others were about a third left. People who smoke either puff their way to the filter – that would be Jack while he watched his brother use a cigarette as a wood burner. When Lacey's ash eventually got pushed down into the tobacco, he's flick the hot ash off of the butt which also discharges the tobacco from the paper and dropped the rest into the street."

"That's cool, Nick," Lacey said, punching his brother in

the arm. "Ain't that cool, Jack?"

"You're an idiot, Lacey."

Billy slapped his hand on the bar top to get their attention. "Both of you. Get some sandpaper and fix the wall out there. Like new. I'll be back in a couple of hours to check. Now git."

The brothers ambled out, Lacey licking the smudge off of his fingernail, getting rid of the evidence, I suppose.

Turning to Billy, "Now tell me the real reason you wanted me to come to town? I know you. You would have just had both of them repair the building. You learned from Forte and that's what he would have done. The old 'Andy of Mayberry' solution."

Billy's face flushed. "The city council is talking about me becoming chief."

"You'd deserve it. You've proven yourself."

"But I don't want the job if Chief Forte is coming back." He was silent for a beat. "He is coming back, isn't he?"

I shrugged.

"Nick, I can't find him. Where is he? And where's Sal? I haven't seen either of them for weeks."

"The Chief is recuperating and in good hands."

"Recuperating from that ghost ship thing?"

"It was a bit more than that, but yes. As for Sal, he's just away."

One of the problems of knowing an adult since he was a snotty nosed kid is never remembering he's grown up both physically and mentally. Billy wasn't the Billy I had stuck in my mind. The glib, home-run hitting first baseman whose practical jokes on teammates were legendary and his ability to dig bad throws out of the dirt just this side of amazing. It was time to treat him like a man instead of a high school jock.

"Tell you what. I'll buy you dinner at The Station and bring you all the way up to speed. One condition."

"What's that?"

"Stop calling me coach and start calling me Nick. High school baseball was a long time ago."

He smiled, "Only if you quit using 'Billy.' My mother calls me that."

CHAPTER SEVEN

The man standing in the doorway was around 5-foot-10, slim, south of 40 years old, dressed in a dark suit, white shirt and blue silk tie with some weird squiggly pattern on it. Not having worn a tie for, oh, ever, I'm no fashion maven so I'm not versed in neckwear styles.

"Mr. Drago?"

"You found me. I give up."

That went over his head like a cotton ball in a typhoon.

"I'm Special Agent Ken Versalio. FBI."

"And I'm not-so-special unpaid consultant to the Bandon Police Department Nick Drago. What can I do for you Special Agent Ken?"

It was nice having a conversation with another human being after the current drought of companionship here at Willow Weep.

"Care to come in?"

Versalio unbuttoned his jacket – I presumed he was expecting an ambush and wanted quick access to his gun – walked into the living room and turned toward me. "I don't want to take up much of your time Mr. Drago…"

"Nick."

"Nick. Okay. I don't want to take up much of your time, Nick, but I was asked by headquarters to answer some questions you may have about D. B. Cooper."

"Like in FBI headquarters? The Hoover Building? Like in Washington D.C.?"

"Yes, sir."

"And how did they know I was asking about Cooper?"

"I'm in the Portland field office and HQ's request just came in on the morning's Cram List."

"Cram list."

"Projects we have to get done quickly. Cram is what we call it at the office because we have to cram it into the day regardless of what we're working on."

"And you couldn't just call me?"

"It had a high priority tag."

"How high?"

"Really, really high." Ken was unwinding.

"Need some coffee?"

"You bet."

He followed me into the kitchen. I pointed him to the cupboard with the mugs and the sugar bowl on the counter top.

"So you drove down this morning?"

He poured a mug full, passed on the sugar and eyed the refrigerator. "Milk?"

I nodded. He popped open the fridge door, scanned the bare shelves, found half-and-half I use for my Frosty Flakes when Cookie isn't watching, squeezed open the cardboard

container, sniffed at the opening and tipped about a
teaspoon full into his mug. I held my breath and watched
the coffee to make sure the cream didn't curdle. It didn't.

I led him back into the living room where he sat on the
couch, crossed his legs and finally smiled.

"You must have some friends in very high places to get
D.C. to send me down here. What's on your mind Mr.
Drago?"

Smiling to myself, I guessed the phone call to Artemus
generated a bit of response.

"Nick."

"Nick."

"You've arrested a man you think is D. B. Cooper."

"Correct."

"Mind telling me how you settled on this particular
guy?"

"Well, I can't get into specifics because the case is just
now with the Justice Department lawyers, but I can tell you
it's pretty open and shut."

"Open and shut."

"Sure is, Nick."

"Missing toes? Maybe the tip of his nose or a finger?"

Ken nearly choked on his coffee. "How the hell did you
know that?"

"Jump from a plane into a storm with the temperature at
minus 7 degrees, wearing loafers which would come off as
soon as he left the aircraft, landing in sub-freezing weather,
walking around the wilderness in only a pair of nylon

socks, no gloves, no hat or ski mask, frostbite is a likely outcome, don't you think? That makes me believe the real D. B. Cooper could have lost a couple of body parts. You just confirmed it."

"Good guess, I suppose."

"Let me ask you something else. Is or was the guy an expert parachutist?"

"Yes."

"Military?"

"Yes."

Scratching my ear, "Certainly not married, at least not when he jumped; didn't have any close friends to speak of and didn't hold down a very public job."

Ken hesitated long enough to let me know I was probably right on most counts.

"So, he's what, about 75 or so now?"

"Close."

"Had a desk job when he hijacked the plane?"

"No, actually, a postal worker. In Portland."

I shook my head. "On a mail route?"

"Yes."

"Not likely your man."

Ken's eyes narrowed. "Why not?"

"Ever try walking without a toe or two? He would have been off work for at least a couple of weeks after losing any body part, probably more. Did your guy say they were amputated some time ago?"

"I'm not sure we asked."

"Probably not. So let me see if I have this right: The right age, expert chutist, no alibi for where he was at the time of the hijacking, suddenly begins spending money or at least buying stuff for around the house. Maybe a new lawnmower or oven or windows in the living room. That kind of stuff. But nothing big. Nothing ostentatious. Right?"

"You're telling the story, Nick."

"Yes I am. A couple of hundred thousand bucks in 1971 was a lot of cash. But he could cash his paycheck, put it in the bank and use the 20 dollar bills for little things in little stores or in rural areas. Buy gas at an independent brand station, for example. Who'd check the serial numbers? He'd buy what he needed, preferably stuff costing less than 20 bucks, with his Cooper Loot and write checks out of his bank account that's been stocked with regular pay for everything else.

"Kenny, my Special Agent friend, a snap. Someone could use real currency a little at a time and the chances of getting caught if he didn't splurge or try to buy a car with a couple hundred 20 dollar bills, are about zero."

"Mr. Drago," we were getting FBI formal speak, "the attorneys prosecuting this case have more than enough evidence to convict our guy of being D. B. Cooper."

"Like you did Mr. McCoy back in '72, a few months after Flight 305?"

Ken looked puzzled.

"You know, the guy the FBI accused, the justice system sent away, who broke out of medium security lock up only to be shot dead as a mackerel a week later. That McCoy."

"We did?"

"You bet your tin badge. How old are you?"

"34."

"No wonder. You weren't even born when the hijacking took place. Let me ask you a question: If the FBI was convinced it had the real D. B. Cooper when it arrested McCoy, why did the Bureau keep the case open all of these years? I even read there's an agent to this day who is responsible for keeping tabs on all of the Cooper-related activities."

"That would be Agent McCullough. I called her before coming down here. There's even been a forensic task force in place since 2002, to be honest."

"Think about it, Kenny. Spending valuable resources and manpower to keep a case open that was considered solved 40 years ago. Does that make sense to you?"

Ken Versalio, Special Agent with the FBI, finished off his coffee in a single *glug-de-glug* and stood.

"I have to get back to Portland, Mr. Drago. I hope I've answered your questions."

On his way out, "I have one more."

He turned and waited.

"You've arrested this guy for being D. B. Cooper..."

"We're about to close the case. That's all I can tell you."

"Did you have a fingerprint or fingerprints?"

Versalio sighed. "Mr. Drago, let me just say we have

Art Spinella   Drago #4

enough evidence and, yes, a fingerprint is among that evidence."

"Didn't you also have a fingerprint of Mr. McCoy?"

Versalio's face flushed.

"Oh, that's right, you didn't even know there *was* a Richard F. McCoy, Jr. So let me fill you in."

Versalio stood at the FBI's version of attention, buttoned his jacket and waited.

"He was a Vietnam War helicopter pilot who was also a skydiver. The FBI said his Army fingerprint matched one found on a Boeing flight hijacked a few months after the Seattle plane. One of those seat-back magazines. And of the 66 fingerprints found on the Cooper flight, none was his. But the FBI made it seem there was a link. Was that a fib, Ken? Did the FBI feel so embarrassed that it blew the investigation on D. B. Cooper that it made up that little piece of evidence?"

Ken rankled, his posture becoming rigid.

"So if the FBI lied about one thing, what other tidbits are being hidden away in the deep recesses of the J. Edgar Hoover building?"

Versalio's face turned even redder. He was about to argue with me, but sucked it up and simply said, "Again, Mr. Drago, this is an investigation I can't really talk much about. The little I could tell you, I hope was helpful."

"Oh, more than you know."

Page
69

Clear sky and lots of fallen limbs, piles of brush left here and there by Cookie, and old rotten timber waiting to be part of the dust-to-dust cycle of life.

FBI HQ's quick response sending an agent to little ol' Bandon from Portland – a good four hour drive each way – seemed they wanted to shortstop any scrutiny of other government agencies or people who had friends at Homeland Security. I wasn't fooling myself, they would have shined me on had I called them directly. Even Sal might have had a problem getting through to the right people inside the Hoover Building. But an inquiry from Homeland Security lit a fire under someone's hip pocket.

I piled the brush in the burn pit, tossed a bit of diesel fuel on top and flipped a kitchen match into the mix. A whoosh, followed by crackling licks of flame and billowing smoke.

The off-ocean breeze took the smoke through the trees and hazed out the sun, but that was the downside. The dry heat from the fire and the smell of wood burning soothes my soul.

With three *Dos Equis* in the cooler and a bubbling pepperoni pizza on the table next to my lawn chair, I watched flames consume small limbs and boil the moisture out of damp leaves before they ignited. The only sound, little pops that sounded like mini-gunshots, a battle of Lilliputians somewhere under the burning rubble. The radiant heat felt good.

One beer and two pieces of pizza down, a rustling in the brush. First Lilly's nose, pointed upward sniffing the smoke then in her baseball sized raccoon brain recognition of hot cheese and pepperoni. She scampered across the lawn giving wide birth to the expanding fire and pulled up short in front of me. Her eyes stared into mine.

"I know, I should have sent you an invite, but I forgot."

She sidled closer to the chair, keeping an eye on me. I picked out a piece of pizza and handed it to her, then poured a quarter cup of *Dos Equis* into the empty coffee mug I'd brought out earlier. Lilly sniffed at the mug, still holding the pizza slice, and settled on her haunches alternating between bites of pie and slurps of beer.

"What do you think, girl? Are the clues really from D. B. Cooper or just a hoax?"

She looked up, widening her eyes just a bit.

"I've got a hunch they're real. And to start, I'm going to use *Chutes and Ladders* as the keystone clue. That just makes the most sense, although Monopoly isn't bad.

"So if it's *Chutes and Ladders*, what is Cooper trying to tell me? Was it a matter of choice or a matter of necessity? If a parachute is the 'chute,' what does a ladder have to do with it? The rear exit of the 727 is a stairway, not a ladder."

Lilly finished the pizza and was putting a solid dent in the brew. Climbing from the chair, I retrieved the clue cards, a magic marker and returned to the fire pit, tossed on a few more big limbs and re-settled in the lawn chair. I highlighted *Chutes and Ladders* on the top card in yellow, indicating my first choice; an underline for least likely.

An appropos child's board game
<mark>**Chutes and ladders**</mark>
Monopoly
> Where's Waldo
> Guess Who
> <u>Old Maid</u>

I was about to move on to the next card when, from behind me, "You Drago?"

The voice was high pitched, nails on a chalkboard. Turning in my chair, a bandy rooster about 6-foot-two, 235 pounds stood 10 feet from me, hands on his hips, face redder than a hooker's lipstick. A bit flabby around the middle and on the downside of athletic.

Some people you instantly like. Others you immediately dislike.

"Nick to my friends, but Drago to you."

"What the hell are you doing?" I didn't believe it was possible, but his voice went up a notch.

"Beg your pardon?"

Sputtering and flapping his arms, he pointed at the fire which was now a roaring blaze. "That!"

"The fire?"

"The goddam smoke!"

"Comes with the fire."

I climbed from the chair, patted Lilly on the head and turned to face the little guy.

"You're smoking up the whole neighborhood!"

"That's what smoke does. Happens every year. Has happened since the first Indian cooked up a salmon." Scratching my head, "And who are you?"

"I live on the corner and that smoke is coming in my house and making my asthma act up!"

He was yelling now and the words were close enough together to almost be impossible to decipher.

"I'll ask again, politely, who are you?"

"All you got to know is I live down the road and your fire is disturbing my health and home!"

"Let me try this in English. Do you have a name?"

"Robert Collins!"

"Okay, Robert Collins, what do you want me to do about it? This is something everyone who lives in Coos County does at least a couple of times a year. It's the only way to get rid of the brush."

"Then you shouldn't have so many damn bushes! Or you should take it to the dump."

My patience was wearing a bit thin. "Where they burn it and charge 25 bucks a load. That fire right there is about a hundred and a quarter's worth with at least 10 more to go. Why would I do that when I have my own matches?"

"I can see I'm getting nowhere with you!" he screamed. "I'm calling the cops!"

I consider myself a pretty good neighbor. Mind my business. Make sure I don't fire up the tractor before 10 in the morning in case someone's still sleeping. Idle down the road so the Harley or the Crown Vic's exhaust doesn't disturb anyone.

Still trying to keep my temper in check, "You from a city?"

"So what."

"Thought so. So you moved from where?"

"Portland. What's that got to do with anything?"

"And you have asthma? I bet you have other allergies, too."

"Yeah, so what?"

"And you moved to rural Oregon."

"I wanted peace and quiet," he snuffed, voice still as grating as sand in a clam. "Not some bozo hicks smoking up the neighborhood!"

"And you moved to a rural area where the pollen count is higher than almost anywhere in the universe, sit around with your windows open and suck on one of those woofers so you can breathe."

"It's a rescue inhaler, you dolt!"

"And you're gonna call the cops?"

"Damn right!"

My patience was gone. "Well, listen up, pal. You want to bring Portland to Coos County, you're gonna be hip deep in shit. People come here for what Coos offers, not to turn it into another Multnomah County. People come because they like the lifestyle. Like the idea of no one telling them how many horses they can own or if they can have cows, pigs, goats, sheep, rattle snakes if they want."

I stepped a foot closer causing him to back away.

That's a city boy's reaction. Country boys stand firm or *close* the gap.

"If you don't like neighbors who shoot guns on their own property and do it with care, move somewhere else. You don't like people burning their brush, take a train back to Portland. You want the freedom to run a business out of your house, build a shed with a minimum of hassle, have a big mean dog, raise orchids, have a fruit stand or a lemonade stand, then you've come to the right place. You want to regulate all of that, then move on, princess. As long as it doesn't interrupt my sleep, aggravate me like a barking little mutt or threaten my family, I'm okay with it."

I could hear my own voice rising.

"And if it does bother me, I let the person who caused the aggravation know. Personally. Neighborly. And if they're really Coos County folks, they'll take care of it without the threat of cops or guns or low-life bureaucrats."

Out of the corner of my eye, Lilly was back on her haunches watching, seemingly enjoying the scene.

"I'm tired of city people who come here to change things. When my parents came here, they came because they wanted to be part of this kind of rural lifestyle. They fit into the Coos County shoes. Not the other way around."

I stepped closer. He backed away further.

"You don't like me burning brush, hold your nose, bud, because it happens every year around this time. And it's damn legal. I don't like cars on blocks, but, hey, if it's on their land, that's their prerogative. You don't like my country lawn and want me to grow weed-free Kentucky

Blue and keep it trimmed nice and neat, tough shit. *I don't want to.* You want that, do it yourself on your property or move to a condo in Santa Barbara. You don't like me hanging an American flag on a 20-foot pole in my front yard, if that offends you, take it up with your armpit because that's what you're talking out of. You don't like my Christmas ornaments on the front fence, stuff a cork in it. I celebrate CHRISTMAS, not some generic holiday."

Taking a deep breath, forcing myself to calm down, "You've come to the wrong county and the wrong road. This isn't a principality of Sacramento or Portland or Phoenix. It's Coos County. We've had enough of people trying to turn this into something it's never been and hopefully never will be: An overbearing, nitpickin' place where government sticks its grubby fingers into every part of your life. Salem and D.C. do enough of that. So my advice to you? Head back to the 'burbs, princess, or become part of the program."

It was as if he just realized I was taller, heavier, meaner and getting really p.o.'d. His voice fell an octave.

"Yeah, but I have a right…"

I matched his tone. "You have a right to express your opinion. No doubt and I'll defend it. You exercised that right when you came into my yard. You crossed the line when you started threatening me with 'cops'. When your opinion means you want to interject your idea of what's 'right' or 'wrong' with how I live, I have a right – at least in Coos County – to plant a boot in your ass and toss you off my land."

Trying to regain some high ground, "You're just a hick,
Drago."

"And you've just earned your first demerit. The second
one gets you a few loose teeth. The third, a long stay in Bay
Area Hospital. Don't ask what happens with the fourth.
You don't want to know."

Waving a "shoo" gesture at him, "Next time, come
down here and ask nice and I'll accommodate you if I can.
But for now, get the hell out of here. My *Dos Equis* is
getting warm."

Boy, not having anybody around was turning me
mighty prickly.

Bandy rooster backed out of the driveway, leaned
forward like he was facing a headwind and scurried down
the gravel road.

I watched him for a minute, turned to Lilly, and asked,
"Did you leave me any pizza, you cross-eyed rodent?"

CHAPTER EIGHT

The bleached bones of long-dead trees wash ashore with every high tide. There aren't as many since mills found ways of using scraps for other products from particle board to toilet paper.

Mel and Barbara Salazar hunted the southern Washington shores for small limbs of driftwood, glass floats from old Japanese fishing vessels, sea shells and other treasures, but didn't expect to find the silver bundle intertwined in knots of kelp and tossed on the beach as if the ocean were cleansing itself of unwanted waste.

Mel poked at it with his walking stick, made of an alder limb and topped with a carved Tiki head.

Using the point of his stick, he attempted to scrape away the kelp so he could see the actual bundle. He was sorry he did.

Barbara screamed when through the translucent wrapping an emaciated face stared at her, eyes open.

Three more days of boredom. Time to put a few rounds through the Taurus .357 Magnum.

When Cookie and I bought Willow Weep, there was a small eight-by-ten workshop the previous owner used to make huckleberry wine. It was a place of solace for me; where I'd build cabinets and furniture and doors and small wooden toys that would make the kids laugh. Stilts had become a specialty of mine.

Since that time, other buildings were constructed, each with a purpose. At least that's what I told Cookie. Batting cage needs a building for the equipment. She'd say, "Okay." Workshop is too small, need a bigger one. She'd shrug and say, "Okay." Storage, we're out of storage room. How about a building? "Okay." And the list went on until eight outbuildings dotted the Weep.

The last was greeted with "Enough. We're looking like a construction zone."

So when the "need" for a shooting range struck my fancy, I went back to the original workshop, cleared it out, sawed a hole in one wall, installed swing-away window panels and insulated the walls. About 30 yards away, a target board made of timbers, mounted on metal legs. I could shoot in any weather.

Heaven.

A friend loads the shells and puts an extra bit of oomph in them for me.

Laying the Magnum and a Walther on the shooting bench, I pulled on ear muffs, pushed the window panels outward. Each is heavily insulated so they would absorbed the sound of the muzzle-blast at least enough to keep the neighbors – as distant as they were – from becoming too alarmed.

The recoil of the Taurus is minimal. A hefty push-back even Cookie found pleasant and controllable.

Slugs ripped into the target, each within the bull's eye. First right handed. Then left. Same result.

A hundred rounds later, switching to the semi-auto Walther, a new gun given as a gift for a favor. With each shot, the brass ejected into the shooting room to be collected later. The sound was not nearly as robust, the kick slight. I also missed the bull's eye by a couple of inches to the left. Adjustment. Rounds 30 to 40 were closer, but still off the mark. Another tweak of the rear site. Closer.

Cell phone vibrated in my shirt pocket.

"Drago."

"Nick, it's Special Agent Versalio."

"What's up, Special Agent Ken?"

FBI guys don't have much of a sense of humor. They take the "special agent" tag very seriously. He cleared his throat. "I've got a problem."

"And what might that be?" clicking on the safety and putting the Walther on the bench.

"I'm getting some very strange vibes from the honchos about our conversation. They want to know why you are looking into D. B. Cooper and how Homeland Security plays into your questions."

"And?"

"Well, to be honest, one of my colleagues and I were talking about the case and realized someone is pushing hard to close it. No reason given, other than perhaps it's an embarrassment to the new Special Agent in Charge."

"Special Agent in Charge. That's the top guy locally, right?"

"Right. He wants it to go away. It's a case that should have been closed years ago and people back in D.C. don't like open cases. Especially ones where a guy was killed because he was supposed to be the perp but we could never really prove it."

"So they found this new guy to blame."

"Built a case around him, arrested him and are ready to put the rubber 'Closed' stamp on the file."

Mulled that for a second. "Okay, so what do you want from me?"

"Did some checking. You're known for solving some interesting puzzles. That thing with Red Ball was a big gold star on your file."

"I have a file?"

"A foot tall."

"Taller than the tallest tree…"

"What?"

"Donnie Brooks. Gene Pitney did a version. You know, 'Higher than a mission bell, deeper than a wishing well…'"

"I have no idea what you're talking about."

"Never mind. So what can I do for you?"

"Can you get up to Portland? I want you to look over the Cooper files and see if you can make sense out of what may be a rush to judgment."

I gave my head the two-finger scratch, "Better than being bored around here. Sure. When?"

"Tomorrow?"

"Can do. I'll be there around 11."

"Do you have a dark suit, dark tie and white shirt? I want to get you in as a Special Agent from, say, Los Angeles."

Looking at the gun bench, "I've got a dark Magnum, black Smith and Wesson and a silver Walther. Will that do?"

Silence. No sense of humor.

"Uh, white shirt? Tie? Does that mean I got to shave off the beard? I just grew it."

"Beard's okay. Trimmed. Some agents have them. Not many."

"I'll have to work on the suit and tie thing, though."

"Eleven a.m."

"Cool."

Raiding the clothes closet, I found the one dark suit I bought for a funeral some years back. I'd have to pick up a white shirt and dark tie at Fred Meyers on the way to Portland. Maybe one of those clip-on jobbies since I was a bit rusty in the knot-tying department.

The Crown Vic settled into a nice even rumble on the trip up Highway 101 and the stop at Freddies lasted only a few minutes. What's with women needing to shop for

Page
83

hours? White shirts in a pile. Got it. Ties on a table. Picked out a blue one. Done. It took longer for the cashier to ring it up than for me to make the selection. Elapsed time: Under six minutes.

Back on the highway to Reedsport, the Cooper clues popped up one at a time. The intriguing tidbit to me was the Song Writing Invisible Rabbit. Obviously a reference to Harvey. But what made him a song writer?

It had to be part of a dual clue. It was the object to another clue's subject. Probably the reference to "Not a mountain, not a saint." That was also clearly "Helen." But which Helen? Not Troy or Helen the Barbarian. Both were too obscure. Helen Hunt had to be out of the running. Few people knew her name even though they'd recognize her as an actress if they saw her.

Helen Reddy? That would go with the song-writing clue.

Reedsport came and went as I headed inland on Highway 38. To the left, the river, brown with runoff from the adjacent hills; the tree and brush choked rocky cliff walls on the right. The CV rumbled through the twisties on the way to Drain, the Sirius/XM signal cutting in and out.

On one of the long stretches, I passed a loaded log truck and recognized the driver as Michael Bowman, a good guy who drinks MGD, but I don't hold that against him. Gave him a double rap of the exhaust as I passed with a return air-horn blast.

Quick stop in Drain for gas and back onto 38 for the short stretch to I-5.

Punched up the country station on satellite radio and sang my heart out to Billy Ray Cyrus, Garth Brooks, Pistol Annies, Toby Keith, Taylor Swift. The usual gang. Glad the windows have a dark tint so no one can see me belting out the tunes.

10:43 a.m.

The GPS led me directly to the FBI offices on SW 1st Street in Portland. The white building with darkly tinted glass sits across from an empty, semi-landscaped parcel that couldn't be described as a park. The street intersects a fast-entry point to I-5, presumably so someone in a hurry can get somewhere else.

I pulled the Crown Vic into the ground-level parking lot, grabbed a ticket and hoped the Feebies validated. Took the wide entry stairs two at a time, adjusted the clip-on tie, tampered down my cowlick and walked toward the reception desk.

"Can I help you?"

The man behind the counter looked a bit rough around the edges, not like the typical rickety guard who in an emergency would take a full minute to find then pull a weapon from his belt.

"FBI offices."

"You expected?"

His eyes squinted at my dark suit, white shirt and dark tie then landed on my beard and gave a once over to my shaggy haircut and motorcycle boots. (Hey, at least I shined them.)

"I'm with the Sacramento, California office. I'm here to

meet Ken Versalio."

"Have any ID?"

He was hung up on the beard. Don't know why. Half
the population in Portland have one. The other half is
female.

Putting an edge into my voice, "Just call Special Agent
Versalio."

"Procedure says I need an ID."

Lowering my voice, "Procedure says nothing of the
sort. You don't like my beard. You don't like my spiffy
haircut. You don't like my big shiny boots. Not regulation.
Tough. Call him."

The guard hesitated then relented and punched in a
couple of buttons on his phone system.

Looking at me, "Name?"

"Special Agent Nicholas Emanuel Butterworth."

Into the phone, "There's a Nicholas Butterworth…"

"Special Agent," I interjected.

Guard sighed, "Special Agent Nicolas Butter…"

"Emanuel. Nicholas Emanuel…"

"Special Agent Nicholas Emanuel Butterworth here for
you." Looking at me, steely knives in his eyes, "Like the
pancake syrup."

He hung up the phone. "Special Agent Versalio will be
down in a minute."

"You're a peach."

The wait wasn't long. Ken strode across the lobby, put
his hand out and in a voice loud enough for the guard to

hear, "Agent Butterworth, good to meet you."

Versalio was protecting his ass pretending to be meeting me for the first time.

Grasping his hand, "You're shorter than I thought."

Ken almost choked.

"Right. Please come with me."

In the elevator, Ken asked, "Butterworth?"

"I was thinking of having waffles for breakfast. Love Mrs. Butterworth syrup."

We were silent the rest of the way to the fourth floor. I followed him down a narrow hallway to a small conference room overlooking Naito Parkway. He waved for me to have a seat then left the room.

The surroundings were sparse. Large wall-size white board with an assortment of colored markers in the narrow tray underneath it. The opposite wall was cork, thigh-high to ceiling, front to back. Black push pins were stuck in a grouping at the lower left hand corner, the cork obviously used frequently, hundreds of pinprick holes pockmarking the surface.

Ken returned followed by a slim blonde woman dressed in a blue blazer, blue skirt, white shirt and chunky heeled shoes. Maybe mid-30s. Perky. Bouncy hair to her shoulders and cute. She was carrying a large document case like those used by lawyers.

"Nick Drago, this is Agent Francis Blue."

"Mr. Drago." No smile, but a warm twinkle in her azure eyes like she was suppressing a smart alec comment.

"Francis."

"Most folks call me Frankie." No accent in her voice, but a soft mid-level tone that made it soothing.

"Frankie Blue. Like it. Reference to Frank Sinatra?"

"Dad was a big fan."

I put my hand out and she took it. "Nick Drago."

"I know. I've read your file."

"Higher than a mission bell…" Somehow I loved that line. Besides, I couldn't get the song out of my head.

She shot back, "Richard Michael Patrick, EMI Music."

"Beg pardon?"

"He wrote it," she said with a smile.

Ken said, "She's our resident music history wonk. Can we get on with this?"

We sat around the conference table.

The two Feebies sat across from me.

Ken started. "Nick, this conversation isn't taking place."

I glanced around the room.

"And, no, it's not mic'd. There are no voice recorders of any sort."

I nodded.

Ken continued, "We – Agent Blue and I – started looking into the Cooper file after our conversation in Bandon and, quite honestly, we're stumped as to why this new suspect suddenly surfaced." His voice was low and almost conspiratorial. "We've had more than 1,000 suspects in this case since 1971. And Andrew Malcolm

Carney never once appeared."

"Was he on the flight?"

"Yes, in fact, he was. Under an assumed name, actually. Had a girlfriend in Portland he was visiting for Thanksgiving."

"Parachutist?"

"Yes."

"And the girlfriend?"

"Died in '93."

Blue broke in. "The file basically claims he stole the money because he couldn't afford to keep the girlfriend and his family and wanted to have a cushion to make sure his wife didn't know about the mistress."

Bandon head scratch. "So he didn't rob a bank or hold up a liquor store, he decided to hijack a plane?"

Ken, "The theory is he wanted one big chunk of change and Flight 305 would be his only caper."

"Caper?"

"Sorry, too much TVLand. His only crime. That would give him enough money to live comfortably and still maintain both a girlfriend and family."

"He must be nearly 80 by now," I said.

"78," Blue responded. "Spry as a puppy, though."

"And what about his financials?"

"Postal worker, which I told you, and modest house, eight-year old car, college loans for his kids long paid off, nice pension from the government."

"So he spent the $200,000 on his dalliance."

Blue laughed. "Dalliance? Is that still a word?"

My face warmed. "Well, yeah, I guess it is."

She looked at me with her sparkly blue eyes and a smile crossed the young, pretty face. "You a prude? That's such a prudish word."

"Not necessarily a prude, but I do tend to revert to old standby verbiage. Habit of mine."

"From your writing?"

"Yeah. Guess you did read my file."

Ken interrupted, "Okay, so what we have is a man who is even keeled enough to not blow a couple of hundred grand on a new Ferrari or lavish trips to Tahiti, but stashed the money somewhere that gave him easy access and allowed him to keep a friend on the side."

Another Bandon head scratch, leaned back in my chair, "Seems so. But tell me this: Does he look like the sketch of D. B. Cooper?"

Blue reached into her satchel and pulled out a half dozen folders, each yellower than the previous. In the oldest – and yellowest – a piece of paper. She slid it across the table at me.

"He looks vaguely, and I mean vaguely, like this version of D. B. Cooper."

I smiled, "That could just as well be this guy…" I reached into my inside jacket pocket, pulled out an envelope and rummaged through the folded sheets of paper and 3x5 cards I'd brought with me. Selecting one of the photocopies, I laid it on the table next to the sketch.

Ken choked and laughed. "That's Bing Crosby!"

I nodded. "Yes, it is. Old joke about the sketch you guys came up with for Cooper. But the similarities are striking, don't you think?"

Even Special Agent Blue chuckled.

"The point," I said, "is that there are literally hundreds of thousands of people who look like that sketch. Does your man?"

"Actually, no," Ken said. "After you and I talked, Frankie and I put a search on Carney's history. We found his high school year book picture, some other photos that were printed over the decades for outstanding civic service and such. To be quite honest, he never looked like Cooper."

"Then I don't get it. How did the FBI settle on Carney?"

Both agents shook their heads and shrugged.

Blue said, "It's as if the Bureau searched for someone who met certain criteria – age, parachuting ability, knowledge of the 727 aircraft, where he lived, other profile pieces. Then our side went out looking for a man who met those criteria."

I perked that one around for a second. "I don't buy it. You said this guy actually had money stashed away to provide enough cash to support a family and a girlfriend. Where'd it come from?"

Again, both agents shrugged.

"And the Justice Department filings to the Grand Jury don't give a clue?"

"Not a one that we can see. They're sealed at the moment. Only the attorneys have all the info."

"How'd the girlfriend die in, what'd you say, 1993?"

"Mugging," Ken said.

"Mugging."

"Mugging," Ken repeated.

"In Portland?"

"Not unusual," Blue said, a bit defensive.

Ken cut Frankie a look.

"Okay, let's say we buy the fact she died from injuries sustained in a mugging. Is that right?" I asked.

Both agents nodded.

"So, we have a woman who was supposedly the girlfriend of D. B. Cooper, a skyjacker the FBI had been hunting at this point for nearly three decades, being killed in a random – and I assume it was random – street crime in Portland, the city of love and good manners."

Waving a hand toward Ken, Blue said, "That was our thought, too. Seems odd. At least coincidental. When I pointed it out in the files to Ken, he felt the same way. Odd."

He nodded, "I haven't been in the Bureau for that long – only eight years – and there are people who have been on this case for a decade or more and they don't seem to have a problem with the mugging and death of Cooper's girlfriend. What was I supposed to do? I want this to be a career, not a pit stop on the way to night manager of a 7-Eleven."

Frankie Blue unconsciously put her hand on his then quickly took it back when she noticed I had seen the exchange.

I pretended to ignore the obvious relationship between the two.

Now it was Frankie's turn. "Nick, what made you ask Homeland Security for access to the files in the first place?"

How to answer? Shrug and say it was just a hobby of mine to look into old crimes? Admit to a letter from someone who was probably crazy as a loon claiming to be Cooper and I was stupid enough to take it seriously? Yeah, that would work. Or I called Homeland Security on a whim. Like they didn't have better things to do.

"Let's just say I'm looking for truth, justice and the American way."

"Superman," she chuckled. "You may be big enough, and your file says you dodged enough bullets, but can you fly?"

"I can't. My Crown Vic can. I'm hungry. Is there a good place to eat around here?"

The Three Degrees Waterfront Bar and Grill is in the RiverPlace Hotel on the Willamette River and barely a mile walk from the FBI field office. With a view of the river and the Esplanade – folks with their nostrils aimed toward the ground instead of straight ahead call it a boardwalk – the food is high-brow and the ambiance certainly isn't like the Minute Café. For a country boy like me, even in a blue suit, white shirt and tie, I feel way under dressed.

"So tell me, Nick, how's Cookie?" Blue asked.

"Doing better, thanks."

"Second marriages often last longer than first," she said.

"And now on to other subjects, okay?"

She shrugged and looked at Ken. "Ken and I would like to know more of the background on your interest in D. B. Cooper, assuming you don't mind sharing."

The waitress approached the table and smiled. "Good afternoon."

Ken glanced at his watch then, "Could we have two white wines and…" looking at me, "a *Dos Equis,* please?"

I squinted at the two agents. "Guess my file is pretty thick."

"Higher than a mission bell," Blue said.

I was feeling like this was more about me than Cooper.

"Okay, then, spill it. What do you want to know about me so we can get on with the real business?"

The waitress returned with a sad look. "I'm sorry, sir, we don't have *Dos Equis.*"

"What do you have?"

She ran through a list of brews that meant nothing to me. *Ninsaki, Trumer.* My quizzical look made her clear her throat and lower her voice. "We also have some bottled beers you might like." Budweiser, Coors Light, the regular fare, then Corona.

"Beggars can't be choosers, do the Corona."

You'da thought I'd asked for ketchup for my *Tofu Udon Noodles*. Both Feebies laughed.

"And before you go, what do you have that's deep fried?"

The waitress rolled her eyes. "I'll check, sir," and walked away.

To Blue and Versalio, "Okay, here's the deal. I received a letter and some clues that basically say the guy you're about to hang for being Cooper is the wrong dude."

"We hear that a lot," Blue said.

"Yeah, I bet you do. But I have reason to believe the

person who wrote the letter may be telling the truth. Don't ask me why I feel that way, I can't explain it. But there's something in it all that has a sense of urgency and fundamental veracity that gives me a feeling."

The two agents looked at each other, then Blue, "Do you have the clues with you?"

I pulled the envelope out of my pocket, slipped out the second set of clue cards and passed them across the table. The two agents thumbed through them. Each shaking their head.

"Don't get the connection," Versalio finally muttered, still looking at the cards. "I mean, I guess the *Chutes and Ladders* makes sense, but the others are a mystery to me."

Blue wasn't quite as quick to dismiss the clues. "Ken, I see what Nick means. There's something about this that's curious. I mean, the allusion to David Copperfield's sleight of hand and Being One of the Three but Not Being One of the Three. Someone put a lot of thought into these and there is definitely a thread."

I watched some of the boats cruising down the river. A white day cruiser drifted past about 100 feet off shore. It slowed to a near stop. My affinity for boats of any sort, especially trawlers, sent me back to the Coquille River and the near disaster Sal and I had in *Dragonfly*. Then I caught the glint from the flying bridge. Someone was using binoculars and peering into the restaurant windows. My hand went to my belt, but the Magnum was in the Crown Vic. Excuse me for being nervous, but the last time I ate in a fancy restaurant a friend was relieved of two fingers, thanks to a Russian special-ops rifle held by a first-rate sniper.

The wake of the cruiser swelled and the boat accelerated past the restaurant and down river.

Blue noticed. "You okay?"

"Yeah. Flashback is all." Back to the conversation, "I agree. There is definitely a thread between the clues."

My Corona arrived and the waitress waited for us to order. She had ignored my request for a list of deep fried food as if I somehow must have been joking.

The final choices were basically burgers all around. She scurried off when I asked if the cook could make my French fries extra crispy.

"Can I see the letter Cooper sent?" Blue asked.

Rummaging around the papers in the envelope, I slid out a copy and passed it to her. She read through it quickly.

"Interesting. Old school. Very formal. 'Dear Nicholas' and 'warmest regards.' Certainly fits the age profile of the real D. B. Cooper. No one writes like that anymore except older folks."

"My thought exactly. The envelope was similarly formal. *Mr. Nicholas Drago.* Not Nick or just Nicholas Drago without an appellation."

"Do you have the originals with you?" he asked.

"In the car. Hoping you'd ask. Maybe you can run some fingerprints or something."

"We can do that," Blue answered.

Versalio returned to the photocopied letter and

envelope, "This formal wording would be consistent with our Mr. Carney. He was a postal worker. Saw a lot of mail. Would have a penchant to be a bit more formal because of all of the days of looking at envelopes and addresses."

Blue frowned, "Don't follow."

I responded, "I get it. Sure, he would have seen address labels with everything from misspellings to inappropriate references. An old logger buddy addresses his Christmas card envelope to me as 'Nick the Prick.' I assume some postal workers would find that funny but others might be offended that the mail service is being used to deliver a Jay Leno joke. Kind of like guys who still carry pocket watches and talk of time being too important to leave to digital green blinks."

"Or guys who smoke pipes and drink brandy out of a snifter," Blue added, a smile in her voice, glancing at Versalio.

Lunch arrived and the cards along with the papers went back in the envelope and my inside jacket pocket.

The burger was big. The waitress hovered until I took one of the fries and bit into it.

"What the hell is that?" sputtering.

The waitress smiled, "Deep fried organic baby carrot sticks. We don't have French fries."

CHAPTER NINE

Waking in an upscale hotel bed is usually a nice experience. Crisp sheets. Multiple pillows. That hint of mint still on your tongue from the little candy left on the duvet. *(Didn't think I knew words like that, huh.)*

Like I said, "usually" a nice experience. Not so pleasant when instead of morning light streaming through the window, the barrel of a big-ass pistol pressed hard between your eyes is the alarm clock.

"Where is your friend?" The voice had a thick accent. Maybe Eastern European, but my bet was Russian.

"Which one? I have so many. And could you lighten up on the gun, it's giving me a headache."

In the dark, when you're prone, it's hard to determine just how large or small your assailant is. My initial guess was big. My second guess was really, really big. Shuffling in the background told me there was at least one other.

The barrel pushed harder into my forehead.

"Where is Mr. Rand?"

Definitely Russian.

"Don't know. Haven't seen him in months. Your guess

is as good as mine. Why?"

My body tensed. Preparing for the next level of what was clearly going to be a physical confrontation. The air conditioner clicked on sending a cold push of air across the room, smothering the smell of the freshly oiled gun.

The silence lasted a few seconds, as if he was trying to translate my English into Russian in his brain. Then he jabbed me with the barrel.

"Hey! That hurts. Knock it off."

"Where is Rand?"

"Why do you need to know?"

"There are matters he has become involved in that are not healthy."

"He eats a lot of donuts and pizza. Of course it's not healthy."

The barrel jabbed me harder.

"You joke, Mr. Drago. But this is not for jokes. Where is Rand?"

The last bump in the forehead smarted. Not bad, but for someone with a conventional pain threshold, it would have caused a yelp. If you've worked in the woods as a logger with guys who are rough as corn cobs, you swallow pain. Otherwise they'll start raggin' on you for being a baby or a girl or a wuss or give you a nickname like 'princess.' It teaches you that unless there's lots of blood involved, smashed fingers, or tree limbs crushing your foot or a choker getting tangled around your leg, it's best not to show outward signs of agony.

There's no crying in baseball.

In this situation, though, when the bad guys are going to get progressively more irritated that you won't answer their questions, it's best to let them think they're really hurting you when, in fact, they're far from it.

"Dammit, that hurts!"

My eyes had become accustomed to the bit of green light from the alarm clock/radio on the side table. The gun is a Yarygin PYa, MP-443 Grach. Semi-auto, Russian-spec 9 mm. Standard military and cop sidearm. Short recoil. Double action. Fairly decent weapon.

To my left, a shadow. Big guy, arms crossed.

"We must find Rand. Quickly. Where is he?"

Another jab. I put my best cowering voice in play. "Dammit! Enough! He's in San Diego, okay?"

The MP 443 Grach has one flaw: an ambidextrous safety so either a right or left hander can click it on and off. The slide stop can be mounted on either side of the gun. This one was set up for a lefty. The Russian was holding the gun in his left hand putting him on my left side.

He jabbed me again with the Grach.

This time I lurched, arched my back as if he really hurt me. My right hand came across, slapped the safety to "on" and simultaneously pressed the magazine release at the bottom of the trigger guard.

Left hand gripped the Grach and twisted it loose. Smashed the stainless steel gun into his nose. Instant blood and grunt. He tumbled off the bed. The second Russian hesitated, caught unaware. Swinging my legs from the

mattress, pushed off. The first Russian was on the floor,
hands and knees, bleeding on the carpet. Hard kicked him
on my way to the second. Too late. The shadow recovered.
Pulled a handgun from under his jacket. No time to aim.
Just fired three rounds. Maybe hoping to scare me off.
Caught him with a long, wide right hook under the point of
his chin. Rattled his teeth, but that was it. The guy was
shorter than me by an inch or two. Bigger across the
middle. Limbs like fence posts. Straight armed me. Gush of
air. My air. Blocked my knee. I came back with a short
hard left-hand jab to the neck. He gagged. Roundhouse
right to the temple. He buckled. Quick and dirty heel-kick
to the ear. Good night, Irene.

When in a fight with two assailants, never ignore the
"other" guy no matter how out-of-the-game he seems to be.

My lights went out.

My legs and arms were stretched to the four corners of
the bed, tied with strips of plastic shower curtain. A towel
had been cut in similar strips and used as a gag, tied behind
my neck.

When you're trussed up like a Christmas turkey, can't
move and unable to yell your head off, there are three
alternatives: First, struggle until your wrists get raw and
bleed; second, make a ruckus and disturb neighbors enough
to encourage them to call the police or, in this case, the
hotel manager; third, do as Cookie does, go to sleep and
wait for help.

The alarm clock/radio showed 6:18 a.m. As a kid I was a teeth grinder. Learned early that the same jaw motion would eventually cut through fabric. Using my tongue, I gauged the towel to be fairly thick. It would probably take an hour or more to grind my way through the material. The Feebies were picking me up at 7 for breakfast to look at the Cooper files, so all I would be doing is getting cotton fibers stuck between my teeth before they found me. Bouncing around on the bed to disturb the neighbors? In a hotel? Guests next door would just take it as a rambunctious roll in the sack, giggle and ignore the noise.

Cookie once led me down a side road in Mexico that turned into a mud pit. In the middle of the night, being "the Man," I attempted to get the Camaro Z28 out of the soup. Rocking the car, scooping mud with a cardboard-covered-in-carpet spare tire cover, cussing and stomping around in the gunk. And what was she doing all this time? Sleeping in the passenger seat. She figured no one was going to find us til daylight, so why fight it?

I elected to do the same.

The click of the electronic door lock woke me. Versalio entered first, glanced around, a sour look crossing his fair-skinned face. Blue was right behind him. When she scanned the room, a little smile crossed her lips.

"Anyone I know?" she asked, walking to the bed and twanging the binding between the bed frame and my left leg.

Versalio pulled the gag out of my mouth.

"Funny girl. Cut me loose, 'kay?"

The manager followed the two agents and gasped. Blood on the floor. Shower curtains sliced to ribbons. Towels with the hotel emblem shredded. A couple of chairs knocked over and three bullet holes in the wall above the headboard. A slight smell of gunpowder still hanging in the air.

Blue untied my legs while Versalio undid my arms. To the hotel manager, "We'll take it from here, Clarence. Damages will be covered."

"Yes, sir," as he scurried from the room pulling the door closed behind him.

"Care to share?" Blue asked, righting a chair and falling into it, placing a large briefcase on the floor next to her. "And, by the way, nice plaid boxer shorts. Really spiffy, Nick."

"Bite me, Special Agent," I said, swinging my legs off the mattress and planting my feet on the floor, careful to avoid the blood puddle.

Versalio grabbed the second chair and scooted it closer to the bed. "What happened?"

"Couple of guys asked a few questions, didn't like the answers and…" waving an arm around the room, "we agreed to disagree."

"Russian?" Blue asked.

"Yeah. How'd you know?"

"Night manager said two guys he thought were Russian were asking about you. Around 4 this morning," Versalio said. "What'd they want?"

No reason to hold back. "They said they were looking for Sal."

"Your buddy Salvador Rand," Blue said.

"The one and only."

"Actually, we were going to ask you the same thing," Blue said.

"And I'd have told you the same thing. One, I don't know and two it's none of your business even if I did know."

Getting clubbed makes me irritable. And I wasn't here to turn this into a *Sallie, Sallie, who's got the Sallie* kind of interview. "I'm here about D. B. Cooper, 'kay? If you can't help me or want information on my friends, let me know and I'll head back to Bandon with a thank you for a nice visit and paying for the room."

"No, wait," Ken said, a bit on the loud side. "Really, we'll get to Cooper in a second. We're trying to get a fix on how you came across this case at this particular point in time."

I reached for the phone, dialed room service. Ordering food is my way of pushing anger back down into my gut. Giving myself a little breathing room to regain composure. The pleasant voice on the other end asked what I would like. "Four eggs, scrambled, two bagels toasted, a double side of bacon extra crisp and lots of coffee." I looked at the two Special Agents. Versalio shook his head. Blue mouthed "bagel, cream cheese, sausage and coffee." I relayed it into the phone. Gave the woman my room number and hung up.

Calmer.

"Sal is away. He has nothing to do with Cooper or my interest in the case."

"He's pretty well known at Homeland Security and in the Bureau," Blue said. Matter of fact, not a question.

"That's my bud. Mind if I take a shower and get dressed?"

In 20 minutes the three of us were sitting around the hotel-room table. I made quick work of the eggs and bacon, dawdled over the bagels. Frankie Blue shared her bagel with Versalio and even gave him a sausage link.

Three cups of coffee later, my plates wiped clean and back on the serving cart. Another call for more coffee.

"Okay, Special Agents Versalio and Blue, what now?"

Blue patted the briefcase, "Copies of some of the more pertinent paper files are in here." She opened the lid and pulled out a small laptop and a thumb drive. "The entire set of files is on this," she said, handing me the storage device. "We can't be away from the office for much longer, this is way off the books, but feel free to hole up here and do what you do best: Analyze and de-puzzle the puzzle."

Versalio, leaned forward, put his elbows on the table. "Nick, the trial is supposed to start within the month assuming there aren't any continuances or other legal maneuvers, so the quicker you can unravel this one, the better. Once the trial starts, there's never going to be a chance to stop it. The Bureau wants this closed."

"Assuming there's something to unravel," Blue added. "In the meantime, I'll grab a sample of the blood, have you transferred to a different room and let the hotel crew clean up this mess. The blood is starting to smell bad. Mind if I take the original envelopes the clues came in?"

I handed her the plastic baggies. "Fingerprints would be helpful."

She nodded and took the packages. She dabbed a Kleenex on the drying blood, put it into an envelope from the desk drawer and the two agents left. Not the best way to transfer or protect evidence, but what the heck.

Within an hour I was in another room, papers spread across the table-desk with the laptop humming quietly. Room service delivered a basket of *real* French fries, two *Dos Equis* in an oversized ice bucket and a glazed donut.

Ah, life is sweet.

Scouring the list of actual facts and matching them against the FBI files took most of the morning. A few items changed and I added them to the 3x5s. A key to deciphering a puzzle: Don't believe everything you read, even if it comes from "official records." As the old saying goes: The winner gets to write the history book.

D B Cooper FACTS ONLY
1971. Thanksgiving Eve.

Page
107

Boeing 727-100

Flight 305

Cooper dressed in dark suit, white shirt, tie and hat (fedora)

ORIGINAL COMPOSITE SKETCH OF COOPER DOESN'T SHOW ENOUGH HAIR.

HAIR WAS MARCELLED (WAVY)

Paid $20 for ticket from Portland to Seattle, one way

37 passengers and five crew

FACT CORRECTION: FBI and OTHERS STATE ONLY FIVE CREW.

OTHERS CLAIM THERE WERE ACTUALLY SIX INCLUDING FIRST CLASS STEWARDESS

Hijack note saying he had a bomb

FBI CLAIM THERE WAS ONLY ONE NOTE.

OTHER CREW SAY THERE WERE TWO.

Briefcase with two red cylinders and wire

ORIGINAL SPECIAL AGENT IN CHARGE SAYS THE BOMB WAS FAKE: DYNAMITE AT THE TIME WAS MANILA COLOR, NOT RED AS STEWARDESS REPORTED

Demanded $200,000

Wanted two parachutes and two backup chutes

ONE CHUTE WAS A PRACTICE FRONT (SAFETY) CHUTE WHICH WOULD NOT HAVE OPENED.

PRACTICE SAFETY CHUTE MISSING AFTER COOPER PRESUMABLY JUMPED.

Ordered plane to circle until chutes and money delivered

Demanded $20 bills — weighed 21 pounds

FBI NOW CLAIMS COOPER DIDN'T ASK FOR $20 BILLS.

WASN'T SPECIFIC ABOUT DENOMINATIONS.

Most bills started with "L" series and dated 1969

FBI microfilmed all 10,000 bills

FACT CORRECTION: FBI DIDN'T MICROFILM THE BILLS. NORTHWEST'S BANK HAD THE BILLS STASHED IN CASE OF A HIJACKING OR EMPLOYEE KIDNAPPING.

LIST OF BILLS PUT INTO A 34 PAGE BOOKLET. NOT IN SEQUENCE. THREE COLUMNS. VIRTUALLY IMPOSSIBLE FOR SOMEONE RECEIVING A $20 BILL TO CHECK AGAINST THE LIST.

Cooper refused military or sport chutes with automatic opening

Plane landed at 5:39 p.m.

Passengers and one attendant disembarked through rear stairs

FACT CORRECTION: PASSENGERS AND TWO ATTENDANTS DISEMBARKED.

Cooper ordered altitude of 10,000 feet, flaps at 15 degrees and speed of 150 knots

COPILOT SAYS THE AIRCRAFT FLEW AT 175 KNOTS

Agreed to refuel in Reno on way to Mexico

WITH FLAPS AT 15 DEGREES, LANDING GEAR DOWN, 10,000 FEET ALTITUDE, 727 HAD A RANGE OF ONLY 1,000 MILES.

Cooper agreed to alter his route to avoid the Cascade Range, Mt. Rainier (14,411), Mount St. Helens (9,677 feet) and Mount Adams (12,276 feet)

Flew west of the high peaks (Vector-23)

Cabin left depressurized

CONFLICTING REPORTS: PILOT SAYS CABIN WAS

DEPRESSURIZED AFTER TAKE OFF.

FBI CLAIMS THE CABIN WAS NEVER PRESSURIZED.

Took off at 7:46 p.m.

No peepholes in cabin door

Aft stairs UNLOCKED at 8 p.m.

At 8:24 Aft stairs deployed, plane genuflected

Captain ID'd the location: Lewis River, 25 miles north of Portland

PILOT LATER SAID THEY WERE OVER THE CASCADES WHEN HE BELIEVES COOPER JUMPED

BUT COULDN'T HAVE BEEN AT 10,000 FEET

Air temperature 7 degrees below zero

FBI FILES SAY SKY WAS CLEAR WHEN COOPER JUMPED.

SAME FILES SAY CHASE PLANES COULDN'T LOCATE 305 BECAUSE OF HEAVY CLOUDS.

Plane traveling at 170 knots 195 mph, according to FBI

Plane touched down in Reno at 10:15

WRONG TIME AND OR DISTANCE AND OR SPEED

Passenger cabin was empty

Missing: Hat, overcoat and briefcase, cash and one set of chutes

ALSO MISSING: A PAPER BAG BROUGHT ON BOARD BY COOPER.

Nylon cords of one parachute missing

In the cabin: Cooper's tie, tie tac, Raleigh cigarette butts, spare chutes.

66 fingerprints left behind. FBI says they led nowhere.

I puzzled over the inconsistencies, ordered two more *Dos Equis* and a cheeseburger. The green lights on the alarm clock/radio blinked to 12:47.

Inconsistencies always make a set of clues untrustworthy, throwing doubt on what seems to be solid information. Piece by piece, any one of the clues could be wrong.

Knock on the door.

Opening it, "Very Special Agent Frankie Blue," tongue firmly planted in cheek, "good afternoon."

She stood in the doorway, alone. Looking very official in her FBI uniform of dark jacket, white blouse and dark skirt. Hard to miss the skirt. It seemed a bit on the short side.

"You have knees."

She ignored me, pushed into the room. Looked around. "Dang it's warm in here."

"Actually, 71 degrees."

"And I presume that's the reason for the shorts and T-Shirt?"

"It's 71 degrees. I work best this way."

Closing the door, "Where's Special Agent Kenny?"

"He got a cram notice this morning. He's on his way to the mayor's office."

She walked around the room, stood next to the desk and looked at the mess I'd created including the 3x5 cards, yellow-pad with notes and the open laptop with the FBI logo on the screen.

"Been busy." Statement, not a question.

"Yes, Agent Blue, I have been very busy trying to unravel what the FBI tangled."

Her eyebrows – as blonde as her hair – rose and a frown came and went from her expression in a blink.

"Such as?" she asked.

I pulled up a second chair and she plopped into it.

"Oh, golly, where should I start?" I can do the harmless country boy routine with the best of 'em. "How about the typical FBI claim jumping. You guys didn't microfilm the cash, the bank did. Conclusion, Nothing important, but Cooper expected the money to be at the airport when the flight arrived. Or shortly thereafter. That means he either knew the cash was being held in reserve for such situations OR he was dumber than a fence post and had no idea how quickly he could get the money."

"So?"

I knew I'd have to start at the beginning.

"Okay, let's do this a different way. From the top. The FBI has spent lots of hours, years, manpower and analysis on tracking down Cooper. But it didn't do its job when it came to the actual crime."

"Of course we did. The man got away with 200,000 bucks. He jumped from the plane. Landed and disappeared."

"See, that's what I mean. You went directly from the crime to the escape. To the aftermath of the crime."

I started again, "Let's say you buy a jig-saw puzzle and the box shows a pretty yellow flower in a red picture frame.

What's the first thing you do?"

Blue thought about it for a second, "You find the edges of the puzzle and put them together."

"Right. You do the easy stuff first. Then build inward. What if you find an edge piece of the puzzle that's blue instead of red?"

"Something's wrong."

"*Correctomundo*. Either the picture on the box is wrong or the puzzle piece is wrong. What we have with Cooper is a blue piece of the puzzle. Lots of blue pieces. But the FBI built the frame – the crime – WITH the blue pieces mixed with the red. Some of the facts don't add up. You guys did the Three Cs. You looked at the crime using *conventional* crime experience. That's the first C. You reached *conclusions* based on that experience. And then you filled in the blanks with *crap*."

"I don't buy it."

"Okay, Special Agent Blue, how long does it take to fly from Seattle to Reno?"

She thumbed the files on the desk. "Isn't it in here? Here it is. 2 hours and 29 minutes from lift off to landing."

I leaned over the computer and clicked on one of the open tabs in my browser. On the screen, a TravelMath.com web site showing a small calculator that allows for point of departure and landing, inputting air speeds in either miles per hour or knots and other user changes.

The flight time from Seattle, Washington to Reno, Nevada is:

2 hours, 50 minutes

"The *co-pilot* says they were flying at 175 knots. See that in the lower right?" She nodded. "That's 201 miles per hour. At that speed, the time to Reno is two hours and 50 minutes. More than 20 minutes longer than the official report.

"Now look at the *FBI*'s 170 knots."

I changed the figure which lowered the speed to 195 miles per hour.

The flight time from Seattle, Washington to Reno, Nevada is:

2 hours, 55 minutes

From: Seattle, WA   1 traveler
To: Reno, NV
Depart: Jan 19
Return: Jan 22
Get: flight + hotel   SEARCH

Get: flight time
From: Seattle, WA
To: Reno, NV
CALCULATE

2012 Chevrolet Sonic www.chevrolet.com/Sonic
Introducing the All-New Chevrolet Sonic. Learn More on Official Site.

Holiday Inn Reno NV www.HolidayInn.com
Book your hotel accommodations in Nevada. Official site.

Reno Hotels Reno.Hotel.net
Deals in Reno Nevada United States. Compare Prices and Save up to 75%.

Eugene Deals www.Groupon.com/Eugene

Change your flying speed:
195.63 mph   170 knots
314.84 km/hr   Update

Travel Math on Facebook
Like 5,795

"The flight time is now 2 hours and 55 minutes. At that speed, the drop zone just moved about 13 miles compared to what the co-pilot said."

"I'm getting it, Nick. And if the plane had flown at Cooper's demanded 150 knots..." she leaned across me and pumped in the lower air speed, "the flight time would have been three hours and 19 minutes."

The flight time from Seattle, Washington to Reno, Nevada is:

3 hours, 19 minutes

She thought about it for a second, "Holy Jesus. That's a solid 30-minute difference from the co-pilot's estimation of air speed."

"And here's the clincher. The actual time from takeoff to landing is, as you said, 2 hours and 29 minutes."

I pumped in a new airspeed to get the time down to the official number.

The flight time from Seattle, Washington to Reno, Nevada is:

2 hours, 29 minutes

From: Seattle, WA | 1 traveler
To: Reno, NV
Depart: Mar 8
Return: Mar 11
Get: flight + hotel | SEARCH

Get: flight time
From: Seattle, WA
To: Reno, NV
CALCULATE

Cheap Flights from $65 RT www.travelzoo.com/flights
Airlines have slashed fares on routes across the US.*

Cheap Fares Up To 65% Off CheapOair.com/Affordabl
Lowest Airfare Guarantee + Get an Extra $15 Off.
Hurry,Book Now!

Reno Hotels Reno.Hotel.net
Deals in Reno Nevada United States. Compare Prices and Save up to 75%.

Payless Car Rental www.PaylessCar.com/Orlando
Save more on Car Rental in Orlando on

Change your flying speed:

230 mph | 199.86 knots

370.15 km/hr | Update

Travel Math on Facebook
Like 6,890

"Does that say 230 miles per hour?"

"Sure does, Blue. Sure does. So all the talk about Cooper being an expert parachutist is bunk. Any skydiver or pilot worth his salt knows the difference between 172 miles per hour and 230 miles per hour. And to answer the obvious question, no there is no time change that would make the length of the flight appear to be longer or shorter by an hour."

Leaning back in my chair, "So, Cooper would have been jumping into a dark, overcast night with a temperature of minus 7 degrees and no chance of seeing landmarks other than major city lights. At a speed he had to know was way more than the one he demanded. Or the FBI reported.

"Now add another blue puzzle piece: The rear stairs were unlocked at 8 p.m. but the pilot says the plane didn't genuflect – which the FBI *assumed* was when Cooper jumped – until 8:24. That suggests he knew where he would be if the plane was cruising at 150 knots, which he demanded. Instead, he was at least 30 and as much as 120 miles from where he thought he should be."

"Or he actually could see in the dark. Stood on the stairs and waited for a siting of, say, Portland," Blue said.

"No, that means he would have been standing in minus seven degrees for nearly a half hour. In a polyester suit? Maybe if he was Special Forces trained for sub-zero weather or if he had a High Country parka and some damn good cold-weather underwear."

Blue frowned, "Which brings up another issue: If he asked for money, a knapsack and parachutes, why not ask for cold-weather gear? Parka and snow pants and wool-lined boots. Gloves."

There's a puzzle piece I missed.

"Good point. Now you're thinking outside of the 'conventional.'"

Here's another blue puzzle piece," I slid the "Facts Only" list towards her. Pointed at the Captain's statement that the jump location was over the Cascades.

"So?"

"Go back to this," pulling a page from the official file. "It says Cooper agreed to Vector 23 to *avoid* the Cascade Mountains, at the pilot's insistence."

Another knock on the door. Room service rolled in a

cart with my burger and beer. Tipped the guy a fiver and pulled the cart to the desk between Blue and me. I cut the burger in half, slid it onto a small bread plate and offered her one of my *Dos Equis*. She agreed.

"This is fascinating, Nick. It doesn't change much, as far as I can tell, but it certainly puts a different light on who the actual Cooper is." She took a long slug of brew and pushed back in her seat. "If he didn't ask for cold weather clothes, was he stupid or just forgetful?"

"At this point, could be either, but I doubt it. But it leads to the third C."

"Which is?" Blue asked.

"Crap. Filling in the blanks as the need arises." Popping the top on the Mexican beer, "With all the manpower and long history of so-called analysis, don't you think someone along the way would have thought about the parka and other cold-weather gear? Or seen the discrepancy between the pilot statements about where Cooper jumped?"

"Sure would seem so."

"But it didn't stop the Super Duper Special Agent in Charge from ignoring a fact that might have led to revised thinking about the entire crime. Just as the Bureau said there were clear skies to explain how he jumped based on seeing landmarks. That piece of the third C would bury the argument about speed vs. distance because it allows Cooper to pick a time and spot to jump.

"On the other hand, your guys blamed stormy skies to explain not being able to see the 727 from chase planes. Even though radar had Flight 305 on screen the entire time to Reno. And the list goes on."

She pulled another slug of *Dos Equis*. "And just this bit of information kills off the notion of an accomplice because Cooper wouldn't have landed where he planned to be picked up."

"Well, actually, he could have had an accomplice in the planning stages, but in actuality, you're right. He would have landed someplace far different from where that accomplice would have been waiting. Besides, he was willing to change the flight path. A clear indication he didn't expect to be greeted with open arms by a friend, relative or co-conspirator."

I pulled out the card with the known fact and slid it across the table:

Cooper agreed to alter his route to avoid the Cascade Range, Mt. Rainier (14,411), Mount St. Helens (9,677 feet) and Mount Adams (12,276 feet)

"Now, if I could punch holes in these so-called facts with a lap top and a few hours of Google searches, what do you think a defense attorney is going to do to the Justice Department case again McCauley?

Blue dabbed her mouth with a napkin, "Poor investigation equals reasonable doubt. And a big false prosecution award." Shaking her head, blonde hair brushing her neck. "Great."

We both went silent for a couple of minutes, only the hum of the climate controlling heater fan as company. Then

I asked, "How long have you and Ken been together?"

She nearly choked on the beer. "Ken and me?"

"It's pretty obvious you two are close. Feeding him pieces of bagel and splitting your sausage. You're constantly touching his arm..."

She laughed mightily. "I've known Ken all my life. Literally. We were *together* for nine months, Nick."

"Not together anymore?"

"Of course we are. We're twins, you dolt. I'm two minutes, six seconds older." She laughed again. "Boy, talk about blue puzzle pieces in red puzzles."

My face flushed.

"I need a chili cheese dog."

One day back a couple of years, Sal got the notion he wanted a Wienerschnitzel hot dog. A quick search of the Internet showed there weren't any in Oregon. The closest was in Vancouver, Washington. A tidy 260 miles from home and, according to MapQuest, a 4 hours and 59 minute drive.

We did it in 4 hours 11 minutes, thanks to the Crown Vic and clear roads.

Blue and I were in the CV pulling out of the parking structure.

"Strange wheels."

"You got a problem with flames and side exhaust?"

"No, and I've spent many an hour in Crown Vics. Cop

versions, though. I get the flames and side exhaust. The chrome wheels. Even that little wingy thingy on the back. It's just not what I expected you to be driving."

"That's a spoiler, not a wingy thingy. And what would you expect me to drive?"

"Jeep of some sort. Probably a Wrangler. Maybe an old Grand Wagoneer or an International Scout. I learned to drive a stick shift in my dad's Scout."

"Did the Wrangler. One of my sons rolled it. I always pictured myself as the Maserati kinda guy."

She snorted. An actual, derisive snort. Not very ladylike.

"How many kids do you have?"

"Five."

"Lot of kids."

"Each has his or her own quirks. Love 'em all. How about you? Blue is a married name, I take it?"

We pulled onto Naito and picked up I5 North. Traffic was light, an oddity for Portland.

"For about six years. Barry was a Sheriff's deputy in Montana."

"That where you're from?"

"Small town. Rural."

"So you married a deputy. Let me guess, your father was in law enforcement."

"County Sheriff. How'd you know?"

"Wild guess. Makes sense." I merged into the fast lane and pressed the accelerator. The CV exhaust bellowed and we rolled up to an easy 80. I really wanted that Wienerschnitzel. "Any brothers or sisters?"

"Older brother. He's the new County Sheriff since dad retired."

"So how'd you and Ken become Special Agents for the F... B... I..."

"You say that like you don't like us?"

"Little arrogant. What's with the 'special' thing?"

She laughed. "They don't tell us that stuff at Quantico. Just that we are."

"So, you married a deputy and, what, it didn't last?"

"Barry was killed when he stopped a speeder who just so happened to be on meth. Shot in the neck. Died on the spot."

"Sorry."

"So am I."

We went silent for at least 10 miles. Thought I'd give her some room.

"Nick?"

"Yeah."

"I read your file, and the file on your wife, Cookie."

"She has a file, too?"

"Everyone has a file. Some are just bigger than others. Remember? Higher than a mission bell. You two, on paper, are pretty compatible, it seems. But why is that? What makes..."

"Holy crap! Say that again!"

"You two are compatible?"

"No, about the Mission Bell. Higher than a Mission Bell. It was sung by Gene Pitney."

"And Donnie Brooks, why?"

"Helen. Not a mountain, not a saint. Helen Reddy. What's she known for?"

"Easy. *I Am Woman*. That's what launched her career."

"*Correctomundo*, Blue. The clue about Helen. Could D. B. Cooper be a woman?"

I could hear the doubt in her voice. "Well, there was one suspect who was a transsexual. Or at least wanted to be changed from man to a woman. Name was Barb something."

"Yeah. Saw that. A dare-devil small-plane pilot who wanted to get his commercial wings. It's in your FBI files." My voice was getting that excited edge I never try to show. "He became a woman. Hated the FAA for not giving him the chance to fly the big planes."

"Uh, name… name… name…" She almost had it. "Dayton! Barbara Dayton!"

Running the files through my head, settling on the Dayton guy/woman.

Bobby Dayton, a real bad-ass from way back, would spit on your shoes just to see how'd you react then beat the hell out of you regardless of what you did or said. As a merchant Marine, he would take middle-of-the-night trips to the bow of the ship and slip on a dress and high heels. Said he felt more like a woman than a man. Started living as Barbara Dayton.

As a woman, he was *uhg-lee*. Tattoos, bad teeth. But on

her deathbed, she claimed to be D. B. Cooper. Friends – the few she had – believed her. Her personality fit that of someone who would be willing to hijack an airliner and jump into minus 7 degree weather to escape.

"Yeah, but she's dead."

Blue's voice went soft. "Doesn't rule her out, though, right?"

"No, guess not. But then who sent me the package?"

We crossed the Interstate Bridge across the Columbia and under the only stoplight between Mexico and Canada on I-5.

We picked up NE 78th and headed east past farms, flat lands and grassy fields. The occasional barn made it feel like the rural Midwest as much as Washington or Oregon.

Within a few minutes we were pulling into the Wienerschnitzel, a tidy off-white and red building across a side-road from a Shell station sandwiched between the W and a Krispy Kreme Donuts outlet.

Sal would be in heaven. Cookie would recoil in abject horror.

Parked, walked into the empty restaurant, the smell of W-Dogs filled the air. I took a long inhale and wished Wienerschnitzel had a beer license. I could spend hours in a place like this if *Dos Equis* – heck, even Budweiser – was available and ice cold.

Caught Blue taking sideways glances at me.

"What?"

"I can't believe you live on this stuff."

"There are people who live on bugs."

The kid behind the counter was maybe 17. Thin as a rail and a tad over five and a half feet tall.

"Can I help you?"

"Three chili cheese dogs for me and a large drink."

He dutifully wrote it down on a pad then looked at Blue.

"Uh, one chili cheese and a small drink."

"Name?"

"Nick." He scribbled that on the pad. Told us the price which I paid. Took my change and remained on the customer's side of the counter since no one else was waiting in line.

He snapped off the sheet from the order pad, turned and hung it on a spiral twirly thing, raced behind the half wall to the kitchen, spun the twirly thing to the grill side, pulled the order from the clip and carefully read what he had just written as if he had never seen it before.

Blue and I watched as he built the dogs, put them in their paper sleeves and slid them under the heat lamp. He then scurried to the customer greeting counter. Put the dogs on a tray. Reading the name on the order sheet, turned to face the empty restaurant. Looking past us, "Nick! Your order is ready!"

"Uh, kid, I'm right here."

He smiled the perfect food service grin. "Thank you for eating at Wienerschnitzel."

We sat at one of the plastic tables. While I opened the

dogs one at a time and downed big bites with some orange soda, Blue picked at her W-Dog as if it had raging botulism, first tasting the chili with her tongue then nibbling at the wiener.

"Not bad, actually," she said, finally taking a healthy bite.

"Nothing like a Wienerschnitzel."

Finishing the dogs, scrunching up the wrappers and leaning back in the plastic bench, "I want to go over the clues with you and Ken. Run my thoughts by both of you."

From behind the order counter, the kid looked across the still empty restaurant, "Is there a Nick here?"

All I could do was shake my head. "Over here, pal."

He swung his gaze from the empty tables to ours. "Are you Nick?"

"Yes, I still am." Climbing from the booth, "What do you need?"

"There's a guy at the drive-in window asking for you."

Alarm bells. I turned toward Blue and signaled her to go outside and around to the drive-thru.

I walked behind the counter and edged toward the window. In a tan sedan, two men. The same two who trussed me up in my bed. The Russians. Both had their hands in plain view, telegraphing no guns were involved.

I still pulled the Magnum from my waist band holster in the small of my back. Pushed the kid aside and with the Taurus below window-sill height, leaned toward the opening.

"Could I interest you in our bacon wrapped, apple-wood smoked Street Dog?"

"Mr. Drago, we got off to a bad start."

"You think?"

"We want to apologize for the rudeness we showed in your hotel room."

The talker wore a gauze bandage on his nose where I'd hit him with his own gun.

"We are in dire need to talk to your friend Sal Rand. Can you help us find him?"

I could see Blue circling behind the sedan, gun at her side. A Glock 9 mm semi-auto. Standard FBI issue. Nice weapon.

"Tell me what it's about and we'll see."

"Mr. Drago, my government needs Mr. Rand's assistance. Please."

I'm all for politeness. The 'please' got me. "Okay, across the street on the other side of the gasoline station is a donut shop. Ever eat a Krispy Kreme?"

He stumbled over the words. "Krispy…"

"Never mind. It's over there," pointing in the direction.

"Da."

The sedan pulled away. Blue squinted and turned her hands palm up. Well one hand. The other had the Glock in it. As if to ask, "What's up?"

She met me at the Crown Vic, climbed in and we drove the couple of hundred yards to the Krispy Kreme, parked and went inside. The two Russians were standing in the middle of the store looking around as if it were their first time at the rodeo.

Blue and I walked to the counter. I ordered a dozen glazed and four coffees. Paid and moved to a table, Blue and the Russians not far behind. Lifting the lid, snagging one of the donuts and downing it in a couple of bites, I pushed the box toward the bigger Russian. He took a bite.

"Da. Good."

Blue and the second Russian grabbed glazed and napkins.

"Okay, tell me why you need to find Sal."

The Russian gave an abrupt nod and wiped donut from his mouth. "You know woman Tatiana Malacova?"

"Sure. Sal's one-time girlfriend. She saved my hiney once."

"Da. She disappeared. She uncovered some very sensitive information about an old Soviet, um, situation. We believe…"

"Disappeared when?"

"Three months ago. Poof. Gone to wind."

"In the wind," I corrected. "Or gone to ground. One or the other."

"In wind. She holds very important post inside Russian government. For her to disappear is not good."

"Thought she defected or something?"

"No, never suspected a lack of loyalty, but we had no answer to why she was missing."

That puzzled me. Tatiana's new position inside the

former Soviet Union was crime investigations. Not knocking over a deli or regular police matters, rather big crimes. Lots of money involved. Mob-connected. Often international. The tall, leggy Eurasian had hooked up with Sal, but wanted to get home to the Moscow.

"What's her family say?"

The Russian's eyes went dark. "I am brother. She is sister. She said nothing about leaving. Just not there anymore."

"You're Yuri?"

"Da."

"She talked about you a lot."

"Da. We are close. She and I."

"You work in the Internal Security Section, I think she said."

"Da. Similar to your Homeland Security."

Blue asked, "What was she working on?"

Yuri shook his head. "Tatiana not one to talk about job. Too, um, hush."

"Hush, hush. Two hushes. One hush means to be quiet. Two hushes mean it's a secret."

"Ah. Then hush, hush."

I turned to the second Russian. "And you are?"

"Other brother. Marcus. I, too, work Internal Security Section."

"Seems the whole family is on the government payroll."

Marcus smiled. "As was our father and his father. Very

good jobs. Very hard to get."

Blue interrupted again, "And you have no idea what your sister was working on?"

"None. Just disappeared."

My turn. "And you think Sal can help find her."

"Da."

"Sorry, guys, but I have no idea where Sal is. He's in the wind, too."

The disappointment spread across both men's faces. "You will help us find him?"

"Absolutely. Tatiana is a close friend of mine."

Blue said, "I'll help, too."

Yuri said, "You are FBI. Agent Francis Blue. We have file on you."

Blue flushed. "You do?"

"Da. Have file on all FBI agents."

I shook my head. "One of these days I've gotta find the building where all these files are kept. It's gotta be the size of New Hampshire."

The glazed donut box exploded. A slug also about the size of New Hampshire tore through the plate glass window, ripped through two coffee cups, the donut box and took out one of the pastry display cases.

The four of us hit the floor, almost simultaneously. Guns drawn. The glass was still cascading from the window frame when a second slug creased the top of the table and plowed into the floor.

Yuri and Marcus scrambled left. Blue and I scrambled

Page
131

right with me heading for the door on my hands and knees. Caught a glimpse of a silver SUV peeling out of the parking lot, electric window going up. It bounded onto the street, cutting off traffic, and raced north. No other threats, as far as I could tell.

"Clear!"

We all stood up and stared out of the window.

I turned and looked around the store.

"Everyone okay?" receiving nods from the employees and a couple of customers, some still standing, others peeking out from behind display cases. Everyone with their mouth open.

"Good. Then donuts and coffee for the house on me."

CHAPTER TEN

The Russians wrapped a couple of Krispy Kremes in napkins, left a cell phone number to reach them and said they were going back to their motel in Salem to decide what to do next.

Blue and I returned to Portland, grabbed some of the files from my hotel room and walked down to the waterfront. We packed into a couple of seats overlooking the marina at a RiverPlace coffee shop and spread the clue cards on the table. I ordered some onion crisps and a Colombian coffee. Blue picked out a Kona blend.

RiverPlace is one of those developments that work. Unlike Detroit, which never has been able to figure out how to best utilize its spectacular waterway, Portland succeeded in making urban living less overpowering with places like this. Condos, green space, loads of gardens and lots of retail shops using boardwalk-style exterior siding instead of steel and glass. Pretty impressive. At least to a country boy like me.

While Detroit overwhelms its river with high rises and lots of concrete, Portland uses its tall buildings as a distant backdrop to waterfront development. Good plan. Good execution. Too bad they have to raid the piggy banks of every rural community to do it.

But that's politics, I guess.

"Mind if I join you?"

Ken Valerio stood next to the table. Dark suit, white shirt, dark tie all neatly pressed and crisp. J. Edgar would be proud.

"Hey, Blue, it's Very Special Agent Kenny."

He took the seat across from me. "Agent Butterworth. Agent Blue. I hope you've had an enjoyable day."

Blue put her hand on her brother's, "You ever have a Wienerschnitzel hot dog?"

"And I can live long and prosper without ever trying one. Why?"

"No reason, but I have to tell you, Nick's file is correct. He is a cowboy."

Ken raised an eyebrow.

She filled him in on our trip to Washington including the Russians and the one-sided shoot out.

"You guys okay?"

Taking a long swallow of coffee, "No problem, Kenny." Patting the cards on the table, "I'd like to get your thoughts on these, though. Here's where we are."

I pulled one card to the side and pushed it toward Ken.

Not a mountain. Not a saint.

Helen of Troy

Helen the Barbarian

Helen Keller

Helen Reddy
Helen Hunt

"Your sister and I both think this refers to Helen Reddy, specifically the song 'I Am Woman.'"

"So you're saying D. B. Cooper was a woman?"

Blue answered. "Maybe. First hear this all out. It gets pretty interesting."

"There was this transsexual who claimed to be Cooper, but died some years ago. Meets the profile in most other ways, though. Name was Barbara or Bobby Dayton."

Skepticism crossed the Valerio's face.

Bandon head scratch. "Yeah, I know, it's slim. Let me continue and remember this is only a theory. We may be totally off base, but give it a second."

He asked, "Assuming for a second that Cooper was a woman, how did she pass as a man when everyone including passengers and flight attendants were certain she was male?"

"Marcelled hair. Olive complexion that could have been makeup. Who knows? Maybe she like Dayton was a transsexual or transvestite. Either way, it could make this clue pertinent."

I moved another card in front of Valerio.

Vestus virum facit
Clothes make the man (Latin)
What I'm wearing

What others are wearing
Uniform

Ken tapped the card. "A woman in a man's attire. Thus the Latin *'Vestus virum facit.'*" He pursed his lips, "Okay, let's go with that for the time being. You have a woman who is D. B. Cooper. Dressed as a man. If you could prove it, then the guy the FBI is about to hang clearly isn't the real Cooper. Still thin, though."

I pushed the photo copy of the letter across to Ken.

"Dear Nicholas:

As you may have read, the Federal and Washington State authorities have arrested Clarence G. Oates claiming he is D. B. Cooper, the famous skyjacker. They are wrong. I know this because I am the real D. B. Cooper.

You may well disbelieve my claim, but that doesn't make it any less true.

"I've enclosed eight cards with individual clues that will prove to you I am who I claim. It is imperative you decipher these clues and insist the authorities release Mr. Oates immediately. He and his family are innocent victims.

"Please hurry, Nicholas, before a serious injustice takes place.

"Warmest regards, D. B. Cooper."

"Note the salutation. 'Dear Nicholas.' Where I'm from, no guy is going to address another guy as 'Dear' and certainly wouldn't use his full first name. It would have been something like 'Hey, Nick' or 'Drago' or even 'Mister Nick Drago.' But 'Nicholas'? Not likely. It's something an older woman would say. Someone like a teacher from the '50s or '60s." Then pointing to the signature, "Nor is it likely a man would end the letter with 'Warmest regards.' At least not in the boondocks where I live."

"A woman, though, would use 'Dear Nicholas' is what you're saying."

"Correct." I pushed the photocopy of the envelope. "The writer also used the 'Mr. Nicholas Drago' in the address. Same argument."

Blue slid another card forward.

An appropos child's board game
Chutes and ladders
Monopoly
        Where's Waldo
        Guess Who
        Old Maid

She said, "Everyone assumes that this one is *Chutes and Ladders*. But is it? Someone suggested 'Old Maid.' Another reference to a woman."

Ken stretched his back against the chair. "Boy, that one really is slim. Who would have thought of Old Maid, for God's sake? Why's it underlined?"

My turn, "Because I thought it was the least likely answer to the clue. Now I'm not so sure."

"Besides," Blue pressed, "What does *Chutes and Ladders* have to do with the hijacking? Sure he used a parachute, but what's the ladder got to do with it that makes it 'appropos'?"

Ken pressed back. "Maybe if there was a partner, Cooper took the parachute; the partner went down the ladder." He shook his head. "Man, let's not overcomplicate this. We're verging on being too smart by half." His eyes ran over the rest of the clues. He was warming up to this little exercise of arm-chair crime fighting. "But this one…"

He reached across the table and thumbed another card to the center of the table.

Joe Friday has one
Gun
Partner
Badge
Distinctive voice
Acting ability
Monotone voice

"I'd take out the 'acting ability' because Joe Friday was a character. If it said 'Jack Webb has one', then I'd lean toward that possible answer." Ken stole an onion crisp from my plate. "From all the reports, Cooper didn't have a distinctive voice. In fact, no one recognized any accent at all. Nor was he a monotone."

I picked it up from there. "That leaves 'gun', 'partner',

'badge,' or some other answer we don't have yet or didn't think of."

Blue, "Of what's left, I'd go for 'partner.' There's always been a suspicion. One of the flight-deck crew or one of the stewardesses. And that goes better with the *Chutes and Ladders* thing."

Ken and I thought that over. With my yellow marker, I highlighted "Partner" but added a question mark. "Gun" didn't fit because there was no indication in any report or from the flight attendants that Cooper had a weapon at all, except for a couple of red sticks presumed to be dynamite (which the original investigation doubted because of the color).

Nor did he pass himself off as a cop or in-flight air marshal. Badge became less likely, as well.

"This is making me tired," I finally said. "And thirsty for a beer. How 'bout it?"

Ken cut Frankie off. "Agent Blue needs to come back to the office. People are beginning to wonder where she's been."

"Spoil sport," she said.

"That's my job." To me, "And you're gonna do what?"

"Get my stuff, go somewhere where they have beer and think. Head home and take a nap."

Ken nodded. "Well, think quick. This Cooper thing is coming to a head."

Blue was first to rise, put out her hand which I took. "Nice meeting you, Nick. Thanks for the hot dog and gun fight, as short as it was."

Back at Willow Weep. Shorts and a t-shirt, big ugly feet unfettered by shoes or socks, thermostat turned up to 72. Aroma of pizza filling the house.

Where was Sal? I needed the bearded giant to bounce ideas off of.

My cell phone buzzed. Text message.

"If you love me, you'll do what you know is right."

That was a woman's almost last resort. The old "if you love me" gambit. I wasn't playing.

"If you love me, you'll respect my decision not to."

Okay, it's a lame response, but geez, give me a break. I don't want the procedure.

The cards lay on the table.

I crossed out the probable losers and highlighted the most likely choices, underlining the least likely, but still active. Where nothing was determined, I left the list alone.

Not a mountain. Not a saint.

~~Helen of Troy~~

~~Helen the Barbarian~~

<u>Helen Keller</u>

Helen Reddy

~~Helen Hunt~~

Vestus virum facit

Clothes make the man (Latin)

What I'm wearing

~~What others are wearing~~

~~Uniform~~

An appropos child's board game

Chutes and ladders

Monopoly

~~Where's Waldo~~

Guess Who

Old Maid

Joe Friday has one

Gun

Partner

Badge

~~Distinctive voice~~

~~Acting ability~~

~~Monotone voice~~

I am not one of the three, but one of the three.

God

Religious reference

Out of the loop, in the loop

Three letters one of which is the letter "I"

Pilot, co-pilot, navigator

Three-in-one oil

Three wheel motorcycle

Trident

Little Bo Peep sheep
Black sheep of the family
Pitch fork
Kitchen fork
BBQ fork
WWII 97th division

Trident patch used by the 97th.

You can't find me. But I am there.
Hide and seek
Ghost
Peep hole
Hidden
Magician David Copperfield
Cute *(that had to be Mary Ann)*
Sleight of hand
Card tricks
Poker
Black Jack

Pick a card, any card
Four stacks, four aces on top
Something seems it's not there but is
Rabbit in a hat
Blood to water
Wine to blood

A song writing invisible rabbit
Harvey

I stared hard at the remaining cards. Lots of
alternatives, but when solving a puzzle, it's necessary to
turn a blank mind to the problem and let the answer come
to you like a memory you just can't grab hold of.

Putting the cards back in a pack, I flipped on the TV
and decided to watch some senseless sitcom. Settled on
"Big Bang Theory."

Dozed off and tipped over.

The thunderous sound of a small plane shook the Weep
and rattled the knick knacks on the shelves. I came off the
couch, rushed to the front window in time to see the dark
outline of a single-engine plane climb into the moonlight.

It was barely at 75 feet, skimming the roof of the house.
Nothing to distinguish it in the dark. Running lights off.
Smell of exhaust. Tree branches rustling in the backwash.
A single-engine prop plane the only real sense I got.

Art Spinella   Drago #4

Grabbing the Magnum, I slammed out the front door onto the gravel drive and watched the plane disappear over the trees, the sound of its engine fading.

Then the signal.

The strobe on the tail blinked on and off. On and off again. Then again. Three long streaks. The plane circled and dove back toward the Weep, buzzed the house and lifted over the trees once more.

I raced into the living room, exchanged the Magnum for a pen and a notepad and returned to the drive.

The plane's strobes repeated the three long flashes.

In the dark, the pilot swung the small craft toward Old Town to the south. I couldn't see it, but heard the engine evaporate into the night evolving from raucous to nearly silent. Then the vibration and buzz began a second crescendo. The pitch was lower. The pilot throttling back to a low speed. Barely enough forward motion to stay aloft.

Flying north, the lights blinked four short, paused, then four short. The light extinguished as the plane made a quick circle. Then groupings of five short, six short, one short, seven short, nine short and seven short. Each sequence separated by a second of darkness.

I was blindly making dots and hash marks onto the note pad hoping I wasn't overwriting or missing the page entirely with the pen.

As it passed overhead, I could barely make out the squared-off wings tipping east as the sound again disappeared; the pilot turning and taking a run toward the ocean.

Page
144

This time the strobe gave one long streak followed by two short blinks, four shorts, circled overhead with the light continuously on; one short followed by one short and three short, five short and two short.

The pilot spun the small plane into a circular pattern. I raced back inside and grabbed the flashlight from the desk, barreled back to the drive and aiming the LED toward the plane clicked the light on, held it for two second, off, then back on for another two seconds and again for two more second.

"Sal, you son of a gun!" I shouted at the disappearing plane. "Glad to hear from you!"

CHAPTER ELEVEN

"Yuri, you have been a loyal soldier for decades here. Unfortunately, some would say you have also become too friendly with our visitors."

The Russian thought, "*Visitors. Nyet. Prisoners, Da.*"

His superior could not be more than 40 years old. The most recent of only a few such men in charge of this facility. Uniform trim, tidy. Buttons only somewhat dulled. Hair a bit longer than at first, but the only barber an American named Joyce, now dead these three months. This God-forsaken place, Yuri thought. Born after the 169 prisoners were transferred in the dead of night to this confinement. Stripping them of their lives.

"As a friend, you have provided some of the visitors with amenities they would not otherwise have been allowed," the young officer continued, pacing wall to wall in his tiny office while Yuri stood at rigid attention. "We haf allowed such interaction because you were among the first to be assigned here and proved an influence in keeping the visitors compliant."

His voice rose as he spun on his heels and stared at the older Russian. "But this missing visitor. He was close to you, da?"

Yuri nodded. "Is true, a friend. After 30 years, one would naturally become close to others in this place. It would be impossible to do otherwise."

The officer exploded, "But he is now gone! He has escaped! And command will not understand how this could happen!"

Yuri flinched. "He has nowhere to go, Captain. As you know, over the past 30 years, others have attempted to escape. All have failed. Mort Brodsky will be no different."

"What kind of tattoos did you pen on this man?"

The question startled Yuri. Tattoos? He wants to know about tattoos? "Varieties," Yuri answered quietly. Obviously other *visitors* had told the Captain about the tats.

"What kind of tattoos, Yuri! Numbers, letters, words, birds, what?"

"Whales, Captain. Always whales."

"Whales?"

"Always whales, sir."

"Did he ever say why he wanted whale tattoos?"

Yuri shook his head. "Only that he found whales to be interesting creatures. As you know, he was allowed to watch movies. His favorites, he said, were sea creature related movies. *Moby Dick*. He talked often about *Star Trek IV – The Voyage Home*. It was his favorite. I watched it with him one time."

"Star Trek." The Captain mulled the title.

"Star Trek IV. The one about whales, sir."

Changing the subject, the young officer asked, "When did you see him last?"

"The day before he disappeared, sir."

"And he had you scribe another tattoo?"

"Yes, sir."

"Of?"

"A whale, sir. Another whale."

The officer closed his eyes and shook his head. His voice softened. "This is not going to go well for any of us, Yuri."

"No, sir."

"This could well end this facility."

"Yes, sir."

"And the remaining 16 visitors cannot be allowed to talk about their experiences here."

"No, sir."

The young officer allowed himself a long sigh. "That is all, Yuri. Dismissed."

As the old soldier began to leave the room, the captain asked, "Was there anything you assisted Brodsky to get that you haven't told me about?"

Yuri tumbled the question through his mind. Then, "Gorilla tape, Captain. He asked if he could somehow get a roll of Gorilla tape so he could bind his prayer book."

"Gorilla tape."

"Yes, sir."

"And whales."

"Yes, sir."

I tossed the notebook onto the side table, grabbed a *Dos Equis* and fell into the lounger. Staring at the hash marks and dots, I knew it was from Sal. The reason for the odd method of communication didn't matter. At least not yet.

As kids, Sal and I would devise codes that let us talk to each other in Mrs. Sworthberg's class. Called to the blackboard to decipher a math problem, we had a code using toe taps.

One of us would develop a code and dare the other to decipher it. Most were pretty lame. Some of our buds, knowing about our secret messages, tried to sneak a pig into our trough by writing a gibberish code and making one of us believe it came from the other.

To counter that move, Sal and I devised a simple plan. Coded messages would be sent in a letter. Under the stamp, hidden from view, would be the number 111 if it were from Sal or 222 if it were from me. Without the "signature," it meant the letter was a trick or the content of the letter was false.

The three long lights were Sal's way of saying "111."

If the stamps on our letters were upside down, whatever the note said was precisely the opposite. "Meet me at 5 p.m." actually meant "Meet me at 5 a.m." The opposite of "church", to our pre-teen minds, was the cemetery. We often sent notes praising Mrs. Sworthberg ("She has nice hair"), hoping she would capture the envelope and read our assessment, but not notice the stamp was upside down.

As for the rest of the mid-night message, I hadn't a clue.

On the notepad, I transcribed the dots and dashes from scrawls to precise hashes and dots.

- - - = Sal

.... = 4

.... = 4

..... = 5

...... = 6

. = 1

.... = 7

.... = 9

.... = 7

- = ?

.. = 2

.... = 4

O = 0

. = 1

. = 1

... = 3

..... = 5

.. = 2

The dash puzzled me. What was Sal saying? Was it a place saver or the beginning of a new message or what?

Putting the numbers into order, I wound up with:

44561797 dash 24011352

and converted those to letters with the "0" being a space.

DDEFAGIG dash ABD AACEB

No dice.

Pulling up an anagram solver program, I plugged in the first twelve letters and came away with 98 words.

FIDGED FIGGED GADDED ABIDE ADAGE ADDED AGGIE AIDED BAAED BADGE BIDED DAGGA FADED FADGE FIDGE GADDI GADID GAGED GIBED ABED AGED AIDE BADE BEAD BIDE DADA DEAD DEAF DEFI DIED EGAD FADE GADI GAED GAGA GAGE GIBE GIED GIGA IDEA ABA ADD AGA AGE AID BAA BAD BAG BED BEG BID BIG DAB DAD DAG DEB DIB DID DIE DIG EGG FAD FAG FED FIB FID FIE FIG GAB GAD GAE GAG GED GIB GID GIE GIG AA AB AD AE AG AI BA BE BI DE EF FA IF

The remaining five letters gave me:

ABA ACE BAA CAB AA AB AE BA BE

That was worth a whole lot of nothing. Sal wouldn't come up with a code that turned into mostly gibberish or was overly difficult to decipher or had so many loose ends it could be the proverbial ball of twine. Except for "badge", "dead," none of the words would lead me to Sal's meaning.

Pushed it aside, took another long swig of beer.

The gravel road gives an early warning of cars and trucks. Vibrations in the ground. Crunch of tires.

Opening the front door, Bill, the acting police chief, had just climbed from his Crown Vic and was walking up the drive. He waved.

"Hey, Billy. Sorry, Bill."

"Hi Nick."

"Reason for the late night visit?"

"Got off duty and thought I'd stop by."

He came into the living room and I pointed to the couch.

"Beer?"

"Sure."

"Help yourself to some pizza. Forte always does."

Bill leaned over the coffee table, slid a slice with one hand, a napkin with the other. He inhaled it before I got back with the *Dos Equis*.

"What's up?"

"Got a call saying someone tried to land on your roof. Santa, maybe?"

"You taking banter lessons from someone?"

He smiled, "Hanging around the Chief and you guys, it kinda rubs off."

"The plane didn't land, fortunately, but it gave off a strange set of dots and dashes using its strobe light."

"Morse code?"

"Nope. That was my first thought, but too many dots, not enough dashes. It was definitely from Sal, though."

"Sal's a pilot?"

"Strictly a passenger. Would rather be flown than drive the beast. Won't take a commercial airline because if one passenger out of 600 stops believing a 747 can stay in the air, it breaks the spell and sure as heck, it'll crash."

"Sal thinks that."

"With all his big, fuzzy heart." Another elbow lift of brew. "Want you to take a look at something."

Climbing from the lounger, I grabbed the notepad and tossed it across the room. Like any good ballplayer, he caught it with one hand while the other balanced the pizza slice. He put it on his lap and scanned the dots, dashes and anagram.

"Weird, Nick." He took a short swig of beer, spun the bottle to read the label, "Above my pay grade. I'm a buy-it-on-sale beer guy." Back at the notepad, "The words don't seem to mean much. I gather the highlights are common words?"

I nodded.

"How do you know this came from Sal?"

"The first three dashes are a code we set up when we were kids."

"Really? So, you finally heard from him."

"He loves me. Couldn't stay away."

Bill laughed. "If you say so. Could it be something other than letters?"

More crunching on the gravel. A knock on the door.

"Door's open!" I yelled across the room.

"Nick?" Blue asked, walking into the living room. Dressed in tight jeans, baggy sweatshirt and loafers, blonde hair showing that just-washed shimmer. She looked stunning. Bill noticed, choked on a bite of DiGiorgno's, blew nose-dribble onto my notepad and spit out the piece of offending pizza.

To Blue, "I think he likes you."

She stared at Bill, his uniform and said, "We Feds have that effect on small town cops."

Bill raised a hand, getting his throat clear, "Hi," he squeaked.

Blue scrunched up her nose, "Hi, back." Looking at the table, "Is that pizza?"

"You know anything else that comes in a box like that? Help yourself. Everyone else does. Beer's in the fridge."

As Blue passed Bill she ran a finger across his cheek which made me swallow a guffaw (yeah, that's a word) and Bill turn redder than a stubbed toe.

He silently mouthed at me, "Who's she?"

Blue returned to the living room with a *Dos Equis*, top

popped, and sat on the couch next to Bill.

"My friend wants to know who you are."

Bill shot me dagger eyes.

"I'm FBI Special Agent Francis Blue. Friends call me Blue." Seeing how easily Bill blushed, she leaned toward him and added, "Lovers call me Frankie. Or, OH FRANKIE!"

The look on Bill's face sent me into hysterical laughter. That hadn't happened since Cookie and Sal left.

Even more gravel crunching. Even more door knocks.

"*Heir ein!*" in my best German.

The door slowly opened. Two Slavic faces peered through the crack.

"Mister Drago?" one tentatively said.

Recognizing them, "It's okay, guys. You beat back the Germans in '42. Come on in."

Tatiana's brothers edged inside, eyes scanning both the room and the three of us.

I waved a hand to Yuri and Marcus to have seats.

"Gentlemen, this is Bill Monroe and you already know FBI Special Agent Frankie Blue. Mr. Monroe is acting police chief here in town. A good cop who learned the trade from another good cop. Bill, these are Tatiana's brothers Yuri and Marcus."

Bill beamed at the praise, shook hands with the Russians.

"What can I do for you?" I asked.

As in the Wienerschnitzel, Yuri did the talking while

Marcus struggled to mentally translate the conversation from English to Russian.

"We are at bitter end." (I didn't correct him.) "Between stone and harder rock." (I didn't correct him this time, either.) "We traced Tatiana to U.S.A. But after the shooting at the German sausage restaurant…"

That one I couldn't let pass. "Wienerschnitzel. It's an American fast food chain that makes hot dogs. And at the Krispy Kreme."

"Hot dogs, donuts, da. After shooting we drive to this village. It is where Tatiana stayed for a time last year."

"With Mr. Sal, yes?" Marcus added.

I nodded.

Yuri continued, "So we check Mr. Sal's house. It is empty." A puzzled looked crossed his face. "Why is there big gun in front of house?"

"Oh, the lawn ornament. Tatiana sent that to Sal as a present." I reached into the side table drawer and pulled out a photo.

"It's an FN Herstal medium remote weapon station," I explained, passing the picture to the Russians who passed it to Blue who whistled.

Bill just closed his eyes and said, "I didn't see that, okay?"

I pulled on my *Dos Equis* and continued. "Totally remote controlled. And that's an M3P machine gun your sister sent with the weapon station. Shoots roughly 1,100 .50 caliber rounds per minute. The turret can angle from minus 42 degrees to plus 73 degrees."

I took the picture back and stuffed it into the drawer.

Marcus nodded and pinched his lips together. "Tatiana like guns."

"Clearly so," Blue said, leaning back and draining her bottle.

Yuri asked, "Can you help us find her? She is very much in danger."

"What kind of danger? Do you have any idea at all?"

Both Russians shook their head, but Yuri said, "Serious."

My turn to sigh. "Okay. I got a message from Sal tonight before all of you showed up."

I passed the notebook sheet to Blue. The two Russians leaned over to read it.

"Looks like the anagrams are useless," Blue said. "Too

many short words. Not enough verbs. It would take longer to decipher a message from that than to just send a carrier pigeon or a note in a bottle."

More beer. More pizza. More head scratching.

"Anything in your high school codes that might apply?" Bill asked.

Thought about it. "Not really."

Blue's blue eyes blinked, then dimmed. "Thought it might be a lock combination, but there's nothing there that looks like a simple lock. Does Sal have some sort of super computer key code, maybe?"

I read the number out loud. 44561797 dash 24011352.

"Nothing I've ever seen him use, but who knows? It's not a birthday or social security number. Not enough digits for a phone number..."

"Is map coordinate!" Marcus blurted.

"Da," Yuri added. "Longitude and latitude. Make dash a number 1."

"Cripe, of course." I said, taking the paper from Blue. "Look. The plane was flying north when it gave these dots, then West with these." I circled each grouping. "That translates into..." scribbling on the pad:

44.56'17.97N

124.01'13.52W

"Is where?" Yuri asked.

I grabbed the laptop, plugged in my "Sal Wire" went to Google Earth and typed the co-ordinates.

Everyone stared at the screen. On it, the image of a beat

up building with a sign reading "Storage" and a phone number. I put a place mark on the photo.

Zooming out, "Lincoln City, Oregon."

Bill asked, "Sal's in Lincoln City? What the heck for?"

Blue blew out a long breath. "Is anything with you *not* a puzzle?"

Shrugging, I picked up my cell phone and began to dial.

"NYET!"

Marcus had come out of his seat and waved me off. "Not to dial!"

If I've learned anything in my recent dealings with covert ops people, they don't often panic and it's always better to heed their directions and ask questions later.

Disconnecting, "Why not?"

"If Tatiana or your friend wanted you to call the phone

number, the elaborate method of sending you a message would have been unnecessary."

"Marcus, my commie friend, you're right. So why did Sal go to the trouble of sky writing the location?"

Blue answered, "So it couldn't be traced. Electronic mail, land or cell phones, snail mail, teletype, all of those and more leave a digital or paper trail of some sort." The two Russians nodded. "You call that number, if your phone is tapped or even if it's not, someone somewhere can find either you or where the call was directed."

Digging deep into the crevices of my memory, "Echelon, right?"

Blue nodded. "It's able to intercept phone calls, faxes, any data that uses a satellite transmission, microwave or public telephone network," she explained.

"And it's real?" Bill asked.

"Yes it is, sweetie," she replied, still flirting. "There's even a thing called the Quantico Circuit which allows for direct access to all content and information about where a call is placed and who was called. The QC can also access the actual contents of calls. You may have just blown it by using Google Earth."

I shook my head. "No, this computer is hardwired directly to Sal's encrypted servers at his house." I lifted the Sal Wire. "He long-ago downloaded all of the Google Earth data. Along with most every other data base from Wikipedia to every government statistic known to man."

Leaning back, Blue shook her head. "A little paranoid maybe? Smart guy. So I think Marcus just saved your bacon. Or at least didn't let you unravel Sal's carefully conceived method of getting in touch with you."

I tumbled the info between my ears for a minute, "I'm hungry. Anyone for a grilled steak?"

Blue sighed, "We just had a giant pepperoni pizza."

"And your point?"

Buttered steak cooked on an open charcoal flame, garlic bread oven toasted, frosty beer and a handful of lettuce smothered in French dressing make for a great meal.

The two Russians ate like wolverines. Blue grunted her way through her pound of cow. Bill kept glancing over his plate at the FBI agent which caused her to give an occasional smile between slugs of beer. Me? I was the first one done, provided a silent burp in satisfaction (which, of course, everyone heard) and waited for the rest to finish.

Back in the living room, "Well, what now?" I asked. "Fly up to Lincoln City or drive?"

Yuri was first. "Drive." Marcus nodded agreement. "You think Tatiana is with Mr. Sal?"

"If anyone knows where she is, it'll be Sal."

Bill begged off, saying he had to get back to the daily Bandon police grind of chasing rabid raccoons. "Besides," he said, "I have to give the city council my answer about the chief job in a couple of days. Gotta have time to think about it some more."

Blue said, "I'll hitch a ride with you, Nick. Fly or drive,

if that's okay."

"Fine by me. I'm for driving even though I'd prefer to fly. If Sal went to the trouble of keeping his location off the books, it's likely the plane left from a private or government airfield. I'd have to file a flight plan. At the least, I'd leave a paper trail anyone could follow because the Cirrus will need to be fueled up. Someone interested in knowing I'm on the move wouldn't have trouble finding out if they know I own a plane."

"It's in the file," Blue said, only half jesting.

"Of course it is. And probably in the Russian files?" looking at Yuri and Marcus.

"Da."

"Guess we drive. We'll leave around 5 tomorrow morning. Be in Lincoln City for breakfast. That okay?"

Everyone nodded.

"Good. The Russians can stay at the Bunkhouse next door. Blue, you can take the guest room. Reveille at 04:30."

A survey of the top execs at the Fortune 500 companies found virtually all were early risers and always had been. Some people are wired to wake up early making the old English proverb, "The early bird catches the worm" an apt saying. For me, my best thinking is done way before dawn. Certainly before noon. After that, mental capacity shrinks to the size of a pea.

As the Crown Vic tunneled its way through the early

morning fog on Highway 101, all manner of thoughts went in and out of focus.

When Sal was called to secret duty and left me with that strange message about goldfish, I knew it was a heavy assignment. This trip to Lincoln City had to be part of whatever he'd gotten himself into.

D. B. Cooper hung by parachute cords in my mind's eye. A woman? Hard to believe.

Poor Karl with his horns of a dilemma about the true killers of the Coquille River paddleboat crew and what to do about revealing the family behind the murders.

The Cubs' restructuring the team to make another run at the World Series.

None was a complete thought, just pieces of a jumble, my mind skipping from one to the next to the next and back. A tangled extension cord.

Cookie's demand rankled me, even though I knew she was right. The Procedure is for, well, someone else, not me.

Coos Bay, Lakeside, Winchester Bay, Reedsport, Dunes City. All coastal towns that slipped by before the sun came up. All, in one fashion or another, now relying on tourism rather than logging or fishing to survive. Hourly wages that once tipped toward $30 an hour when that was 10 times minimum wage, now mostly a third or half that. Hard men and hearty women who once lived by sweat and calluses and muscle now hitched up their Wal-Mart britches to tackle motel room cleaning, lawn maintenance, or standing behind the counter of a trash and trinkets store hoping visitors would buy one extra set of tumblers with a lighthouse etched in the glass.

God love tourists who love t-shirts.

"Are we there yet?"

Blue was riding shotgun, half asleep, seat jacked all the way back, curled up like a cat. The two Russians in the back, eyes slammed shut, heads tipped onto the side window glass, thankfully not snoring.

"Couple more hours."

"Pit stop."

"We'll stop at Honeyman just before Florence."

The Honeyman State Park has a building on the lake deep in the woods built in the 1930s by kids shipped in from cities as far away at New York as part of the Civilian Conservation Corp., one of those programs to get folks back to work during the Great Depression. Stunning stonework and typical Oregon Parks Department first-rate maintenance make the 80 year old facility a gem. The visitor center has a plaque dedicating the building to those kids.

I pulled into the park, wound my way through the tall pines and pulled to a stop in front of the visitor center.

The Russians woke up, shook themselves and without a word piled out of the CV heading straight for the men's room.

"You don't think Sal's gonna be a bit upset with an FBI agent and two Russian homeland security thugs showing up?"

"Hey, two's company, four's a party."

She smiled, "You're not going?"

"Bladder of an elephant. Bet that's not in my file."

"I'll have to check."

She pushed open the door and headed inside the building.

When you're on a mission, it's always wise to keep an eye on the vehicles around you or never seem to be far behind. The silver SUV with the tinted windows tried to hide in the before-dawn darkness by staying at least a few hundred yards back. But in the dark even an observant klutz like me can ID a vehicle by the spacing and height of its headlights, its jiggle over bumps, the driver's constant attempt to match the speed of my car or maintain a set distance. I didn't want to leave the CV because of an enlarged bladder, rather to see if the SUV tagged along.

The Chevy Tahoe pulled into a parking slot a dozen spaces over. The doors didn't open. No one was making way to the restrooms. The shadows behind the dark glass remained motionless. Undefinable.

I had two choices. Confront them or let them continue following us. Confronting guys works if you have an idea of who or what they are, what weapons they're carrying, their number and skills. That requires a visual. Something I didn't have.

Yuri and Marcus returned first, climbed into the back and grunted some greeting which I hoped wasn't "Good morning" in Russian. Why was that an obsession with me and Sal? Okay, so Mrs. Sworthberg would enter the classroom and say "Good morning", but somehow coming from her it was a threat. Like, "Good last damn morning of your life. The firing squad will be here in a minute." Made me shudder. Sometimes the words not said are more worrisome than the ones that are.

Blue climbed into the front passenger seat. She had obviously run her fingers through her blonde hair. Looking in the rear view mirror, it was just as obvious the Russians hadn't bothered.

I backed out and headed for the highway. The Tahoe wasn't far behind.

Blue noticed my glancing in the rear view mirror. "Company?"

"Maybe."

Fortunately my windows are pretty darkly tinted, too. The two Russians turned to get a gander at the SUV. Neither said a word. Both pulled weapons, dropped the magazines to check the load. Blue reached into her handbag, pulled the Glock, setting it in her lap. Flipped down the sunvisor and opened the vanity mirror so she could see the Tahoe.

I pressed the accelerator and edged up to 75. The SUV ramped up its speed as well.

"Well, that answers that. They're definitely tailing us," I said to the others.

Across the Siuslaw River Bridge, the SUV stuck a hundred yards back. Florence gives the impression of being a bigger town than it actually is. Old Town District on the river is sprawling and has an assortment of businesses, bars and restaurants as good as any place on the Coast. The main drag through town feels like Orange County, California with trees pushed back from the highway and ample off-street parking.

I kept to the speed limit through the heart of the city and came out the other end on the same kind of two-lane blacktop that makes up most of Highway 101. Douglas fir hard up against the roadway, mixed with Alder, shore pine and the typical bramble brush.

A couple of miles north of Florence come the twisties through coastal mountains, almost always with a view of the ocean. For the travel trailer crowd, it's spectacular. For motorcyclists, it's a thrill. For someone trying to get away from men with guns, it's a pain in the ass.

The first bullet took out part of my spoiler. *Cha-ching.* There's a couple hundred bucks, I thought. Pushing the pedal halfway down and clicking off the overdrive, the CV's V8 spun up into the heart of its power curve putting some distance on the SUV. But the Tahoe's big V8 has torque. And on twisties, that's as important as horsepower. Maybe more so.

The Chevy closed the gap quickly. Now there were two arms sticking out of its windows, each hand with a gun. Each gun blinking flashes of gunpowder. Each slug punching a hole in the CV's deck lid. *Cha-ching.* At least a hundred bucks for each hole. This was getting expensive.

Yuri, Marcus and Blue each pushed down on their window switches. Thrust their arms out. Began a salvo of fire at the Tahoe. Me? I was hoping the CV could stick to the road through the curves at 80 miles per hour. Hoping the Tahoe couldn't keep up.

I was wrong.

Marcus took one in the hand. His nine-mil MP-443 Grach flew out the window, spinning wildly, clattering into the bushes along the road.

Yuri yelled, "Are good?"

"Da. Need weapon!"

"Under the seat!" I shouted over the wind and gun fire. Blue reached down, felt around and came up with my antique Colt.

She held it then looked at me. "A Peacemaker? Really?" Then handed it back to Marcus.

"Won the west! Yahooo!"

I always keep the Peacemaker under the seat. Habit. Big slugs. Lots of noise. Accurate as hell. Marcus put it to good use.

The first booming shot tore through the SUV's windshield, left of center. The hand out of the passenger-side window went limp, gun falling to the roadway.

It turned into a slalom race. Koni shocks, hefty anti-sway bars, Michelin tires won't turn a Crown Vic into a Porsche, but it's a hell of a lot more stable than a Chevy Tahoe. Hard left. 35 mph limit. Taken at 65. Blue and the Russians holding on like Velcro. The Tahoe fell back. Only to close the gap on anything that looked like a straightaway.

Another slug in the truck lid. Another in a taillight. One more in the bumper. *Cha-ching.*

"Hang on!!" I yelled as I stood on the brakes, the anti-lock system chattering the tires. The SUV swerved left to avoid a rear end collision. Caught a tire in the dirt, tucked it under and sent the Tahoe into one of those rolls where the roof never touches the ground until the last thundering crash. I wanted to get away from the scene as quickly as possible so I kept my foot on the gas and scurried through the curves as fast as a weasel in a drainpipe.

My cell phone rang.

Blue fumbled around the front seat, found it and answered, "Nick Drago's line."

You could smell the adrenaline and hear it in her voice.

"Just a second, please."

She handed the phone to me and whispered, "Cookie."

I hit speaker so I could talk and drive at the same time. "Hey, hon." I tried to sound calm.

"Who was that?" she asked.

"Special Agent Frankie Blue of the FBI."

"And she's answering your phone, why?"

"I was busy."

"What are you into, Nick?"

"Nothing important." I slowed down to 50 mph. My voice was quivering and I could see Cookie's eyebrows scrunch up, little slits of disbelief.

"You have a woman answering your phone?"

"And two Russian homeland security types in the back seat."

"Two Russians."

"And the FBI Agent."

The sarcasm was thick as pea soup. "So you're hanging out with government law enforcement these days. Care to share?"

"Uh, I'm just one of gang, you know?"

"Nick, you are a writer, not a cop or special agent or KGB spy or whatever they call themselves now. You are not one of them. 'Kay?"

Blue turned her head away from me, looked out the side window and began to giggle.

"Roger, that, boss. Can I call you back and explain?"

"Nick, there probably isn't a good explanation."

"No, really, there is."

"Whatever." She hung up.

Now I knew she was pissed.

Sal and I, after years of experience, found there are some key words women use.

1. *Whatever.* Is a woman's way of saying, "Go to hell."

2. *Fine.* Women use this to end an argument when she's right and you need to shut up.

3. *Nothing.* The calm before the storm. This means something, and you should be on your toes. Arguments that begin with "nothing" usually end in "Fine."

4. *Go ahead.* This is a dare, not permission. Don't do it!

5. *Loud sigh.* While not a word, it is a non-verbal statement often misunderstood by men. It means she's thinking you are an idiot and wonders why she is wasting her time standing here and arguing with you about nothing.

(See number 3 above.)

6. *That's okay*. This is perhaps the most dangerous statement a woman can make to a man. It means she wants to think long and hard before deciding how and when you will pay for your mistake.

7. *Thanks*. A woman is thanking you. Do not question or faint. Say "You're welcome." Caveat: If she says *"Thanks a lot"* this is pure sarcasm and she is not thanking you at all. DO NOT say "You're welcome" in response to "Thanks a lot." It will only get you a *"Whatever."*

8. *Don't worry about it. I'll do it.* Another dangerous statement meaning this is something a woman has told you do several times but is now doing it herself. This will later result in a man asking "What's wrong?" and getting a *"Nothing"* response.

"Trouble on the home front?" Blue asked, a laugh in her tone.

"Oh, yeah."

CHAPTER TWELVE

If a tsunami hit this part of the coast, the mayor of Lincoln City would be Captain Nemo. At only 11 feet above sea level, the town lives off of tourists and retirees, although it is one of the nicest destinations for inland Oregonians. Tidy and well run, with a great lake and two rivers nearby.

As with all rural towns, keeping the cash inside the borders always plays a major role in a community's survival. In Lincoln City's case, someone had the smarts to break down a major recreational area project into bite sized pieces that allowed local contractors and businesses to win bids and keep the bucks in the city limits.

We stopped at Mo's restaurant for breakfast. The Russians ate their way through two helpings of waffles, bacon, sausage, a half-pound of butter, hash browns and a pot of coffee.

"Don't they feed you in Moscow?" I asked.

Blue scarfed down nearly as much which would have made Sal proud. I didn't do badly myself.

Sal. Was he really here? He's as close to a brother as I'd ever get and I gotta admit, I was anxious to see the big man.

I paid with cash and we climbed into the CV.

A kid was walking around the car. "Hey, mister, are those real bullet holes?"

"Naw, my garage has a mice problem. They'll eat through anything."

"Really?"

"Cross my heart and hope to die."

"Wow. If it wasn't for those holes, that'd be a really neat car."

He wandered off taking an occasional glance over his shoulder at the Crown Vic and shaking his head.

The GPS showed the way to the spot we were looking for. Down a side street out near the high school. We passed a bright blue plumbing supply building and a lot filled with commercial trucks. On the right, the storage building with the sign attached, surrounded by a ratty chain link fence topped with barbed wire. The metal structure had maybe a dozen large garage-style doors and rusty rain gutters that were overflowing with debris. The adjacent dirt lot was littered with a half dozen travel trailers and motorhomes, most in scruffy repair.

We stopped at precisely the longitude and latitude in Sal's message, pulled to the side of the black top, rolled down the windows and waited.

For about an hour.

"Well, now what?" Blue asked.

"It's Sal. There's a reason. Not to worry."

The Russians were wiggling in the back seat, Yuri cleaning his semi-auto, Marcus spinning the wheel on the Peacemaker.

"Is good gun," he said.

"That one's from 1903. The first Colt Peacemaker was made in 1873."

"Cowboys used them?"

"Indeed."

"I wanted to be a cowboy when a child," Marcus said. "Shoot buffalo and fight with Indians and Jesse James."

The kid from Mo's parking lot, hands deep in his pockets, walked toward us, stopped next to my window and gave a hard stare.

"You Nick Drago?"

"Sure am."

He nodded. "Okay, pull into the lot and drive into the last stall. I'll meet you there."

"Who are you?"

He didn't answer, just walked along the chain link fence, around a short weatherworn wooden fence and into the lot.

I looked at Blue who shrugged, fired up the CV and idled to the designated doorway. The kid waited for me to nose up before pressing a button on the jam. The door slid up and he waved me in.

The interior of the storage unit, maybe 20-feet by 25-feet was painted gloss white and empty. Shutting down the CV, we all climbed out. The kid waved for us to follow him. He led us to a narrow door in the back wall, punched in a key code and I heard the metal click of a magnetic lock releasing. He held the door open as we single-filed onto a stairway leading down. Dim light of bare 40-watt bulbs spaced 10-feet apart. Just enough illumination to keep from tripping down the treds.

The magnetic lock latched and the kid squeezed past us to take the lead.

"Where we going?" I asked.

He didn't answer, just continued down the stairs.

About 30 feet below ground (my best guess), the stairway ended in a narrow corridor. Same light-bulbs, same dimness. Concrete walls, floor and ceiling. More bunker than hallway.

Echoes of footfalls the only sound. No one spoke. I nearly hit my head on the hanging lights so the ceiling was maybe 6-feet-10-inches tall. Anyone with claustrophobia would have begun screaming after 5 minutes. The smell of dank air, the slight downward slope of the floor, the shadows that repeated themselves each time we passed under a light.

After 15 minutes of walking, we reached another door. The kid punched a code into the key pad next to the handle, stood back and opened the door for us. Brilliant light beamed from the other side and in that light a big man with a big beard and a big smile.

"Hi, Nick. Glad you could make it. What's with the beard?"

Crossing into the brilliance of the room forced me to

squeeze my lids nearly shut.

"Took a trip to Ensenada. Felt like a gringo so I grew the beard to fit in."

"So now you look like a gringo with a beard."

My face was cracking with a stupid grin. I walked up to Sal and threw my arms around him. "Man, I thought you were gone forever!"

He thumped me on the back. "How are my goldfish?"

"They'll be happy to know you're still alive." I turned to the others, "Let me introduce you."

"No need," Sal said, putting his hand out to Blue. "Special Agent Francis Blue. An unexpected pleasure." To Yuri and Marcus, "Gentlemen. I think you will want to come with me."

It was my first chance to look at where we were. Walls concrete block. Ceiling, concrete poured. Floor white hospital tile. Two doors, one on each end of the opposite wall. No furniture, just a 12 by 12 foot cube.

"Where are we?" I asked.

"In time, Nick. In time. First, this way."

Sal led us to one of the doors and opened it with a key-swipe card. On the other side, a homecoming party.

Tatiana threw herself at her brothers, squealing in delight, chattering in Russian. A tall, sandy haired man leaning against a conference table.

"Holy Jesus, Chief!"

"Hi Nick. Good to see you."

I grabbed Forte by the shoulders, stared into his eyes.

He laughed, "I'm fine. I'm back. I'm sane, thanks to you, Sal and the U.S. military."

"And you're the one who flew over my house?"

"Of course. And Sal was my co-pilot. He was quite adamant I couldn't deliver a message to you without his able assistance."

Another voice, this one coming from a hallway in the left wall of the room.

"Hey, Nick, good to see you old pal, did you bring the *Dos Equis* or do I have to make a run to the store?"

Artemus popped out of the hall, same tan slacks, black Harley shirt, loafers and argyle socks. To Blue, "And you are the FBI's Special Agent Blue. I've read your file. Quite impressive." He took her hand and gave it a gentle shake. "Your pictures do you no justice."

Tatiana and her brothers were still chattering when Artemus broke in. "Yuri and Marcus. I've heard much about you two." He shook their hands, but his eyes had changed to hardened steel in a fraction of a second. "Your files are equally impressive." The tone said the Homeland Security Assistant Director wasn't happy to see either of the men.

Spinning on his heels, looking at the assembled crowd, "We should get down to the reason you're here, whether invited or not."

We were taken to a large conference room, at least 40

feet long, 30 feet wide. More like a small gymnasium. Tables lined one wall, drapes of plastic sheets covering whatever was on them. An electronic white board took up a third of one short wall with a dozen chairs set in a semicircle so occupants could see whatever was displayed.

I caught a whiff of air-freshening deodorant as I walked past one of the tables. Artemus directed me and the rest of the crew to a long conference table centered precisely in the middle of the space, surrounded by a dozen chairs, each position having a yellow pad, pen and water glass.

"Coffee?" I asked.

Sal pointed to a small alcove. "Get a big mug. This is going to take a while."

We stood in a raggedy line pouring coffee into plain white mugs and returned to the conference table. The low hum of HVAC filtered air and the sterile smell of a sub-basement. The lack of soft furniture in such a large space made even the slightest movement of a chair or the clink of a coffee cup against the pot reverberate off of the concrete walls.

"I'll bring our new arrivals up to speed," Artemus said, clearing his throat and losing his usual light-hearted, bright-eyed look. "We have an international situation that cannot go beyond this room. Period. Sanctions are in play. Do I need to explain what that means?"

"You talk, you die," Blue whispered. "Do I really want to be here?"

"Too late," Sal said. "Already cleared with your Director." To the Russians, "And you are now off the grid.

Even your bosses don't know where you are or what you will be doing. Clear?"

Tatiana repeated Sal's words in Russian to assure they fully understood.

Marcus looked at Yuri. Both nodded, "Da."

"Good." Sal stood and began pacing. "Let me fill you in. It all begins with files. Everyone has one."

He scooched back and looked at the ceiling. "It starts with a birth certificate. Then comes the Social Security number." He looked at me, eyes dim, "Ever had an inoculation for polio? Of course you have. More for the file. Over the years, medical records, school records, job and credit reports. Applications for college, speeding tickets, Facebook, God forbid, a police record. How do you think they make up that 'no fly' list used by airlines and Homeland Security?"

Artemus snorted. "That's the tip of the iceberg, Nick. Everyone needs a passport now. Bang, into the file. Pay for a meal with a Visa card. Send a 20 to your favorite political candidate. Skip a property tax payment. Like to Tweet negative comments about the President? Zap. In the file."

Breaking in, "Yeah, I get it, but that's just overload," even though I knew they were right. "How the hell do you keep all that info available? Pretty soon there's so much, even the biggest computers in the 'verse get stressed with too much information."

"That was a problem, sure, when it was on paper or early computers," Sal interrupted. "Within the past five years, most all of it is in the clouds. Server farms as big as a small state. Sucking gigajoules of power just to keep up."

Sal's voice had changed. Usually glib and almost mocking, it now contained stress and a hoarse note associated with not enough sleep.

"And if you think the info isn't there, you're wrong. It's all there. Every black wart and good deed and all manner of in-between is assigned to you and, you know what? I can get it all. Anytime I want. I can build a file on any human being in this country. Doesn't mean I know where you are at any given time, but once I have a name, the rest is a piece of cake. Most times I don't even need the name."

Artemus picked it up. "There are folks who want to be 'off the grid' by going solar or using only a generator or paying cash for everything. What happens when you, for example, stop using the power company for electricity? It's put in the file. A marker. Something our software can identify as a change of status. Sometimes that's a great indication of what you're up to."

He scratched a note on the yellow pad in front of him. Perhaps a reminder. "Only pay cash? Not a problem. We now can track cash flow down to a single street in a single small town. The slightest increase in cash sales or cash deposits from stores or services will send a signal that someone may be attempting to go off the grid. How do you think we know the size of the underground economy?"

He stood and walked to one of the tables.

"That said," he continued, we have a problem and a mystery which is why we had the military officer fetch Sal. And now we want to have you, Nick, as part of the team that finds a solution."

"Sorry, but what's the problem that needs a solution?" I asked.

"About eight months ago, Tatiana discovered something in the archives she was searching related to government funds being diverted," Artemus said, then looked at her. "Care to take it from there?"

"My job is now to trace criminal activity within the country. Oil barons and such. Many billions of dollars are missing or sent to what you Americans call 'safe haven' banks. I track so government can tax according to laws."

Tatiana rose and walked to the head of the conference room table where she could see all of us. As she passed Sal, her hand traced a path across his shoulder. It was an unconscious act, but one that clearly indicated the two had rekindled their relationship.

"In the ledgers for one of the oil companies, I found appropriations making no sense. These appropriations were unsubstantiated expenditures totaling more than $120 million each year since 1984."

"What was the company?" I asked.

"Also interesting. It was started that same year by two former KGB officials."

Marcus and Yuri looked at each other, the former frowning. "You said nothing to us?"

Tatiana smiled. "Brothers are for loving, not confiding." To the rest of us, "There seemed to be no source for this expenditure. The oil company had only a few minor assets and no debts. The two officials received funds from unknown places, turned and spent it on supplies."

"Supplies?" I said.

"Da. Food, clothing and what was listed as miscellaneous."

"Did you interrogate these guys?" Blue asked.

"No, no. Could not. One died in 1997. The other returned to government. Became deputy director of economic office. Very high powered circle of friends."

My turn. "How high?"

"Too high for my lowly position to question."

"And the company?"

"It was sold to another oil baron. Also with high contacts in the central government."

"But the payments kept being made," Sal said.

"Da, until the old Soviet Union collapsed," Tatiana replied.

"Then what?"

"Payments for supplies disappeared from books. Dead end."

"And what happened to the oil baron and the KGB guy?" Blue asked.

"Is good question, of course. Oil baron became even more wealthy. Was man behind Russian-Chinese oil pipeline. The former KGB official was sent to new position in energy bureau."

"So he and the oil guy were still in touch."

"Yes, Nick. But Boris Nicovich is more than energy

czar. Is responsible for international information gathering on other countries' energy plans. Has many moles in U.S., Chinese and European oil industries. It is said he has one Saudi prince on his payroll. Even has direct line to your President."

Tatiana pushed her dark hair away from her ear as if to explain what she was talking about. "Oil pipeline from Canada to Texas is example. Nicovich opposes. In long term, he believes the U.S. will buy oil from China which, of course, is bought from Russia. If Canada sells to Asia, then U.S. has to purchase oil from other sources."

I shook my head. "So this is just a big game of geo-political Monopoly. What a world." I climbed from the chair, walked to the coffee urn and refilled. "I'm just a dunce when it comes to this kind of political intrigue, you all know that. So why am I here?"

"To solve a puzzle."

"God, no, not another puzzle."

"There's another?" Sal asked.

"Yeah, a D. B. Cooper thing. I'll tell you about it later."

Sal's beard moved. He was smiling. "D. B. Cooper. You got enmeshed in that particular wild goose chase?"

"Not so wild, Sal my friend." Pulling from my coffee mug, "So what puzzle needs solving here?"

"Long story short," Artemus broke in, "Tatiana recently picked up a thread that the supplies payments were still being made. More like the middle of a thread. She couldn't see either the beginning – where the money was coming from – or the end, where it was going. Her instincts, which you know I trust implicitly, said something was way wrong."

"But we could not discover what," Tatiana added. "So I mentioned to Artemus as a courtesy in case it involved an American oil company. Considering Nichovich's reputation and history, it was not farfetched he was spying on the U.S. energy industry. He is very secretive man. Even Putin worries about him."

"So you guys back burnered it, I'd guess."

"Da."

"Again, so what am I doing here? What's the puzzle?"

The kid from Mo's Restaurant stuck his head in the door. "Mr. Rand? A minute, please."

"What is it Joey?"

He glanced around the room, settling on me and the other newcomers.

Sal nodded. "It's okay."

"Snoopers in the lot."

Sal's eyebrows rose. "How many?"

"Two. They came into the office and asked if they could rent a bay. Told them we were all full up. Started asking about the kinds of bays they were. If they were heated or insulated. That kind of stuff."

"And you think they're snoopers?"

"Suits and ties. Eastern European accents. Bulges under the jackets. Oh, they're snoopers, alright."

"Tell Marty to deal with them. The usual. When do they need the bay and for how long, yada, yada."

"Yes, sir."

The kid disappeared, closing the door behind him.

"Trouble, Sal?" I asked.

"Maybe. Could just be fall out from your little chase earlier today."

"You know about that?" Blue asked.

"Files, Agent Blue. Everything goes into a file. Police and ambulance reports. Nick's car is hard to miss and easy to describe. Some of the eyewitnesses even had a partial on the plate. By tagging Nick's file, anything related to him automatically updates and we get instant notification. Done all the time."

"Crap. Sorry," I said.

"Not a big problem, Nicky. We can deal with it."

"Can we deal with it over a pizza or something? I'm starved. And a pint of something cold and made of hops. This is beginning to sound like a long story."

The pizza was delivered by two guys with big necks in white aprons. Bubbling cheese, full-fat pepperoni, fresh mushrooms. Couldn't ask for anything better.

Sal and I sat at one end of the conference table.

"You haven't lost a pound, big man."

"Are those a couple of gray hairs I'm seeing in that mess you're calling a beard?"

"Stuff it."

Chuckle, "Same old adult responses, I see."

"So what is this place, Sal?"

"We jokingly call it Area 51 West. When Lincoln City decided to build a new high school back in '96, we..."

"The CIA."

"Don't interrupt. Never was CIA, never would be. Now listen up for a change. In '96 we were looking for a location on the Pacific to support our submarine tracking operations, specifically as it related to improved detection."

"Those planes that fly up and down the coast looking for subs aren't enough?"

"Not quite." Sal folded a third piece of pizza and bit off the pointy end. "While Area 51 looks at ways of creating stealth, this operation was tasked with uncovering stealth."

"Why not do that at Area 51, then?"

"Someone who has bought into certain technology is not the right person to find ways of unraveling that technology. You need a counter, independent view and scientific minds that reject or at least oppose something like detection invisibility."

"And that's what this place is."

"It's around 10 acres 75 feet below Taft High School. Labs, testing facilities, the whole shootin' match."

"Go Tigers." I had seen the reader board in front of the school and thought how common feline mascots are. Bandon, like Taft, uses the tiger. "So the aircraft searching for subs are outfitted with stuff made or developed here to detect stealthy submarines. About right?"

"And more, but that's the general idea."

"Why Lincoln City, aside from the fact they were building a new high school."

"Can you think of anyplace more perfect? Out of the way on a national basis. Lots of car traffic because it's a tourist town. You can't get any closer to the ocean. Low-cost housing throughout the county so our people can live here unlike Area 51 where they have to be flown in every day."

I scanned the table. Tatiana and her brothers were laughing and talking Russian. Family reunions are always lighthearted at first. Artemus was sharing some kind of international intrigue stories, but Blue and the Chief were paying little attention, instead huddled together swapping cop tales, I guessed.

"Where's Sam?" I asked.

Sam is Artemus's muscle. Big, mostly silent, carrying a huge gun.

"We call him Marty around here. As in the old Disney show 'Spin and Marty.' Don't ask why. Anyway, he's up top taking care of our snoopers."

"And Artemus is 'Spin' then."

"You got it."

"And we leave the security of our nation to Spin and Marty. That's disturbing."

Sal laughed. "And guys like you, too. Which is even more disturbing."

"By the way, the Chief is looking pretty good."

"Our recuperation facility in Eugene did a splendid job. He's a hundred percent. Sprung him about three weeks ago.

He's not key to this project, but I thought it would do him some good. He'll be back police chiefing Bandon soon."

Sal straightened in his chair and slapped the table with an open hand.

"Okay, people, back at it."

CHAPTER THIRTEEN

The young Russian officer stood at rigid attention even though he was on an encrypted radio-phone with his superior. The headset rarely used but always available.

The deep, resonant voice of the old warrior was clear. "You must do this, Captain. All remnants of this operation are being expunged."

"General, sir. We have only 16 remaining. All are the children of the original 169. None is older than 20. Is this the wisest decision?"

A sigh came over the line, one of either concern or annoyance, the young officer couldn't tell. Finally, after a lengthy silence, "It is out of my hands, Captain. It is a secret that must be kept. You will receive a location to carry out the order within three days. Someone must tell the Prime Minister."

The Captain gasped. "He does not know?"

"Only two of the deputy prime ministers know of your visitors, Captain. All will be dealt with accordingly before the Prime Minister is informed."

The Captain shuddered. This was more than he wanted to know. "Yes, sir."

The General sighed again. "Stay strong, Captain. You will be home soon."

Perhaps, the young officer thought, but this horror would be on his head until his native soil was tamped on his grave.

I banged the information Artemus and Sal outlined like the old pong game.

"So you're saying that in 1983 when the Soviet Air Force shot down the Korean Airline's 747, that plane was on a stealth mission?"

Both Sal and Artemus nodded.

"And it was a Korean, not an American operation."

Sal answered. "You have to recall the times, Nick. South Korea was just beginning to test its economic muscle. It was raiding U.S. companies for technology to advance its industrial base. It wanted badly to become a dominant economic power in Asia and the world."

Artemus added, "This was way before Hyundai or LG refrigerators or electronic gadgets. They figured if they could break the stealth aircraft barrier using electronics, rather than designs like the F117 Nighthawk, it could be installed on any aircraft or ship or land vehicle."

"Pretty ambitious," Blue said.

"And it worked," Sal answered.

That raised more than a few eyebrows.

The big man continued, "KAL Flight 007 was invisible to Soviet radar which is why it was able to penetrate Russian airspace and couldn't be spotted on Soviet fighter radar. It was pure luck 007 was finally found after literally hours of crossing some of the most sensitive Russian military installations."

"But why an airliner with civilian passengers?"

Artemus answered, "A miscalculation. The Koreans believed that if the flight had civilians on board, the Russians wouldn't dare shoot it down. They forgot about the Soviet hierarchy. If the top people in the government saw that its military commanders were unable to catch a commercial airliner, heads would roll. Literally. And when 007 *was* finally discovered, it was about to leave Soviet airspace. They didn't have time to force it down. Instead, they felt they had no choice but to shoot it down."

"Jesus, Mary and Joseph," Chief Forte muttered. "And we knew this?"

"The U.S. was just as surprised by the Korean action as the rest of the world," Sal answered. "After all the political rhetoric and incriminations settled down, though, we insisted on seeing the technology the Koreans used. Needless to say, they shared it all."

My turn. "At Area 51."

Sal nodded. "At Area 51. Correct. We needed to know how the Koreans put stealth technology into a huge aircraft so we could make sure we could see a Russian's military aircraft if they used the same technology."

"Every code needs to be developed with a way to decipher the code," I said. "That enables our side to interpret it if the other side gets it. Doesn't this just make your brain ache?"

I went to the fridge, pulled a beer from the shelf and returned to my seat. "Don't tell me you tried to penetrate Soviet airspace with this Korean stealth tech, Sal."

The big man turned to Artemus who nodded. "Yes, Nick, we did."

"Holy crap, Artie. You guys ask to be hit in the chops then wonder why someone would be so cruel and do it." I pulled from the bottle, watching Artemus's face. It remained calm.

"About a year and a half after the KAL flight was shot down, we sent another commercial airliner along the identical path 007 took with the same equipment – tuned a bit by our side – to see if the Russians could detect the plane."

"And…?"

"They did."

"Shot it down?"

"They did."

Tatiana flushed. Embarrassed for her country. Blue took a deep inhale and let it out slowly, then asked, "How come no one knows about this? Another commercial airliner gets blasted out of the sky by the Soviet Union and it didn't make front page news anywhere in the world?"

Sal and Artemus exchanged glances.

"Let's just say it was best forgotten by both the

Russians and us," Sal answered. "We certainly didn't want anyone to know we'd put civilian lives in danger and the Russians couldn't take another international hit like they did with the Korean flight."

"So no one said anything to anyone," I said. "You guys need to be taken behind the barn and taught a very big lesson."

Sal ignored my comment. "The good thing about the Korean stealth technology was that none of the usual flight control towers – Japan or elsewhere – could see the plane either. No one knew it was there except us."

"And the Russians," Blue added.

"Well, they found it, like KAL 007, by accident."

"How many on board?" I asked.

"Including crew, 169."

"How come families didn't...?" Blue's face fell. "You used people without families."

"Correct," Artemus said. "Recruited by the government. Well, rather, by a government agency."

"At Area 51," I said.

Sal just gave a short, almost imperceptible nod.

"President Reagan knew nothing about this?" Blue asked.

Artemus cleared his throat, squeezed his eyes together then opened them. "No. Most Americans don't understand that there are many levels of security clearances. About 25, actually. The President of the United States is a level 17."

"Are you saying that the President can't access

information above level 17? I find that hard to believe," Blue scoffed, voice rising, anger tingeing her tone.

"Agent Blue, did you see the movie *Independence Day*?"

"Yes."

"The President is told there are aliens. He demands to know why he wasn't told. Well, that was a truer scene than most people can imagine. He didn't know because he wasn't cleared to know."

"Who the hell makes the decision about clearances above the President?" Blue's voice was now getting harsh. She was clearly a died-in-the-wool law enforcement officer with a patriotic streak a mile wide. The President should know everything, in her mind.

"Agent, I suggest you tone it down," Artemus scolded. Chief Forte put his hand on her arm. I expected her to shake it off, but she didn't. Instead she simply groaned in frustration and clamped her lips together.

I looked at Homeland Security's Assistant Director. "What do you make of this? It sounds like there are powers well beyond the President."

Artemus folded his hands under his chin. "Ever hear of a big corporation's chairman being fired?"

"Of course. Happens all the time."

"Wait a second," Blue argued. "Are you saying there's a board of directors in the U.S. government?" Snorting, "That's ridiculous."

Artemus unclasped his hands then re-laced his fingers on the table. "Agent Blue, there are secrets labeled 'Born

Classified.' Simply put, no one can declassify those documents, not even the people who wrote them."

Blue sat in stunned silence, then, "You're kidding."

"Agent Blue, many of Area 51's projects were developed under that Born Classified designation. Not only is it true, but some of the documents will forever be lost because no one has the authority to open them and the original writers are long dead."

Pulling from my *Dos Equis*, to Sal and Artemus, "Enough. Let's argue about that some other time." To Sal, "All passengers perished, I presume."

"So we thought," Sal said. "But then the unexpected happened."

Artemus continued, "A body washed onto the beach in southern Washington State." The Homeland Security assistant director walked to one of the long tables and pulled off a plastic sheet. "It was wrapped in this."

Under the sheet, folded neatly, the stuff used to keep merchandise from breaking in transit.

"Bubble wrap?"

"Yes, Nick, bubble wrap," Sal said.

Fingering the corner of the plastic, "I don't get it, guys. This bubble wrap has nails through it. Did someone torture the guy before tossing him in the ocean?"

"Nick, those nails were pointed sharp-tip out, not in," Sal said. "And each nail, and there are more than 800 of them, was welded with some sort of industrial-strength black goop to make sure water didn't get into the cocoon."

"Cocoon. You mean the body was inside this thing with

the nails pointing out. That's nuts."

"Like a big porcupine. But that's not all. There were five industrial size desiccants inside the cocoon," Artemus said. "To keep the body dry. Absorb the moisture as the body decomposed. Suck the juices out of the decaying flesh."

"Can you do that?"

"He also had these packets of sodium bicarbonate in with him," jabbing a pencil at 2x6-inch cloth envelopes. "The desiccants pulled the moisture out of his body and the bicarbonate bumps up the pH to a level hostile to bacterial. Called wet mummification or some such, according to the squints in the lab."

"So the guy was put into a bubble wrap bag and mummified is what you're telling me."

"We think he did it to himself," Artemus said.

"Suicide by bubble wrap?"

That made Blue roll her eyes and got Sal to grin.

"You could say that, I guess. But wait, there's more."

He unfolded the plastic and put three pieces next to each other. "Pants, jacket, helmet or hood," Artemus said. "All joined by Gorilla Tape."

I spun around and headed to the fridge. "You don't get a suit like that at Macy's. You guys live in a very weird and disturbing world. I need another beer."

Pulled three long necks from the box, popped the tops and returned to the table, handing one to Blue, another to the Chief and a third to Sal. To Artemus, "You don't get one. I think you're already drunk."

"Well, then, you're gonna think I'm really off the deep end," he said as he pulled the plastic sheeting off of a second table. "What do you make of this?"

On the Formica top, what looked like parchment between two sheets of glass.

"Is that skin?" Blue asked.

Artemus nodded.

"Christ, is that his belly button hole? Where's the rest of him?" Holding up her hand, "No, don't tell me."

"And all the tattoos. There must be a dozen or more," I said.

"Fifteen, to be exact. Ranging in age, according to the analysts, from fresh to at least a dozen years old," Artemus said.

I took a closer look. The inks had been muddled in the mummification process. Some of the tats were impossible to see clearly.

"What are they pictures of?" Blue asked, also unable to make out all of the designs.

"We'll get to that, but first back to the issue of files," Sal said. "We were able to get fingerprints. We hunted the files and found they belonged to a Mort Brodsky."

"Am I supposed to know the name?" I asked.

"Wouldn't think so. He was a low level government accountant. He was also one of the 169 people aboard the Jumbo Jet the Russians shot down in '85. Our jet."

I leaned over the encased skin. "He hasn't been floating

in the ocean for 30 years, I bet."

"More like six weeks before washing ashore," Artemus said.

'How'd you estimate six weeks?"

"Blood and body juices. The autopsy puts time of death at about a month and a half. Put the other way, one of the passengers of our stealth 747 that was presumably shot down 30-plus years ago has been alive somewhere. An autopsy showed the body is of a man about 60 years old, which fits, considering he was 28 when he boarded the 747."

I stared long and hard at the tats.

"Have you guys put this through some magical thing-a-ma-bobbie and cleared up what these tattoos are? They look like fish."

Sal nodded. "Come here."

At the electronic whiteboard, everyone grabbed a seat while Sal clicked on a rear projector. The screen bloomed into a blue-hazed outline of each tat.

"Whales, Nick. Each is a whale."

"All different?"

"No, some repeat."

Sal clicked the remote and the outlines went through a series of colors. "Different filters to bring up the designs," he said.

"Okay, now let me see each one individually, then put

the clearest of each on the screen at the same time." My brain does tricks on me, which is why puzzles are so simple. It's probably due to the fact my sister at age six hit me in the head with a croquette mallet. She claims it was an accident. Sometimes I wonder.

No doubt about it, there were eight different whales with five multiples.

"Have you identified each of the whale types?" I asked.

Artemus took the remote from Sal, fast forwarded through more slides and ended on one showing each tattoo, the type of whale and the number of each.

Sperm 1

Humpback 1

Pygmy Blue 2

Blue 3

Killer 4

Right 2

Gray 1

Fin 2

"What can you tell me about Brodsky?"

"Like I said, a government accountant," Artemus started. "Went to NYU. Came from an upper-middle class New Jersey family. Smart but not motivated, according to his evaluation reports."

"In the files," I said, perhaps with a bit too much sarcasm.

"Yes, in the files."

Blue asked, "Majored in accounting?"

"Actually, no. He was an art-history major much to his family's distress. Dropped out during his Junior year and spent two years in Europe."

"Drawing and painting, I presume," Blue said.

"Correct. After a couple of years he returned to the U.S., went back to NYU as an accounting major which was more acceptable to his family. Guess he figured there was no money in being a good but not great artist."

"You have any of his artwork?" I asked.

"In the fi…" Artemus caught himself. "Yes we do. Not much, but his mother had saved a few pieces before she died."

Sal went on to explain that Brodsky's family was killed in a private plane crash in '81, had no siblings, never married. "Not even a steady girlfriend. No close friends, lots of acquaintances. Pretty much a loner."

"Have the artwork?" I said.

Artemus reversed the slides until he came to a series of paintings and sketches. All were street scenes. Paris. Rome. London. The proportions were good to my uncritical eye, but nothing compelling. Sparing use of color over pencil sketches.

Blue hunched forward and absorbed the paintings. "These resemble the style of the tats. Simple lines conveying accuracy but no extraordinary detail. A few hash marks tell you the wall in this painting is brick, but he didn't draw each brick. Just the illusion."

I hadn't noticed, but now that she had said it, my mind made the connection. "Do you think he tattooed himself?"

Blue stood and took the remote from Artemus, quickly going back to the tats. "What do you see, Nick?"

"Just like you said. The illusion of whale types, but not extraordinary detail. I just assumed that was to make the tattoo simpler to do. You're saying it was on purpose."

"And not only on purpose, but done from a drawing, not freehand."

"Whoa," Sal said. "Are you telling us that he drew the whales first, then tattooed them on himself?"

I shook my head. "Couldn't have. Some of those tats are simply impossible to self-inscribe. On his breastbone, for example. He would have had to do it upside down or in a mirror. No, I'd guess he gave the drawing to the tattoo artist who did the actual work."

Blue added, "And he was probably left handed. The heads of the whales are all aimed to the right. Most, if not all, righties will draw the head to the left."

"Bet that wasn't in his file, Artie."

"Stuff it, Nick."

"Consider it stuffed. Do you guys have some magical way of determining the age of the tats?"

"Not with any accuracy," Sal said.

"Okay, then. Have your analyst guys look at the blood under the skin that's mixed with the ink. Get me a reading on the level of melanin."

"The stuff that makes you tan?" Forte asked.

"In a round-about way, yeah. Need a reading for each of the areas with a tattoo and a few places where there aren't any tats. Also from his butt." To Artemus, "You have a picture of Mr. Brodsky?"

Artemus retook the remote, clicked a couple of buttons and an index of the slides came up on the electronic white board. He scrolled to "Brodsky, Mort" and clicked again to get to a submenu. Another click and a photo of a young man filled the screen.

"Mediterranean heritage," I said. "Jewish?"

"Yes," Sal answered.

"Darkish skin so the levels of melanin will be reasonably high. How quick can you get me those readings?"

"An hour, maybe less," Artemus said. "What are you thinking, Nick?"

"Not yet. I have an idea, but it's gonna take a bit of research first. An hour might do it. I need a printout of each of the tattoos. Clearest you've got." I could feel my shoulders tightening; gave them a stretch and to Sal, "Can we do some catching up in the meantime?"

"Sure. I'll have Joey show everyone their rooms. There are fresh clothes for you, but we weren't expecting the KGB or the FBI to drop by for a visit so we'll have to scrounge something up."

Marcus took offense. "No KGB. Am with Homeland Branch."

Tatiana laughed and said something to her brother in Russian. His flat Slavic face relaxed, "Is joke. You Americans have odd sense of humor. You have any of those crispy donuts here?"

Sal looked puzzled so I translated, "He wants some Krispy Kremes. Can you call up one of those special black helicopters of yours and have the pilot make a donut run for a few dozen?"

Sal grinned, "No, but the kitchen staff has a great file on donuts. We'll find something that'll make due."

CHAPTER FOURTEEN

The room each of us was given measured 12 by 15 or so. A desk, computer, printer, queen-size bed and a couple of lounge chairs. More Motel 6 than the St. Regis, but adequate.

I pulled out the desk chair and flipped on the Dell. After a minute of whirring and wheezing, a black screen with the words, "Keylogger enhanced." No porn sites without the government knowing.

Tapping into Wikipedia, I hunted through the whale entries, finding what I needed, scribbling notes on the print-out of the tattoos. Called up a world map and put each of the whales in their dominant habitat. Stared at the screen for a dozen minutes, moving electronic pushpins here and there.

Satisfied with what I'd done, I punched the print key and a small Minolta spit out a page.

The rest would be up to the melanin analysts.

My watch said I still had time for a power nap. I climbed onto the covers of the bed.

Now how many puzzles was this? D. B. Cooper. Where in the World is Sal? Brodsky, Brodsky who's got the

Brodsky? And now this thing about whales. That's too many for a country boy to deal with at one time. And with Cookie a bit miffed at me, my mood had turned crab-apple sour.

Knock on the door.

"Come in."

Sal pushed into the room, suddenly filling up a whole lot of the floor space. He fell into one of the lounge chairs facing the bed.

"Hi, Nicky."

"Your goldfish are fine."

"Glad to hear it."

"Your Volt is charging."

"Swell."

"Your lawn ornament has the neighborhood abuzz."

"Screw 'em."

"Had a run in with that yokel down the road. The one who cut down all the trees."

"Screw him, too."

"That's what I told him."

"Good for you." Sal scratched his beard. "And how's Cookie?"

"Mad at me."

Sal thought that one over.

"Isn't the first time."

I rolled onto my side so I could see the big man. "Madder than ever."

"What'cha do?"

"Went to Mexico."

"Without her."

"Yup. She went to Spring Training. I went to Ensenada."

"Instead of going to Spring Training with her."

"Yeah, I think that was a mistake."

"Ya think?"

"Sat on the beach. Grew this beard..."

"Ugly beard, my friend."

"Grew this beard, which I love to death, and drank margaritas by the bucketful. *Dos Equis* tastes different in Mexico. Even better."

"It's the water."

"The water, sure. That's it."

"Just like Mexican Coca Cola tastes better when it says *"Hecho en Mexico"* on the bottom of the bottle."

"True."

"So she's mad you decided not to go to Spring Training. What were you thinking?"

"I wasn't." Rolled onto my back. "She's also mad because I won't have 'the procedure.'"

Sal laughed. He and I had casually discussed *the procedure* in joking, not serious, banter. "Geez, Nick. It'll take an hour!"

"She's insisting."

"And you're resisting her insisting. Nice rhythm."

"Also true." My beer had gotten warm, held it up and

Sal punched up a number on the intercom phone, ordered two more bottles which arrived with the remnants of ice still on the glass.

"New subject. What do you know about D. B. Cooper?"

Sal scratched at his beard again. "He grabbed the money and jumped. Never found. The rest is beyond my level of interest."

"What if I told you he was a she."

"D. B. Cooper was a woman."

"Yeah. What would you say?"

"Why not. Annie Oakley. Emilia Earhart. Mary Fields. Ida Lewis. To name just a few."

"Mary Fields?"

"Female stagecoach driver in the 1800s. Hard drinking, gun-toting woman who protected a convent of nuns in Montana. Here, look," he said, turning to the computer and putting her name in the search bar. Up came a photo of Mary Fields.

"Pretty cool, huh?"

"And who was Ida Lewis," I asked.

"Woman lighthouse keeper also back in the 1800s. Saved dozens in the waters near Newport, Rhode Island. Her first rescue was when she was 16, if I'm remembering right."

"In other words, you don't think it's a stretch that D. B. Cooper was a woman."

"Not in the least." Sal clicked off the monitor and leveled a gaze at me. "You okay?"

"Frazzled a bit, but otherwise good."

"Want a donut? They're fresh."

"No, I want an explanation."

"If I can, I will."

"Did you work for the CIA?"

Sal laughed, deep and hard. "No, Nick, never did nor would I ever."

"In that case, I'll take that donut."

Back in the conference room, I took my single sheet of paper with the map and whales to Artemus, asked if he could put it on the screen which he did.

Everyone grabbed a seat. Tatiana with her brothers; Forte, Blue, Artemus, and Sal in the front two rows. A man I didn't recognize stood near Artemus and smiled when I looked at him. Pasty in a laboratory worker sort of way.

"Do you have the melanin readings, Artie?"

"Randolph here will go through the findings, Nick."

The lab rat walked to the front of the group, took the remote and punched in a number. The screen flashed a chart with each tattoo image followed by a number from 25 to 35.

"Mr. Drago's idea of measuring melanin was, quite honestly, something we hadn't thought of. The results are revealing in some ways, not so much in others."

Using a laser pointer, "What you're looking at is the Fitzpatrick Scale. It classifies everyone by skin color. Albinos, for example, are Type I and score a zero to seven; Nigerians or other very black Africans are a Type VI and score well over 30 on the scale."

He cleared his throat. "Type I's never sun *tan*. They always sun *burn*. Conversely, Type VI's never tan. The reason for the extremes is the melanin in the skin. To simplify, the more melanin, the darker the skin tone."

"Mr. Brodsky was a what?" I asked.

"Type IV. Beige with a medium-brown tint. Very typical of Mediterranean peoples. The Fitzpatrick Scale puts this group at 25 to 30." He tapped the pointer in the palm of his hand. "By measuring the melanin in the non-tattooed parts of his skin, it appears he was naturally a 26."

"Whoa, you're losing me, doc," Forte broke in. "What's melanin do?"

"It's the body's protection against ultra violet light. You need some sunlight for good health, but people out in the sun for a long time get sun tanned or sun burned. That tanning process protects the body from getting *too much* ultraviolet light. Cultures long associated with Northern Europe, for example, didn't need much melanin because there wasn't that much sunlight or ultraviolet light. I'm fair skinned because my ancestors came from a place where there wasn't much sunlight. Namely, Scotland. Mr. Brodsky, on the other hand, came from a culture in sunnier, hotter climates so he had naturally darker skin as a means of protection from ultraviolet light."

Forte shook his head again. "So a sun tan is a *good* thing? It's not just cooking your skin?"

"Yes and no. It's a good thing in moderation because it produces vitamin D which is essential to ward off many diseases. Melanin production through tanning is your body's way of protecting you from the harmful results of ultraviolet rays."

I interrupted, "Enough of the medical stuff. Mr. Brodsky was a natural 26. What was under the tattoos?"

"He spent lots of time in the sun, Mr. Drago. Many, many, many hours. That 26 figure came from a patch of skin on his hip. The skin without tattoos from his chest and back were 29 and 30."

"And under the tats?" I asked.

"Depending on the tattoo, a 28, 29, 30 and up. A few were even the equivalent of 35."

"So you're saying he spent his time without a shirt on, in the sun a good part of the day."

"That's pretty much what I'm saying, Mr. Drago."

"And none of the tats were done when his skin was at the baseline of 26."

"Also correct."

"Well, I guess that rules out a prison in Siberia."

Almost in unison, the group muttered, "Prison?"

"Sure. Prison. Mr. Brodsky was in prison."

Fore asked, "For 30 years?"

"And his prison was a ship."

"What?" Again, almost in unison.

"Look, the man floated for six weeks in the ocean. He committed suicide by bubble wrap. Why bubble wrap? Because it floats. Why nails with the points out? Because of predators not the least of which sharks…"

Sal laughed. It was not the laugh of someone who found a story to be funny, rather from a man who had just suffered an epiphany. An eye-opening revelation. "Of course! Dammit, Nick, that makes perfectly good sense. It also explains the shark tooth we found embedded in the bubble wrap."

Continuing, "And the constant tan means the ship was mostly or at least very often in the southern hemisphere. South Pacific, South Atlantic. Or along the equator."

Blue said, "So this ship simply cruised from port to port with Mr. Brodsky on board for 30 years?"

"Probably never made port. Stayed in the ocean, supplied from the mainland. If it docked, the chances of escape or discovery increased dramatically."

I turned to Tatiana. "When you were looking into the oil baron and the secret funds for supplies, did you get an indication of what volume of supplies and what they were exactly?"

Tatiana stood and took the remote from Randolph. She punched in a number and a graph came up on screen. On it, a crazy quilt of lines with labels like "medical," "office," "clothing," "food," "personnel transfer" and at least a dozen others.

"Can you break out just the food portion?" I asked.

Tatiana pressed a variety of buttons on the clicker and reduced the hodge-podge to a single chart.

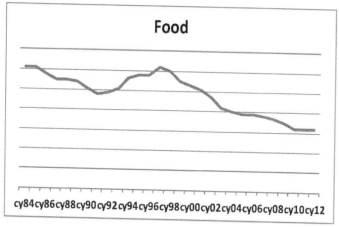

To the group, I asked, "What do you see?"

Blue was first to react. "The prison ship had 169 people on board, plus the sailors, in 1984. Over the next six years, the food requirements diminished or were cut."

"I vote for diminished," I said. "Tell you why in a second. Go on."

"Then it began to increase after, what is that, six years or so. Nick, you're not suggesting the captives began having babies, are you?"

"The initial decline is likely because some of the captives either revolted or committed suicide or attempted to escape. Whatever the reason, the number of prisoners shrank. Food requirements declined. Of those remaining, after so many years, pairing up is natural and that turns into babies. Thus the increase in food requirements."

"Then why the fall off after 1996, Nick?" Forte asked.

"Mortality is mortality. Some probably died of natural causes; others couldn't stand it any longer and, again, tried to escape or simply committed suicide. The leveling off over the past two years probably means the survivors have lived their entire lives on board a ship and their parents are either all gone or resigned to their captivity."

"Christ," Forte said. "Imagine that, if you can."

Blue again. "Ever read *Man Without a Country*? About this prisoner kept in solitary confinement aboard a sailing ship for decades because he was considered a traitor? Well, that's what these people are. Without a country. We have to find the ship and them."

I retook the remote and returned to the tattoos and the world map I'd given Artemus earlier.

"Mr. Brodsky told us where the ship has been and hopefully we can figure out where it is now." Walking to the e-board, I pointed to a small tattoo of a Right Whale. "This was the first. It's more like a prison tat. Rough edges, probably ballpoint pen ink, not tattoo ink. Done with a pin or tip of a knife."

One by one I pointed to the different whale sketches, explaining the ongoing refinement in both the design of the drawing and the advancing quality of the tools used to scribe the tattoo.

Blue, hair becoming tangled from her hands constantly running through it as she both listened and evaluated, "So you're saying that these tats were done over a long period of time and the tattoo artist became increasingly proficient at duplicating Mr. Brodsky's sketches."

"Exactly. And he did these breeds of whales on purpose, not just at random. They tell us where the ship was and tell the story of the prison ship.

"And some of the breeds are not the same as you've ID'd. Some are sub-species found in different parts of the ocean."

I clicked to show a slide of Killer Whales.

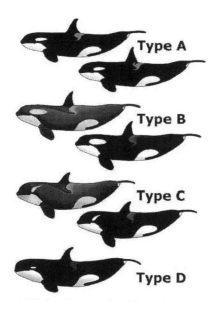

"Some of Mr. Brodsky's tattoos were of Killer Whales, but two different sub-species. The Type A and the Type C varieties. If you look at the tattoos, the eye patches on some of the Killer Whales match the Type A and the other match Type C. One is a transient variety, the other is what's called a 'resident' which doesn't move much. If you look at one of the tattoos, you see it has a hook in the dorsal fin? Very observant of Mr. Brodsky. That's a female. Very accurate drawing."

"Question for you, Nick," Blue said. "Why go to all the trouble of getting tattoos to tell a story when he could have written it out and tucked in a back pocket or something."

"I can answer that," Artemus said. "First, and foremost, we did find some paper on Mr. Brodsky. A single sheet. High pulp content. The gases and fluids from decomp destroyed it. I'm assuming Mr. Brodsky figured that might happen so he devised a more elaborate way of talking to us."

"This is all well and good," Forte said. "But we're still not privy to the ship's current whereabouts. As Nick pointed out, it seems to have spent its time in warm climates, but there is quite a bit of ocean meeting that criteria."

"Chief, we just follow the tats."

CHAPTER FIFTEEN

"Can't you determine where Brodsky jumped into the water?" Blue asked.

"Not really," Sal said. "We can track the currents at this time of year just fine, but there are a lot of variables. First, Mr. Brodsky mummified over the course of six weeks. What was his original weight? How long did it take to expel the gases and did the cocoon move exactly with the current or was it slower? And by how much? Second, let's say we can trace the current to somewhere off the Asian coast. That's literally hundreds of hundreds of miles of potential starting points. Maybe a quarter-million square miles."

"But it's the start," I said. "And we know two additional facts: First, the shark tooth. Your analysts say it's from a Whitetip. They also say it's a warm, deep water shark that can be found from Southern California to Peru and across the Pacific to Hawaii, Tahiti, Samoa."

"Big territory," Sal said.

"Yeah, but look at the map." I clicked the remote and called up the Whitetip's territory.

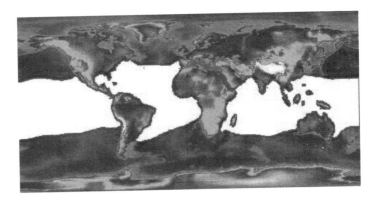

"The white area is that shark's happy hunting grounds. Big territory. So let's eliminate all the places that couldn't reach Washington State."

I called up a cropped photo of the map and moved the section with Australia to the left side, U.S. on the right.

Now let's add some points of interest."

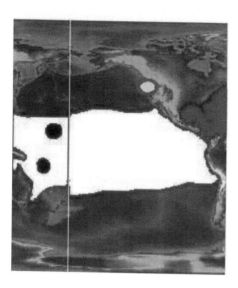

"The cocoon was found in lower Washington State. That's way outside the Whitetip habitat. The top right dot is where the body was found. The two black dots are the outside limits of a six-week jaunt in the Pacific riding the trade currents this time of year.

"And you can virtually eliminate the bottom black dot because to make it in six weeks would require a damn near tsunami heading east and the cocoon picking up the Pineapple Express from the south heading north."

Sal stared at the map for a moment. "So we should start looking for a ship in the Pacific northeast of Australia and below the California parallel."

"Correct."

"The problem I see is that it's been weeks. The ship could be anywhere."

"Assuming it's a large ship, which it would have to be considering the original captives numbered 169, what's its possible speed? That would give us a relative distance and a range," I said. "I know it's a long shot, but what else do we have?"

Tatiana provided some of the answer. "We know the ship is restocked every three months. We can assume that would include refueling to avoid too many contacts with a supply vessel."

Using the yellow pad and pencil on the desk, she scribbled some calculations while talking. "An old ship can travel at perhaps 15 knots for most efficient operation. It would travel 300 miles in a 24 hour period or 2,100 miles a week."

She did some more pencil calculations. "That is impossible because ships from that era would be out of fuel in less than two weeks. The Captain of this prison ship would have to spend many days simply, what do you call it -- idling -- to make his fuel last three months."

I was doing the calculations along with Tatiana only in my head. "So in six weeks, it's not going to be too far from where Mr. Brodsky went overboard. Maybe 600 to a thousand miles at a very low speed to conserve fuel."

Sal scratched his beard, "As good a guess as any. And probably heading south."

"Why so?" I asked.

"Due east takes it toward the U.S., away from the next

supply point which is probably Sahkalin Island since it's the closest to Russian secret bases. West gets into areas covered extensively by Russian, Asian, U.S. radar. The Captain of the ship doesn't want to be seen. In fact, has spent years avoiding scrutiny. South follows the whales, if I'm reading your map correctly."

"That cut down the area from a quarter-million square miles to maybe 100,000," I said, half in jest. "Call out the Boy Scouts."

Artemus gave a jerk of his head. "Good work. We'll get satellite tracking on it right away. See if we can find the ship." To Tatiana, "Do you think you could trace the supplies shipments' ports in case it's not Sahkalin?"

"Perhaps," she said. "But it will be difficult from here. I would need access to my files in Moscow."

Sal grinned. "Not a problem. I'll get you in."

Marcus looked at his sister, "He can do such?"

Tatiana nodded. "Very adept at hacking."

"Even Russian secret files?" He was astonished.

"Yes, Marcus. Even secret files."

The broad face frowned, his big head shook. "Is no wonder we lost Cold War." To Sal, "Have vodka here? And more donuts?"

"Ah, the universal food group," I said. "I'll have beer with mine, thanks."

---

2 a.m. Dinner, talking about the tattoos, sharks, whales

and missing ships done for the day. Sal and I sat in my room.

"Okay, Nick, tell me about this D. B. Cooper thing."

"Strangest thing." I patted the file folder on the desk. "Thanks, by the way, for having my stuff brought down."

"No problem. They needed to empty your car so they could fix the bullet holes and repaint it."

"What?"

"Fix the bullet…"

"I heard you. Repaint the Crown Vic!"

"Can't have you driving around in a silver CV with flames and side exhaust and bullet holes. A little obvious, don't you think?"

"Repaint the Crown Vic!"

"Relax, it'll be fine. Tell me about Cooper."

"But the Crown Vic? What color?"

"White."

"Oh, geez. People will think I'm a geezer. I'll have to dye my hair silver, slouch behind the steering wheel, drive in the left-hand lane at 10 under the limit with my turn signal blinking. You're killing me, Sal."

"D. B. Cooper. Tell me."

Long sigh. Opening the folder, I handed Sal the letter from the supposed D. B. Cooper and the clue cards.

"Dear Nicholas:

As you may have read, the Federal and Washington State authorities have arrested Clarence G. Oates claiming he is D. B. Cooper, the famous skyjacker. They are wrong. I know this because I am the real D. B. Cooper."

"You may well disbelieve my claim, but that doesn't make it any less true.

"I've enclosed eight cards with individual clues that will prove to you I am who I claim. It is imperative you decipher these clues and insist the authorities release Mr. Oates immediately. He and his family are innocent victims.

"Please hurry, Nicholas, before a serious injustice takes place.

"Warmest regards, D. B. Cooper."

Sal read the letter then re-read it.

He turned to the clue cards with the footnotes.

Not a mountain. Not a saint.
~~Helen of Troy~~
~~Helen the Barbarian~~
Helen Keller
Helen Reddy
~~Helen Hunt~~
 Vestus virum facit
Clothes make the man (Latin)
What I'm wearing
~~What others are wearing~~
~~Uniform~~
An appropos child's board game
Chutes and ladders

Monopoly
> ~~Where's Waldo~~
> Guess Who
> Old Maid

Joe Friday has one

Gun

Partner?

Badge

~~Distinctive voice~~

~~Acting ability~~

~~Monotone voice~~

I am not one of the three, but one of the three.

God

Religious reference

Out of the loop, in the loop

Three letters one of which is the letter "I"

Pilot, co-pilot, navigator

Three-in-one oil

Three wheel motorcycle?

Trident

Little Bo Peep sheep

Black sheep of the family

Pitch fork

Kitchen fork

BBQ fork

WWII 97th division

Trident patch used by the 97th.

You can't find me. But I am there.
Hide and seek
Ghost
Peep hole
Hidden
Magician David Copperfield
Cute *(that had to be Mary Ann)*
Sleight of hand
Card tricks
Poker
Black Jack
Pick a card, any card
Four stacks, four aces on top
Something seems it's not there but is
Rabbit in a hat
Blood to water

Wine to blood

A song writing invisible rabbit
Harvey

Sal thumbed through each one, not asking a question. Rearranging the cards.

Then I filled him in on my and Blue's theories and interpretation of the clues.

After a few minutes, "Okay, Helen Reddy I get. The song '*I am Woman.*' *Chutes and Ladders*, a logical choice, but not really a clue. It's a description. Why bother? It's useless as a clue."

"Unless there's a hidden meaning it in."

"Maybe. Here's the good one, though. *Vestus Virum Facit*, the clothes make the man. That isn't a clue unless you take it another step. Why include it? What clothes? Why point out that he or she was wearing clothes? The original Latin meant what a man wore defined his station in life. Dress well and you'll be seen as someone who is from an upper class. Dress like a warrior – again, this was ancient Rome – and people would know you as a soldier. Dress in a weird little toga and you must be a member of the Senate."

Like I've said, Sal sees things in three dimensions.

"So what we have in these three clues…"

"Of course, Sal. D. B. Cooper, a woman, was dressed like a man, but a particular kind of man. Dark suit, white shirt, dark tie, dark shoes. He looked like a businessman or…"

Sal grinned, "You got it. Or an FBI agent. Remember, they didn't wear those blue windbreakers with FBI in big yellow letters on the back in 1971. They wore their work-a-day clothes."

"Which explains the reason Cooper asked for parachutes but never asked for warm weather gear even though he or, rather, she was supposedly going to jump into below-zero weather. She never left the aircraft."

"That makes some of the rest fall into place," Sal said.

"Joe Friday. Badge. She was pretending to be law enforcement. 'I am not one of the three, but one of the three' means she – the 'I' – wasn't one of the three letters in FBI, but pretending to be one of the agents."

"Clever woman."

"We got to get Frankie in here."

"Why?"

"She's a skeptic, or at least a good agent. Need her FBI knowledge for something I'm thinking."

"No, no, no," Blue said, shaking her head, snapping the "Joe Friday" and "Not one of the three…" cards with her thumb. "Why two clues about being an FBI agent? "

Hunching forward in my chair, "Good point. So how else can we interpret the clues?"

Sal looked at his watch. "It's 5:30 in the morning.

Maybe a couple hours of sleep would help."

Blue ignored him. "The Joe Friday clue, one of the choices is 'gun.' I think that may be the right choice, not 'badge.'"

"What did agents carry as weapons back then?"

"Not sure, but I'd guess it was a .38 police special revolver. Most law enforcement were issued those," Blue said.

"So Cooper, probably in the briefcase, had a revolver. For what purpose? She certainly couldn't shoot her way past a crowd of police and Feebies."

Sal returned to the conversation, "Prop."

Blue and I looked at the big man.

"A prop." To Blue, "How many agents stormed the plane when it landed?"

"Don't know. I would guess it was quite a few, though. Between our guys, state police, local cops, maybe a dozen or more."

"And how would they have stormed the plane?"

"Both entrances. The rear door was down, so some would have come in that way. The stairs to the plane up front, that way." She paused, "Oh, I get it. You think Cooper actually waited for the plane to be rushed by all the cops and just mingled with them. Wow, that takes huge cajones."

Blue grabbed one of the clue cards, slid a pen from the desk top and circled one of the notes. She passed it to me.

Magician David Copperfield
Cute *(that had to be Mary Ann)*
Sleight of hand
Card tricks
Poker
Black Jack
Pick a card, any card
Four stacks, four aces on top
Something seems it's not there but is
Rabbit in a hat
Blood to water
Wine to blood

"Remember when Copperfield made that 747 disappear in front of an audience?" she said.

"Yeah, how'd he do that?"

"Who knows? Who cares? The fact is he did it. On TV."

"So Cooper was a magician?"

"Nick, it means she was hiding someplace on the plane. When the cops rushed the cabin, she suddenly appears, gun drawn like all the rest, dressed in a dark suit, white shirt, dark tie, shiny shoes, maybe with a forged FBI identification badge clipped to the suit jacket; assists with the search of the plane then…"

"Takes the ladder off the plane," I added. "Chutes and ladders."

"Not the parachute."

"Holy horse pucky, it fits."

Sal's face screwed into a look I'd known for decades. Like he'd just gotten a whiff of a diaper pail. "Why leave behind the clip-on tie?"

"Oh, I can answer that one," Blue said. "Not allowed."

"Pardon?"

"J. Edgar wouldn't allow agents to wear clip on ties. They had to be hand tied. Half Windsor."

"And he brought the clip-on as a leave-behind prop." I was getting a full picture of Cooper's sleight of hand. "The real one was probably in the briefcase along with the gun."

"One problem," Sal said, still smelling the diaper pail. "Everyone says Cooper looked like a man. Face angular. Hair receding."

Putting on my best smart aleck face, "Many women have masculine features, present company excluded, and someone with a lot of hair can easily shave some of it off. Like your beard, Sallie. You could turn it into a moustache in, what, half an hour?"

"Or whittle it down to a cheesy beard like that moss growing on your chin."

"That hurt."

He smiled. "It was meant to."

"Or it was makeup," Blue said, rummaging through the FBI files looking for the exact report. "She was seen coming out of the lavatory holding a bag and the briefcase like a pizza box. You know, flat. The passenger described him – and she thought he was male – as having a ruddy complexion with jet black hair as if it were dyed." Finding the information she was searching for, "Nancy House. That was the witness."

"Makeup? Why not. Cooper was said to have no discernible accent but was described as perhaps Hispanic or Mediterranean – Italian or Greek, maybe."

Blue interrupted, "Okay, but when you shave off head hair, it's pretty obvious. I mean, the sun hasn't tanned it at all."

"That would explain the makeup," I said.

Sal added, "It's the Pacific Northwest."

I completed the thought. "It rains. The sun hides for months. No one tans in the winter. Christ, it's so damp, *fiberglass* rusts in Seattle."

Cooper had to wait. We regrouped in the conference room at the long table. The same steely eyed, thick-necked guys came in with serving carts. They loaded buffet trays with pancakes, sausage, eggs, toast (three varieties), ham and steaks.

Sal and I were first in line and took our usual. Some of everything.

Back at the table, "You really repainted the Crown Vic?"

Sal had already finished off one steak and was starting on the pancakes. "Yup."

"And you have no remorse?"

"None."

"I'll get even."

"No you won't." Wiping his mouth with a linen napkin, "Nice catch on the shark and whale stuff, Nicky. That's exactly the reason I wanted you here."

"Explain something to me. Why all the secret sky lights to get me here? A phone call would do."

"Easy, squeezy…"

"Japaneezi, yeah I know. But why?"

Between sausages and pancakes, "There cannot be a trace of this operation contacting you or anyone else. We do not exist. What we're going after will be scrutinized internationally and potentially will cause a major rift between Russia and the U.S. No traces can be left so both sides can officially deny knowledge and pass it off as some previous administration's misdeed."

"And a phone call could leave a trail. You're talking about Echelon."

"Echelon is old hat. A remnant of the Cold War. We're way beyond that, now. Ever wonder how your cell phone can work on this side of the Mexican border, but walk 10 feet into Mexico and it doesn't work anymore? Or how Twitter can censor a single message out of millions in one country while not restricting access everywhere else in the world?" Wiping the last remnants of egg from his plate with a piece of sourdough bread, "Remember the movie *Three Days of the Condor*?"

"Robert Redford. Early 1970s. Analysts read everything

and tried to find hidden meanings. Geopolitical or black ops. Sure."

"Computer software today can do that in seconds. I send you a letter. I call your phone. I write an email or use Facebook or Twitter or any other social website, computers spin the info, find links and trace it all the way back to the original source. Then store it in…"

"A file where it lasts forever. That's scary."

"So, what could we do to get your attention and get you here without leaving a trail that someday could come back and bite us on the ass? All it would take is the right reporter and a Freedom of Information Act request backed up by a Ninth Circuit Court judge."

Eyeing the buffet, trying to decide on another helping, Sal continued, "None of the usual means of communications would work. We never trained carrier pigeons to come from here to your house. You'd have to be listening to a CB for citizen's band to work and we'd never know when that would be. Couldn't just walk up to your door and knock. That would break cover."

"So you had Forte light up the night sky. Didn't he have to file a flight plan?"

"Only if he flew from an FAA certified airfield. He left from one of our pastures near here."

"Pastures."

"People who work here have houses nearby. Mostly ranches. Where do you think we put all the dirt we hauled off from this little underground encampment? Staff comes to this facility by walking or bicycling or taking an underground tunnel. We have a labyrinth of tunnels all around here."

Artemus stood from the table and walked to the electronic whiteboard. "Okay, folks, time to get back to work."

Chairs scuffled back and we all took seats at the front of the room.

"Overnight, here's what we've discovered. Tatiana tracked down a few ports where supplies could have been shipped from. But one has bubbled to the surface." He nodded to Tatiana who rose and took center stage.

"When old USSR collapsed, the resulting federation formed the Association of Sea Commercial Ports in St. Petersburg. The purpose was to transition to a market-based economy and to resolve issues in that transition. This was a critical part of rebuilding the Russian Federation economy."

She clicked the remote and called up a map of the Pacific Ocean including territories within a few hundred miles of Russian shores.

"The supplies of food, clothing, *etcetera* were shipped from the Almaz Marine Yard, also in St. Petersburg, to three Russian Federation ports. One on the Baltic, one on the Black Sea and the third at Sakhalin Island."

"Isn't that where KAL 007 was shot down?" Forte asked.

"Correct. Today is the major oil and gas export and import facility in Eastern Russian Federation. Is also location of major military bases."

"And we're thinking this is where the supplies for our mysterious ship are sourced," Artemus added. "Sal's assessment was spot on. Which means a couple of things. First, since the shipments are made only every three months, the transport has to be in a rather large vessel at relatively close range. Two, since the shipments have been made from any one of these three ports, the mystery ship travels a lot."

I piped in, "And third, if the last shipment of supplies came from Sakhalin, the mystery ship was in the Pacific, which makes sense considering Brodsky's body came ashore in Washington. That's actually more confirmation of what we already knew, isn't it?"

Tatiana's face clouded, eyes dimmed. "One problem, Nick. The last shipment of supplies was one third of the usual quantity."

Silence filled the room like cotton balls in a glass jar.

I broke it. "We have to find that ship and fast. The Russians responsible for this are calling it quits. They won't leave a trace."

Tatiana took a quick inhale. "My fault, no?"

"Not your fault, Tats," Artemus said. "Your inquiries may have tipped off these guys that someone was on to them, but they already began to wind it down. The supplies shipments have been getting smaller."

Forte, who had been sitting next to the Russian agent, put his arm around her. Blue leaned across the Chief and took Tatiana's hand. "It's okay." A whisper.

CHAPTER SIXTEEN

The distance between hope and dejection is measured in microseconds. For Captain Vladi Merchenko, the General's morning communications ruptured his fragile belief in the operation's purpose and necessity.

The lanky young officer had become the second permanent commander of the converted oil tanker. His predecessor Captain Petrov never left the Albanian-flagged vessel in 24 years, seemingly content with having his own island to lord over; setting his own courses to see at a distance through powerful Soviet military binoculars places like Tahiti, Samoa and even, on occasion, Catalina Island.

During the first five years, he and his five military guards ruled with an iron fist. His "guests" were limited in their access to any part of the ship save a small space topside, the cafeteria for meals and their own quarters. He denied requests for decorations and his small but deadly guard staff frequently encountered resistance to orders, discovered plans to revolt, uncovered a small makeshift boat made from tarred scraps of sheets over a flimsy cardboard frame.

Ingenious, he admitted to himself. Using the thick residue from the oil this ship had transported to coat all of the little boat. Once found, he tested it in a calm mid-Atlantic sea. He had one of the guests, the troublesome airline Captain, who quickly took control of the captives, sit in it while all the others watched. It floated for more than two hours before a small swell swamped it sending the Boeing pilot into the ocean.

Petrov ordered full power ahead, leaving the guest to the sharks.

The resulting riot cost Petrov severely. Many of the captives had been passive, afraid for their lives, but his action developed into increased attempts to take over his ship. One of his guards had been murdered, automatic weapon stolen and used in a futile attempt to storm the ship's control tower. More than a dozen had died including another of his guards.

His superiors began second guessing every action. His communications with Soviet hierarchy constant, often a dozen times a day.

But that wasn't the reason Petrov changed. His desire for companionship and a willing captive – a woman from a place called Idaho – softened his flinty edges. She encouraged looser reins. Small steps, he realized, but effective. Movies, better quality food, an occasional night of music and drinking.

While a core of the captives remained resistant, many resigned themselves to their plight. Some started cohabitating. Others withdrew into despair. Of the latter, most elected to end their own lives either by jumping off the ship or committing suicide by escape. But there was no escaping from the Mir. One nearly succeeded by slipping over the side and scaling transfer lines to the supply ship. She was quickly returned and later ended her life by ingesting quantities of the now decades old oil-tar.

When Captain Vladi Merchenko was given command of the ship he found 26 of the original guests and 12 children. During his command, four additional children were born, some 25 of the original captives died of either old age, maladies for which the ship had little medical supplies or suicide. None, however, the result of guard actions.

The remaining original captive, Mort Brodsky, proved to be a gentle and wise man who cared for the children, related well to the guards, especially Yuri. He could see the two standing on deck in quiet discussions, laughing, occasionally in heated exchanges probably over politics, but always with the air of friendship.

"Is good," he would say to himself, watching the two, Brodsky always with his shirt off, Yuri always tipping his rifle against the deck rail as one might an unneeded umbrella.

This was not a "happy ship," but it certainly was no longer a floating version of a Siberian gulag.

In mere days, however, it would be relegated to history.

"No," Merchenko thought. *"Not to history. History implies someone would write about it and store it in an archive for future generations to read. No, this would be vapor. Stricken from the minds of humankind forever.*

"As maybe it should be."

"Here's what we know," Artemus, leaning on the small table in front of the electronic whiteboard. "He punched a key on the remote and a numbered list appeared. The Homeland Security assistant director read each one:

1. Flight 776, our Boeing, followed the exact path of Korean Air's Flight 007, crossing into Soviet territory, passing over sensitive military bases, disappearing from both their and our radar, being caught just before exiting Soviet airspace and shot down.

2. Neither side was about to say anything to the world. We were caught spying, using civilians. The Russians were caught shooting down another commercial airliner.

3. We thought the passengers, like KAL007, were all killed when the aircraft crashed.

4. Apparently it didn't crash and instead was captured. We don't know how or what happened.

5. The survivors, presumably all 169, were rounded up and taken somewhere.

6. Tatiana picks up a lead on diverted government funds. Don't know what for or why or even who. She tells me, but we have nothing. The inquiry goes cold.

7. Mort Brodsky's body is found some 28 years after Flight 776 is presumed to have been shot down. He's been in the water for about six weeks. He's mummified of his own making. Suicide by bubble wrap, as Nick puts it.

8. Nick pulls a rabbit out of his butt and IDs the general location of the shark that tried to take a bite out of the

bubble wrap and starts us on this thread leading to a mystery ship because, of all things, whales and melanin.

9. Tatiana IDs the port where supplies are shipped to the mystery ship.

10. Because of the lower volume of supplies, especially a two-thirds reduction in the last shipment, it is clear most of the captives are dead for whatever reason and the Russians are about to end this operation soon.

11. Satellite recon begins. Covering more than a hundred-thousand square miles of ocean.

"Missing anything important?"

Clearing my throat, "Yeah, something I think is important. Someone's trying to turn this entire operation into dust. They need to kill off anyone with direct knowledge of the ship. That means everyone on board including their own people.

"That means Tatiana and by affiliation everyone in this room. They've tried to get Yuri and Marcus at the donut shop; they went after me, Blue and the Commie Brothers on the way here. They've sent what you call snoopers to this facility. And they won't stop unless, and it's a big 'unless', we can get the captives off of that ship and back home. That would effectively shut the lid on both sides."

Tatiana's face lost the waxy look of self-incrimination, "This was not the work of anyone in official Russian government today, I believe. It was the action of one tycoon run out of power after the collapse of old USSR."

I took a long pull from the coffee mug, "You're saying it was an operation that *couldn't* be ended. Sometimes you get in so deep, even if you want to set the record straight, it's going to have tremendous repercussions. So you simply keep up the façade and every day it gets worse, deeper, more dangerous to reveal."

Another pull of coffee. "The current government knows nothing about this. It's now only the operation of this oil tycoon and maybe a single remaining energy czar from the old regime."

"Da. Saying anything today would mean prison or a firing squad."

Sal asked, "Then who are the snoopers working for? Oil tycoon or energy czar? Are they Russian military or private contractors?"

Artemus provided the first smile of the day. "Let's ask one of them."

Sam, aka Marty as in Spin and Marty, stood in the back of the room in a corner. His usual *modus operandi*. Big, brutish, a suit making him look like a big, brutish guy in a suit. A shade shorter than my 6-foot-5, he outweighs me by a few pounds, all of it hard muscle.

The bulge in his jacket hid, well, sort of hid a Desert Eagle .50 caliber semi-automatic. He rarely says much, but his eyes capture everything around him, process it quickly and generate the appropriate reaction.

At Willow Weep he'd shown his metal in two shootouts over the past year.

He walked to the front of the room and explained that

when the snoopers came to the facility, he first talked to them as if they were potential customers. Clearly, they weren't.

His voice had the soft confidence of someone who enjoyed his image and the fact he could back up that image. Deep, resonant, "When the three snoopers left, two went north, one headed south." They were the most words I'd ever heard him speak. A slight New Jersey accent. "I intercepted the majoke heading south and brought him back here."

For fun, I asked, "Blindfolded or unconscious?"

Sam smiled. Never answered me.

Artemus said, "He's been cooling his heels in one of our guest rooms. Perhaps Tatiana and her brothers would like to have a conversation with him?"

All three nodded. Sam led them out of the conference room.

Looking around, "Where's Sal?"

Artemus just gave a head bob, "He's devising a way to rescue the folks on the ship. Setting up the appropriate, uh, stuff."

"But we don't know where the boat is." Blue said.

"No, we don't. But there's still a lot of prep that can be done."

Tipping back on two chair legs, I asked, "Where do you think the snoopers were going when they left here?"

Forte had become more animated and entered into more conversations just in the short time I'd been in Area 51 West. "Southbound guy back to your and Sal's places, I'd guess. Northbound guys, Portland, maybe." He hesitated, a thought entering his mind. "Where was the body found?"

"On the beach near North Cove, Washington," Artemus answered. Light dawned in his eyes. "You think they were heading there?"

"My cop instincts tell me yes."

I'd worked with the Chief for quite some time and knew his thought processes pretty well. "You think they're going to clean up some loose ends by making the people who found the body disappear?"

"My guess, yes."

To Artemus, "The only way they'd be known is if they talked to the press…" It dawned on me, "Or simply emailed someone about their find. The Russian version of Echelon?"

"Christ." Artemus barreled from the room.

That left me, Forte and Blue in the room.

My stomach growled.

"Poker, beer and chips while we wait?"

Geo, as her fellow captives called her, grew up onboard the Mir. She knew nothing else in terms of her physical location in the world. Her knowledge of the basics – reading, writing and math - was thorough otherwise. Toss in a bit of philosophy, artistic forays, economics from the Americans, and her education had been reasonably rounded. But to her, without benefit of newspapers or other media, current events stopped at 1984. That was as much as her fellow travelers knew.

Her father, a loving man, allowed her in the pilot house of the ship. As Captain, he taught her navigation. She was awed by the ability of the small steering wheel to turn such a huge vessel. Of the view from the pilothouse windows across the decks and bow. She had been in the command center of this ship during storms, rogue waves, calm south Pacific seas and the frigid, angry Baltic.

When her father died, she wept. When her mother died, she wept. When Mort Brodsky disappeared, her back straightened and the years of training by the small Jewish man allowed her to take over the reigns as leader of the American contingent.

She entered the pilot house uninvited but never denied. "Captain, a moment please."

She saw the long, drawn worry lines in Merchenko's face. The slouch of the shoulders. The tightly fisted hands.

"Is everything okay?" she asked.

Merchenko closed his eyes, forcing his lips to turn upward. "As good as can be expected, Geo. What can I do for you?"

"Jimmy brought up an interesting point that perhaps you can clarify. We have been circling this area ever since Mr. Brodsky disappeared."

"And James knows this, how?"

"He is a stargazer, Captain. Quite good at it. He says the bow of our ship has been regularly crossing the Leo constellation on 36 hour intervals. We, thus, are circling.

The council would like to know if there is a reason for this."

"Tell James we will be moving to a new location soon and he shouldn't worry." He looked at her and for a flash of a second his eyes went dim, the smile flickered off then back on. Geo nodded, turned and left the pilot house.

Captain Merchenko had become enamored with the 20-year-old having watched her grow from a gawky 13-year-old to a smart, pretty young woman. It would be sad when she died.

As the four of us attempted bluffing a pair of deuces to a winning hand, Forte asked, "You mentioned following the tattoos to discover the whereabouts of the mystery ship. A little elaboration would be welcome."

He raised my three potato-chip ante to eight.

"There were 15 tattoos, right?"

Everyone nodded.

"The oldest and crudest was near his belly button. Remember Blue remarking about that? Well, Brodsky was a government accountant in Washington D.C. Indoor job. Probably never got a tan on that part of his body. The melanin level would be his natural coloration when he boarded Flight 776. And it was. 24 on his hip. But the melanin level under that first tat was 31. That's a lot of suntan. He had been living day to day with his shirt off."

I added eight potato chips to the kitty and then another

two.

"The first tat was of a humpback whale. Where are they found? Pacific Ocean, mostly. Pretty large territory, but only in warm water – where the sun shines and Brodsky could have gotten a tan – when moving from north to south or vice versa to or from regular breeding grounds."

Forte bumped me another eight which Blue matched.

"By looking at the other tattoos and the underlying melanin level we could track the ship to mostly sunny and hot locations. Some hotter than others. By putting those on a world map of whale populations and movements, we get a fairly good idea of the path the ship had been taking over the previous 15 years."

"Why 15?" Blue asked, turning over her pair of fours which easily beat my pair of threes. She swept up the chips, ate two, and collected the cards. Shuffled and dealt another hand.

"This is a guess, but Brodsky was smart enough to plan the suntan and the whale tats, so I figured he also planned the time between tats. Say every year on a specific date. After all, he was trying to tell us where he was or had been so pinning the tats to a particular date would be logical. On March 30th of 2000, for example, I was here. On that date in 2001, I was here."

"So the last tattoo was a Sperm whale, it had to be at this location." Blue said. "Clever. But those whales are everywhere, from Washington State to Japan."

"But what the tat showed was not just any Sperm whale. It was a male, according to my rather abbreviated research. And under it, the skin had a melanin level of 35 putting it, in March, somewhere in the southern hemisphere where Sperm whales can be found. That's pretty much off the coast of New Zealand or Australia."

"You need three points in order to find a location," Blue said. "You have the whale breed's approximate location, the melanin which gives us an approximate time of year. Add the shark hunting grounds and the length of time Mr. Brodsky was dead..."

"And that puts him in a location about where we had the one dot on the map."

"Confirmation, again, only a bit narrower area to search," Forte said.

I couldn't help mimicking an MI6 friend as we had done so many times during our last encounter. "Quite." Peeking at my hand, "Ten chips of the potato to open."

No one got a chance to raise my bet. The conference room door slammed open. Sam barged in, "Everyone on deck! We got company!"

Following Sam with Blue and Forte right behind, we crashed back into the original hallway we'd taken to get to the conference room from the garage/stall at ground level. A soft thud could be heard ahead of us. Explosive charge of some kind.

"Saw six on the monitor," Sam yelled back at us. "Dressed in black. Flak jackets of some sort. SWAT headgear and automatic weapons."

We were crowded in the hallway, two abreast. All we had were *pistoles*. Those we each carried like a teenager carries an iPod. Part of our regular attire. But against six guys with automatic rifles, we were badly outgunned.

To Blue and Forte, "Head back. Get us something with guts from the armory!"

"There's an armory?" Blue asked, breathing deep, steady.

"There's always an armory in places like this. Where is it, Sam?"

"Behind the electronic whiteboard."

The two rushed back to the conference room, slapping at the bare bulbs in the ceiling, killing the light, while Sam and I inched forward.

The first slug took a chunk of Sam's ear. Lots of blood. A grunt of pain followed by an expletive and the booming sound of his Desert Eagle followed by a distant gasp. He'd caught a piece of somebody, but we couldn't tell who or how badly. They had broken all of the hallway bulbs up to the point they were shooting from. Between us, a lighted stretch of No Man's Land. Both sides hung back in the darkness.

Moving next to Sam, I flattened to the floor, pulling him down with me. Chatter of automatic weapon fire. Waist high if we'd been standing. Natural instinct is to shoot for the mass which is why I made our mass close to the ground. Rolling onto my back, I shot out the remaining four bulbs, hating to waste the ammo, but knowing a full clip is secondary to staying alive. We were plunged into absolute darkness. The kind that eyes can't adjust to.

"On the count of three," whispered to Sam, "shoot two about medium low. I'll play pool."

One... Two... Three...

Sam's measured shots down the core of the hallway into the dark were deafening. Desert Eagle punching holes in the air as big as cannonballs. The flash from the big-bore handgun's barrel giving quick laser-like light. Enough for me to gauge where along the ceiling I wanted to fire. Six shots at the ceiling, aiming three quarters the way into No Man's Land, hoping to bank a few slugs into the attackers, figuring they were in groups of two, three groups deep. Maybe spread out front to back 10 to 12 feet.

More automatic weapon fire. Again too high. Military hardware. Suppressed noise and flash. Hard to judge how far away. Sam and I belly crawled forward a dozen feet. Another count of three. We put down another layer of lead. Same as before. Faster belly crawling. Someone had been taking my measure and decided to try the same game. A round of eight hit just above our head, ricocheting off the ceiling and bouncing into the floor about where we had been. Deadly fire if we hadn't moved.

Both of us twisted our bodies, putting our backs to the opposing walls. Holding fire. Waiting for the visitors to move toward us. Hoping we'd removed at least some of the contingent. Make the odds a bit more even.

Sam and I held our breath. Arms extended, guns aimed roughly at ankle height.

Nothing. No sounds. No feet shuffling. No breathing.

No swish of pants material or creaking of leather garrison belts or tink of a loose shoulder strap loop.

Rookie soldiers in situations like this begin to panic after five or six minutes. Or figure they're in the clear. Professional soldiers will wait as long as it takes for the other side to make a mistake.

Sam's breathing had slowed to an imperceptible pace. Mine was slightly faster, but hell I'm just a lowly former bouncer-logger-welder turned writer in need of a "procedure."

Stupid argument with Cookie. She was just looking out for me. Oh shit, that could wait.

Another minute of dead silence. Were they still there? Did Sam and I luck out and kill them off? If we'd wounded any of them, we would have at least heard some painful gasps. A man shot does not remain quiet.

The combined brilliance of a thousand-candlepower worklight with the baritone explosion of a grenade launcher was enough to damn-near stop my heart. It took a second, but I realized it had all happened behind us and the result all in front. The illumination put three men in black clothes wearing night-vision goggles in stark outline. The grenade whistled over our heads and slammed into the lead man-in-black sending him backward before exploding and morphing him to mist. The other two were stunned into inaction. Sam took out the one on the left. I caught the one on the right just above the body armor. Their ends came quickly.

Sam rolled onto his stomach. I tipped onto my back.

"You okay, Sammy?"

"You're just a barrel of laughs, Nick."

"Speaking of barrels, how 'bout a beer? I'm buying."

CHAPTER SEVENTEEN

Propping my feet on the conference room table, gave myself a Bandon head-scratch. "Who were those guys?"

Tatiana's long legs crossed and recrossed. A nervous reaction she showed when Mother Russia came under critical review.

"Not government." A bit of defensiveness but also some relief. "Weapons were older Russian military. Government special operations units use the latest, most advanced weapons. These came from the black market, most likely. The men are what Americans call 'soldiers of fortune.'"

"Sure of that?"

"Da. To make sure, Sal is checking Russian military data base to see if these men's faces can be matched."

"I don't understand how they found this place and more importantly how they got in," dropping my feet to the floor.

Artemus, sitting silently after debriefing us on the incursion, suddenly became talkative. "It had to be your fault, Nick. The first snoopers came 'round after following you. They must have told the special ops team. It's not like the Russians don't know about this place. Just like they know about Area 51. But to attack it, that's supersized you-know-whats."

"Yeah, but why?" I asked. "Okay, they don't want us to blab about their prison ship. I get it. But neither does the U.S. government. It didn't send a hit team." Sal walked into the room, pulled up a chair and settled his 299 pounds into the cushion. "At least I don't think they did," raising an eyebrow to Sal.

"No, the U.S. government wants this to go without a hitch as long as its fingerprints are not on any rescue attempt. It wants to hold the whole shoot down and prison ship thing over the Russians' head." To Tatiana and her brothers, "Sorry about that. But it's true."

Yuri answered. "We would do same thing."

Sal nodded knowing the Russian was right. "Indeed you would." Climbing from his chair, he walked to the whiteboard, plugged a USB thumb drive into a slot in the podium. A couple of quick clicks and the image of a strange craft came up.

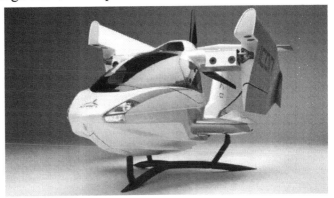

"This is the Icon A5," Sal said. "It will be the core of our plan to get our people home."

My groan stopped Sal in his tracks, brought a smile and a quick headshake telling me to knock it off until he'd finished.

"It is an amphibious two-seater..."

"Looks more like a jet ski." Couldn't help myself. "Aw, come on, Sal."

He ignored me, as Sal often does. "The wings fold, as you can see in this photo. It can take off from either ground or water. It can land on either ground or water.

"Here's a picture of it with the wings extended."

I had to admit it was a pretty cool little bugger. Pusher motor, three-blade prop. "It looks like a snowmobile."

"Well, it's not. It's going to be our entry onto the prison ship."

Sal clicked on the screen, launching a YouTube video of the Icon. Anyone who loves toys would be drooling over the film. It ended way too soon. I gotta get one of those.

Video over, Tatiana pushed herself upright in her chair,

"We don't even know what kind of ship this prison boat is."

"Which is why we went for a small two-passenger aircraft that's amphibious. If possible, it'll land on deck. If not on deck, then in the water nearby."

"This is sounding pretty edgy, my friend. Why don't we just send in Seal Team Six?" Sal shot me hard eyes. "Yeah, I know, no U.S. fingerprints. So who are the wild and crazy guys who will attack a prison ship using winged snowmobiles and confronting guards with guns?"

"You, of course. Why else would we invite you? Pilot. Know your way around weapons. Have been in the thick of some international situations. Can handle yourself pretty well in close hand-to-hand, at your age."

"Gee, thanks for the compliments, but who else?"

"Yuri, Forte and Tatiana. We were going to send Sam until you brought our Russian friends. We worried about using Sam because of his ties to Homeland Security, but didn't have a strong alternative. Now he'll stay home. Marcus will help with any radio translations we need."

Blue raised her hand, "Uh, what about me? I want to go."

Sal looked at her, "Miss Blue, I was going to ask you, but since you've just volunteered, you're now on the team." He ran fingernails through his beard. "Only one problem."

"What's that?" Blue asked.

"No government fingerprints. Your bosses just fired you this morning. All your records have been, uh, expunged."

"What!"

"Don't worry. It had to be done. You'll survive."
Looking at Artemus whose eyes went all official, "Nice
job, too."

She looked at Forte and grinned. He returned the smile
and gave her a short, low fist pump.

Sal continued, "I've taken the liberty of making all of
the arrangements for the assault with the appropriate
military operations. For your information, this is now a
level 22 secret. Once this is over, even I won't be able to
read the files."

Sal's beard moved. A smile? And the look on his face,
which I'd seen many times before, meant he was telling a
big fib. The operation may be Level 22, but Sal would
undoubtedly be able to read about it anytime he wanted.

He continued, "I know we haven't a clue, yet, of where
you will be going, but we have a general idea. And the plan
we've devised is sufficiently flexible to allow for the prison
ship to be anywhere in the South Pacific.

"My only problem, it'll take 36 to 40 hours to get all
the pieces in place and you six have to be in Hawaii in the
morning."

"Love Hawaii, Sallie. Can I buy one of those flowery
shirts like Dick Bentley wears?"

Standing joke between Sal and me. Dick, a fellow
Harley rider, drives a bright yellow Corvette. Wears
Hawaiian shirts and shorts. Has the knobbiest knees in all
Coos County and thinks waking neighbors with his riding
lawn tractor is great fun.

"No."

"How 'bout one of those drinks with umbrellas, then?"

"No."

"Will a pretty girl put a lei around my neck when we get off the airplane?"

"Shut the hell up, Nick."

Flying commercial has never been my idea of fun.

Yes, I know Mr. Boeing builds damn good airplanes. And the guys in the cockpit are reasonably well trained. But the notion of leaving my hind end in the hands of people I don't know is a bit disconcerting. Looking out a mini-porthole above the clouds isn't why I fly. I want to be down on the deck, seeing if there really is a mountain in my path.

My own Cirrus SR is the kind of plane that warms heart cockles. Fast, agile, sleek. Cookie accepts it and feels reasonably comfortable and safe because of the built-in parachute. Sal loves the plane because it's high tech, computer controlled and overfilled with gadgets. For me, its ability to almost anticipate my next flight move with lightning fast response gives me a tingle and an ear-to-ear smirk.

I could fly a 747 even though I've never tried. Landing would be the hard part, but heck, most landings are just crashes that don't happen.

On a cold, windy day in September some years ago, I

flew into the crater of Mount St. Helens just for the fun of
it. Steam was venting from the recent eruption and the FAA
wasn't happy with me. But the updraft of the vent and the
off-shore wind that sent the little Piper I was flying
backwards when I rose above the crater's edge put all
concerns about having my license pulled into a deep dark
lock box. The reprimand went into my permanent file –
there's that word again – and ended any chance of opening
an approved flying business. No sweat. That wasn't on my
bucket list anyway.

Blue and Forte were in the First Class seats ahead of
me, Yuri behind, and Tatiana in the window seat to my
right. The tickets went on my credit cards because Sal
didn't want any government fingerprints. He promised
reimbursement.

Yeah, right.

"You have talked to Cookie?" Tats asked.

"Not in a couple of days."

"You and Cookie okay?"

"Okay." Bandon head scratch. "She wants me to have a
procedure."

It was a word Tatiana wasn't familiar with.
"Procedure?"

"Doctor thing."

"Oh. Procedure is good for you?"

Thinking that over for a second, "Probably not bad.
Done all the time."

"Then why not get this procedure?"

"It's a guy thing."

"Men don't like this procedure?"

"Not particularly."

Tatiana digested my answer. "Only men get this?"

"No, women too."

"Then why not agree to procedure if Cookie also gets?"

I looked at the gorgeous Eurasian, smiled and planted a kiss right on her lovely cheek. "You're brilliant!"

Even though I'd have to wait to land before sending it, I wrote a quick text message to Cookie and stashed it under Drafts.

"I'll do it if you do it."

The Mir, a mid-70s Chinese-built oil tanker, was well beyond its life expectancy. Repairs to the 2480 kW engine were increasingly difficult and frequent. With a range of 3,000 miles, and deadweight of about 7,100 tons, it was the ocean-going equivalent of a Nash Rambler.

Converting it to house prisoners was done in a secret military shipyard. The same yard that upfitted Soviet submarines near St. Petersburg. Early revisions were solely to make room for the 169 passengers, handful of guards and small operations crew. Sparse, dormitory style compartments put 30 prisoners to a room.

After the fall of the Soviet Union, and the realization that the ship would no longer be sanctioned if discovered, it was necessary to either end its duties by scuttling both ship

Page
264

and all aboard or making the accommodations more civil. The latter would reduce the chances of conflicts that would only make discovery that much more politically embarrassing.

With the encouragement of Captain Petrov, the original skipper, the decision was made to revamp both the ship and its purpose. None of the Captain's superiors were aware of his marriage to one of the prisoners, only that he had committed to remaining on board for the rest of his life.

That, and similar commitments from two of the guards meant the Mir could sustain its secret mobile-island status well into the future without needing to dock. Granted the complexity of refueling and resupplying such a vessel posed unusual circumstances, Boris Nicovich, the powerful and feared energy czar, found a willing accomplice in one of the newly wealthy oil barons. For secretly supplying the support necessary to keep the Mir afloat and off shore, the baron's company would receive government contracts worth hundreds of millions of dollars.

The deal was struck. The Mir went on circling the globe, resupplied with fuel and human necessities by quarterly mid-ocean transfers. So well planned were these exchanges, the true nature of the Mir remained hidden from knowledge except for the Russian energy czar and the oil magnate.

"You will make way to the following longitude and latitude," the General informed Captain Merchenko. "Be there no later than 2200 hours GMT." Silence for a second, "That is 21 and a half hours from now, Captain."

"When we arrive, General, what will be the procedure?"

Another silence. As if the General was attempting to decide how much to tell his subordinate officer. Finally, "The Mir is to be scuttled at that location. We will have a small contingent of experts to deal with the passengers. It is something I cannot ask you or your guards to do, Captain Merchenko." Another pause. The voice small and almost sad. "I am sorry this must happen."

"God forgive us, General."

"He cannot. Nor do I expect to ask for that forgiveness." The voice became stronger, "You have done a significant and exemplary service to Russia, Captain. You will not receive praise or a medal or commedation. But Mother Russia will forever be in your debt."

The line went dead. Merchenko cradled the handset, detached the rubber suction cup with its long wire and clicked the off-switch of his micro-cassette recorder.

I punch the overhead button.

Being First Class, a flight attendant appeared almost instantly. I shook the first one off and punched the button again. The same woman came to the seat and I wagged my head a second time. She glared and returned to that little place behind the wall where flight attendants gather and tell jokes about their passengers.

A second later, an older woman in a tailored uniform that enhanced her aging figure poked out of the hidey hole and made way to my seat.

"May I help you, sir?"

"You're perfect."

"Beg your pardon?"

"Mind if I ask how long you've been a flight attendant?"

Moving one hand to her hip and the other on top of the back of Forte's seat, "Is this some snide comment that'll make me throw you off the plane?" The words were harsher than the look on her face. I could like this woman.

"No, I'm curious and I have a question."

"I've been a flight attendant since we were called stewardesses. Now what's the question?"

"Ever fly in a 727?"

"Of course."

"The model 100?"

"The plane that had an exit in the back, yes. I was a rookie back then. Why?"

"Where was the lavatory?"

Deep sigh, "If I recall, there was one in the front, another pair in the back on either side of the rear stairway. Why?"

"Did the plane have cabin access to the luggage or baggage compartment downstairs?"

"Only on the flight deck. Nothing in the cabin. Why?"

Blue had picked up on the conversation and turned in her seat to watch the older flight attendant.

"One last question. Did you ever know Tina

Mucklow?"

Her face showed a mind searching through years of commercial flying with hundreds of flight attendants. The light. "Oh, not really. Knew of her, though. She was one of the stews on that D. B. Cooper flight, if I recall."

"Thank you. Oh, what's your name?"

"Sweeps Sullivan."

"Odd name."

"Blame my Irish dad. Glad I could help."

Blue leaned over the seat back and to Tatiana, "Switch."

The two women changed places, Blue falling into the window seat, legs curled under her.

"You're guessing what, Nick?"

"Okay, let's look at the clues again."

Scrounging into the footwell, I pulled out my duffle bag and slid the D. B. Cooper file onto the fold-down tray. All of that took a bit of doing and would have been impossible in coach, my big feet and long legs in the way.

"Remember what you said about the Joe Friday clue not being a 'badge' because that would mean there were two clues referring to being a fake FBI agent?"

"Sure. It was a brilliant observation, if I say so myself."

"Well, the same can be said about these."

I pulled two cards out of the deck.

You can't find me. But I am there.
Hide and seek

Ghost
Peep hole
Hidden

Magician David Copperfield
Cute *(that had to be Mary Ann)*
Sleight of hand
Card tricks
Poker
Black Jack
Pick a card, any card
Four stacks, four aces on top
Something seems it's not there but is
Rabbit in a hat
Blood to water
Wine to blood

She stared at the clues. The light dawning slowly, but certainly.

"Why two clues about hiding? Is that what you mean?"

"That's the same problem as the badge clue. There's no reason to have two clues saying she was hiding, so one of these is wrong. Let's say that 'Something seems it's not there but is' is the correct clue. Then what does 'You can't find me, but I am there' mean?"

Blue began shaking her head. "Sorry, Nick. I'm not getting anything."

"Okay, let's back up." I rummaged through the cards again and pulled out another one.

Joe Friday has one
<u>Gun</u>
Partner
<u>Badge</u>
~~Distinctive voice~~
~~Acting ability~~
~~Monotone voice~~

"First we thought this one was a badge. That duplicated the other clue about being an FBI agent. Then we figured it was a gun. Good choice. But it conflicts with one of the best scenarios. Yes, she may have had a gun, but is that a suitable clue to prove someone else isn't Cooper? Not really. It tells us nothing about *how* she committed the hijacking. What if the Joe Friday clue actually is a tip off that she had a *partner*."

Blue mulled that, reached up and punched the flight attendant buzzer. As Sweeps Sullivan reached our seats, "Could we have a couple of beers, please?"

"Yes, ma'am."

She returned in less than a minute with two Millers, tops already popped, and a pair of beer glasses. Gotta love First Class.

Neither of us bothered with the glass.

"So, Nick, you're saying one of the flight crew was a

partner to Cooper. That's hard to fathom since the Bureau checked out everyone backward and frontward and sideways."

"Yes, but what of the stewardess who became a nun?"

"Tina Mucklow. Later changed her name to Tina Larson."

"Yeah, that's the one. She never talked to the press. She never gave her take on the hijacking. She became reclusive and later became a nun."

"Oh, man, you're smearing someone who can't answer that kind of accusation, Nick."

"I'm only talking here. And she didn't have to be a real partner in the crime. What if it was after the fact?"

"How so."

"Okay, follow me on this. What if D. B. Cooper faked the jump and stayed on board. In the lavatory. The plane lands in Reno. Before law enforcement comes on board, the crew searched the plane for Cooper. Tina opens the lavatory door. Cooper points the gun in her face and says something like, 'Tell anyone I'm here and I'll kill you.' Maybe threatens her family.

Scared, she gives a quick nod of agreement. Closes the door. The cops come aboard. She and the others are escorted from the plane. Cooper slips out of the lavatory and begin searching the plane for himself. Feebies and cops leave with Cooper tagging along."

"Wow. You think it could have happened that way?"

"It's a damn good bet Cooper didn't jump out of the plane. Not asking for warm weather gear is the best indicator of that. Not caring if the plane took one flight path or another is a second. The plane was clearly going significantly faster than the demanded 150 miles per hour. If Cooper had been, as the FBI suspected, a military jumper sometime in the past, I can guarantee you he would have known the difference between 150 and 195 miles an hour. Or, as our speed calculator showed, in excess of 220 miles per hour. He had access to the flight deck intercom. He would have demanded the plane slow down to the agreed to speed. The fact is, he didn't."

"So what else can we get out of David Copperfield, then?"

"He's an illusionist. Have you ever seen his Lazer Magic act where he cuts himself in half on stage then his bottom half carries around his top half?"

"No."

"Quite the illusion. In fact, what Cooper is telling us is that the entire hijacking and escape is nothing but an illusion. It should have been the first clue, not near the last. Every other clue supports the overall framework of the hijacking being an illusion."

Blue sighed long and slow. "But none of that proves the guy who we have in custody *isn't* D. B. Cooper."

Frustration is a tough emotion to beat back. This was bouncing me between glee at deciphering the clues and depression over not being able to put a finger directly on the person who hijacked Flight 305.

"I need a nap."

Blue patted my hand and laughed. "Poor Nicky."

I closed my eyes and asked, "Have you ever had a procedure?"

"What kind of procedure?"

"The kind that… Never mind."

CHAPTER EIGHTEEN

A pretty little Hawaiian woman in a fake grass skirt and a huge white smile put her arms up in the air as high as she could. It wasn't high enough so I had to bend down to get her to slip the lei over my head and around my neck.

"Thank you."

"No prob," she said with a decidedly southern accent.

Bubble burst. The tourism department for the islands needs lots of bodies to pass out these Polynesian necklaces, even if the giver comes from Charlotte or Dallas. I thumbed the fake flower gift around and found the little tag that someone had forgotten to remove. "Made in China."

Bubble two, burst.

The second greeting for the five of us was a tall skinny kid at the gate with a Seattle tan holding a sign reading, "Drago Party."

"Don't tell me. You're from Detroit or Phoenix."

"No, sir. I was born here."

Bubble three, burst all to hell. Hope the operation goes better.

We were led to a Lincoln Town Car limo, bags stuffed in the trunk and us in the back seat. I remembered to take my phone off of airplane mode and send the text message to Cookie.

Mentally I said, "Take that. Hah."

We pulled out of the airport under a cloudless blue sky and 80 degree temperatures. The air conditioning in the limo was cranked up to freezing.

The cell phone rang in my shirt pocket. "Drago."

"Nick! We found it!"

"What'd you find, Sal?"

"The ship. The prison ship. We know where it is *right now*."

I punched speaker phone so everyone could hear.

"Satellite?"

"Only for confirmation. Echelon Explorer found it! Picked up some encrypted chatter between Sakhalin Island and a ship in the general area of that dot you put on the Pacific map. Hit the archives of communications looking for a different set of key words and son of a bitch, it traced nearly a year of communications."

Cheers and fist pumps all around the limo.

"So we know what we're doing and where we're going? That was fast. I was hoping for a couple of days on the beach or surfing or something."

"We'll talk when you get to the hotel. The op is set for tomorrow and you guys will have to be on the move pretty damn quick to get where we're going."

Sal clicked off. My phone buzzed. A text message.

From Cookie. "*Deal*" is all it said.

I gave Tatiana a sour look. "Gee, thanks."

She smiled. "Procedure?"

"Don't act so innocent. You and Cookie set me up."

She turned her head to the window so I couldn't see her smile.

"Damn cell phones."

Sal was waiting for us in the hotel's business center conference room.

"How the heck did you get here before us?" I asked.

"A little military assistance. I didn't think your credit card could use another first-class airfare on it." He pointed to the chairs around the table. "Sit."

Over the next hour, Sal set out to explain the plan of attack. It was scary brilliant.

There are basically three ways to take over a large ship with some defenses. One is to blow a hole in its side and simply destroy it where it floats, hoping to kill as many of the people on board as possible. The second is to storm it with overwhelming manpower and firepower and make a statement about not taking shit from anyone. And third, send in a small group of commandos who silently kill everyone who could possibly offer resistance.

In our case, we didn't have the resources of government munitions to blow it up, nor the attack battleship necessary to make a statement. And we were hardly commandos, even though all of us had some experience in police or law enforcement or government security. Well, everyone but me. Like I said, I'm a logger-bouncer-welder turned writer who happens to have a nice gun collection.

Nor did we want to kill everyone. Just the opposite.

What Sal was laying out was a spooky attack with lots of ways it could go wrong. It was up to each of us to make sure the others didn't screw up and as titular head of the op, my duty was to keep everyone alive until the cavalry arrived.

What we didn't know worried me most. The number of defenders. The number of prisoners. Modifications to the ship that would have been made to accommodate prisoners for these many years. Were they behind locked reinforced steel doors with a guard always in the hallway? Had they become so accustomed to their captivity they suffered Stockholm syndrome and would side with their captors? Was the Captain a military man or the faux mayor of a colony? Was the ship booby trapped for just such an attack? Or was it booby trapped to keep prisoners from escaping?

I couldn't fret about everything, but that was enough.

Sal had pinned a four-by-six foot wall map of the Pacific to the wall of the conference room.

He moved to an area somewhat south of where my original dot was drawn when trying to locate where Brodsky slipped over the side in his bubble-wrap suit.

"This is where you're going," Sal said, marking a small black X between the Marshall Islands and Hawaii. We'll have a hard point by the time you take off. It's one of the deepest parts of the ocean which makes sense if you're going to scuttle a tanker with all aboard and hope it's never found."

"How deep?" Blue asked.

"More than 19,000 feet. Very deep."

"What kind of message did you get, Sallie?" I asked.

"The key part of the communication was the location the ship was to reach. The ship's Captain seemed reluctant. His commanding officer also saddened by what had to be done. But there was no doubt the end game was to kill everyone on board and sink the ship."

"Type of ship," I said.

"Tanker. Oil tanker, we believe, based on the satellite photos. Once we were able to pinpoint the communications and the starting and ending point, we were able to move the satellite to take a peek at the ships in the area.

"This is well off the usual shipping channels so the only ships were rogues or private. We narrowed it down pretty quickly to the Mir, an old Chinese bucket of rust built in the '70s and small by today's oil tanker standards. We couldn't get much detail of the ship because of cloud cover, but enough to know the decks have been partially cleared of piping, gear and oil or chemical transfer lines and hardware."

"So they've turned it into a what, a cruise ship?"

"Not quite, but I'll tell you the Captain sounded pretty reluctant to carry out his orders. Not so much what he said, but what our voice profilers said the undertone of his comments and inflections gave away."

Blue leaned back in her chair and looked directly into Sal's eyes. She was hard core Feebie, no doubt. "Is there the possibility they consider themselves, including the prisoners, a colony all unto itself and would fight anyone who tries to intrude or interrupt or end their current way of life?"

Sal hesitated a second too long. Softly, "We don't think so, but it is certainly a possibility. The resistance may come not only from the Russians on board, but the Americans as well. It's something you'll have to deal with in real time. As it happens. If it happens."

I wanted this conversation to end and right now. It was putting doubts into the minds of those of us who would make the assault. "We can't worry about that. Not now. We know this: The Russians are going to…"

"Not Russians. Rogue criminals," Tatiana said, a touch of anger in her voice.

"Sorry, Tatiana, I'm using 'Russians' as a simple way of identifying who *they* are. Not intended to broad brush all Russians, believe me."

She crossed her arms and gave a jerk of her head. Point made.

I continued, "The people who are responsible for this prison ship are going to sink it. Period. We agreed?"

Everyone, including Tatiana and Yuri, nodded.

"So our job is to take it over and make sure that doesn't happen. We'll sort out the good guys and bad guys after we've locked down control of the ship and have some protection from the U.S. government or whoever. Maybe it'll mean sailing the damn thing all the way to Hawaii and into U.S. waters, but I seriously doubt our government would like that."

"Pearl Harbor," Sal said. "We need to get those people to Pearl. We have ways of making sure they are debriefed and give us time to figure out what to do with them."

"Like what?" Blue asked.

"Who the hell knows? They can't be talking to the press for sure. They can't be telling their story to Dateline or the Enquirer or the New York Times. We have to isolate them for a time and make sure they understand that revealing what happened to them could cause an international incident of monumental proportions. That's a bridge we cross later."

Squinting at Sal, "Don't tell me there are some in the U.S. government who would prefer the ship be scuttled and all on board wind up dead."

Sal remained silent.

"This isn't a suicide mission, is it Sallie?"

"No." The answer came too quickly, but sometimes that means the person giving the answer is actually convinced his response is correct because he had that discussion before and won an argument.

"Okay, I accept your promise that we'll not be dead tomorrow at this time," I said.

"I didn't promise that," he grinned. "But knowing you, you'll come home in an oil tanker with flames painted on the bow."

"You think they have *Dos Equis* onboard? Or some

stupid Russian beer made from cow dung?"

The five of us – me, Forte, Tatiana, Blue and Yuri – sat with our backs against the thin walls of the fuselage, the smell of dust, axle grease, motor oil, and the motor pool's friend in a can, WD 40.

Major Steven C. Montgomery walked through the cargo area looking like Tom Cruise only a lot younger. Thin, short – maybe 5-foot-six – tan with close cropped hair. The flight suit outlined a fit and lean body and the requisite Air Force pilot sunglasses wrapped around a full good-looking face.

"Hate to tell you, Major, but it's dark out there. Do you need the shades?"

"Mr. Drago, sir, you should see me when I fly this thing with the blindfold on." Light banter that often hides a touch of nervousness. Mine, not his. "We'll get this thing off the ground in five so strap in."

This "thing" happened to be a Boeing C17 Globemaster, meant to airlift cargo into combat zones. A huge door at the rear of an 88-foot by 18-foot by 12-foot bay capable of delivering anything a forward troop contingent needs.

"Major, are you sure you can do this?"

"I put one of these down in the desert. Another in a rice paddy. Hell, on this run, I won't even have to put the wheels down. Of course I can do this."

Raising a hand, "No offense meant."

"Mr. Drago, sir, what you are going to do is far more dangerous than what I'm gonna do. Good luck," he said, walking toward the cockpit.

The four Pratt and Whitneys wound up, the vibration and noise transmitted through the walls of the fuselage. The three Icon A5s strapped down by the Loadmaster, a sergeant named Hopkins. Each sitting with their wheels up on Styrofoam blocks to keep them upright. Wings folded back. Noses toward the front of the C17, tails to the rear loading door. Each painted flat black and, Sal guaranteed, the bottoms and other components fully reinforced.

The Air Force doesn't believe in windows so we had no idea what was going on except by what our ears and rears told us.

As the engines spun up, forward motion initially slow and lumbering, gaining speed and then the release from gravity like pulling your shoes out of mud. The nose of the C17 tipped up under full power using all of the aircraft's 1800-feet-per-minute climb rate. I was guessing more without the usual 275,000 pounds of payload and Tom Cruise at the controls.

"Never been in one of these," Blue said into her wireless headset. Her voice was a bit anxious.

"Piece of cake," turning my head toward her. "Just be glad Forte isn't piloting. You'd be airsick by now."

The Chief snorted, but didn't respond. He and I occasionally flew in his Cherokee when the day was just right and I wasn't in the mood to burn through a hundred gallons of av-gas just to see the sights. Forte flew to Eugene when he wanted a cup of coffee because he loved to fly. Maybe even more than me. Well, probably not more.

Closing my eyes, I could hear idle chatter among the group and began to realize that Forte and Blue were having a bit of repartee. Nice to hear. Gave me a pang of guilt for being so hard-headed about "the procedure."

The engines quieted as the Galaxy's nose flattened out. At the C17's cruise speed of 515 miles per hour, it would be three hours before we were offloaded. That would make it about midnight Hawaii time. Who the hell knew what time it would be on the ship.

I ran over Sal's plan in my head.

Should work.

I trusted Forte as a pilot, but Blue was the unknown. She'd learned to fly back in Wyoming as a kid. Her license was up to date, but she'd only flown rentals and not that many hours. She was checked out at Hickman Field in the Icon. Did pretty well. But that was only two hours behind the stick. This was going to be a lot tougher.

But the Icon is a new breed of light sport aircraft allowed under FAA's recently approved Sport Pilot License. Cheaper, easier to get; planes more car-like with a shallow learning curve.

I decided I couldn't worry about it now. For all the talk about keeping American fingerprints off of the operation, having Blue along – fired or not – seemed contrary to the goal. Didn't quite get it. When asked, Sal just said it was a necessary risk. As was using the C17.

Chatter among the others lasted only an hour as everyone went inside their own heads to either think about what was to come or to simply catch a quick nap.

Three hours after takeoff, Loadmaster sergeant bumped each of us on the knee and made a twirly sign with his index finger.

"Ah, you want to dance. No, wait, you think you're a helicopter."

"Cute, Drago. Get your ass in gear and light these little toy air-ee-oh-planes up. You're going for a swim."

Forte and Yuri climbed into the middle Icon while Tatiana and I took our seats in the front craft. Blue slipped into the rear Icon.

"Everyone locked in?" I said into the stalk coming from my helmet to a dime-sized mic in front of my lips.

"Locked, loaded and lovin' it," Forte responded. If there was any anxiety left, it was now replaced with excitement. The Chief always liked a good fight. The others simply responded, "Here."

The Loadmaster walked past each of us. Individually we gave thumbs up to indicate we were ready when he was. Sergeant grabbed a solid hold on a wall-mounted grip, planted his feet and waited.

Suddenly the C17 became an elevator heading to the ground floor; stomach left behind. P+Ws winding down, the big plane's nose rising a few degrees, letting its wings catch air. The mechanical sound of flaps being lowered. Airspeed drastically cut. Everything shaking.

Rapidly.

Loadmaster sergeant hit a control and the huge ramp-door began to lower. Paying it little attention, he leaned down and released the latches holding my Icon to the in-floor rollers used to dump pallets out the back. They usually had parachutes attached. We didn't. Sergeant Hopkins performed the same procedure on Forte's and Blue's Icons.

The little amphibians rocked on their foam braces.

Sergeant Hopkins walked to the front of my Icon. He could be seen by all of us through Plexiglas windshields. Holding up his hands with all fingers wide spread. 10 seconds. The Galaxy rattled even more as it slowed to what I assumed was near 'brick rate.' When an aircraft is going so slow it falls to earth like a brick, wings be damned.

I pictured Tom Cruise in the pilot's seat. Grinning through a cigar clamped in his teeth. Sunglasses glinting reflections of the cockpit gauges. Co-pilot covering his eyes.

Sergeant Hopkins tossed up a five count with his left hand. Then four fingers. Then three… Two… One.

He hit a button on a remote handle and Blue's Icon rolled backward. In my side-view mirror I saw it disappear into the black craw of night sky through the open doorway. Then Forte's. Then mine.

"Thank you for coming, Geo," Merchenko said to the woman who looked at the others gathered in the pilot house. They included Yuri, the oldest guard, Spivak, the

First Officer who had been aboard for as long as she had been alive and Petrov, the youngest of the group and the most recent addition of the commanding Russians.

The Captain leaned against the navigation console, hands behind his back.

"I have called all of you here because our mission is coming to a conclusion."

He cleared his throat before continuing. "Within hours we will be what the Americans call 'on the unemployment line.'" He didn't expect a laugh but Yuri smiled.

Geo interrupted, "What is going to happen, Leonid? To us and the island?"

Merchenko was always amused by the captives calling the ship an island. They actually referred to it as "Gilligan's Island" for some reason he was not privy, assuming it was an inside American joke.

"Allow me to explain, first. Yuri, Spivak and Petrov and I are here because of the safety it afforded our families. The small contingent of engine-room and systems personnel have similarly been well provided for. By volunteering for duty on the Mir, we were guaranteed permanent jobs and high rewards for the family we left behind."

To Yuri, "As the only one who has been aboard since its first days, you understand this better than any of us. You were enlisted at a time the Soviet Union was in massive economic decline."

"Da. No food. Long lines for even the most common of necessities," Yuri said, eyes leveled at the Captain. "My wife and children and, I am only guessing, grandchildren are well to this day because of that decision."

"And they are, Yuri. And that will not change after today."

Pushing off from the nav console, Merchenko looked at each of the faces in the room he had come to know well.

"But these orders, these commands from our superiors are wrong."

Petrov straightened as if he were slapped. That was not a surprise to Merchenko. The young man was filled with a belief in the superiority of his country. In his duty to Mother Russia. His President's vision of a powerful and economically dominant nation.

Geo tilted her head and asked again, "And what happens to us, Leonid." Not a question, a statement. "We would not have been kept aboard this vessel for these many decades without a reason. Is the reason no longer valid or is it such an embarrassment it requires a final act?"

Yuri intervened, "Geo, lovely lady, this could not go on forever. This day has been written from the time your parents and I came aboard."

"True," Merchenko said, head nodding. "But we do have the ability to define the way we write the final act." He released a long sigh, a signal to the others that his decision came only after long consideration. "I am taking this ship to Hawaii and will ask the Americans for protection."

"What!" Petrov yelled, raising his rifle.

Merchenko snapped his right hand from behind his

back and leveled a semi-automatic at the young guard. "Do not go further. I will shoot you."

"But you can't go crying to the Americans, Captain! We have a responsibility to protect Russia. To honor the desires of our superiors who clearly know what must be done better than we do."

"Yuri, please relieve Petrov of the rifle."

The older guard slowly and gently took the weapon, clearing the chamber and clip of any ammunition, stuffing the shells into a pocket.

"Geo," Merchenko said to the young woman, "tell your fellow Americans they are going home. But we may well require some assistance in doing so."

"What kind of assistance?"

"We are supposed to be at a particular location at a specific time in order to scuttle the Mir and presumably terminate the lives of anyone who is onboard. I have, for the past nine hours been steaming toward Hawaii. Command, however, will undoubtedly track us down and we will need to defend this ship."

"We will help," Geo said.

"Good." To Yuri, "And you?"

The old soldier gave a quick nod. "I have always wanted to see Hollywood."

Merchenko looked at his first officer who exhaled deeply. "I go reluctantly and in protest, but I will not stand in the way of your decision, Captain. Please note that in your log so I can return home."

Merchenko nodded. "Thank you. It will be noted."

Petrov, face reddening, hands trembling in anger, "I promise you I will perform my duties as a soldier of the Russian Federation! You will not get to Hawaii if I can stop it, Captain. You are wrong."

"Then forgive me, Petrov." The small semi-automatic spat twice.

With the Globemaster flying directly into a light wind and barely a dozen feet above a smooth ocean, the drop from the rear of the C17 was quick, hard and damn scary. Once hitting the rear edge of the open doorway, the tail of the Icon dipped, tossing the nose upward. Like being on the bottom-end of a teeter-totter.

The tail slammed into the water at over a hundred miles an hour – the Globemaster's slowest speed while still able to stay airborne. The Icon skittered, leaping from low swell to low swell. Each impact with the ocean at that speed like hitting a Manhattan pot hole, smashing my teeth together, sending arches of pain into the crown of my head.

The small craft dropped its nose, nearly plowing into the Pacific sending it ass over teakettle. Folded wings viciously vibrating under the impact and C17 backwash.

The cinched harness – an X across my chest, two padded straps across my lap – held me tight to the cushioned seat, but the deceleration to zero miles an hour took 20 seconds, my body being slammed forward then backward in micro-second increments, trying to tear the seat bolts from the floor.

Tatiana's eyes were closed, arms hugging her chest, head snapping back and forward with each crash of the Icon into the next swell.

Then silence.

The Icon settled into the ocean, gently rocking. The cacophony of rushing air, deluging water over the windshield and creaking of the hull with each collision with the Pacific now gone.

"Breathe, Tats."

I saw her nod, but she had nothing to say.

Moonshine streamed into the cockpit providing enough illumination for me to find the interior light switch. The white LED beam from the overhead lamp cast shadows. I found the lever for unfolding the wings and twisted it. As the wings groaned, I grabbed the CB and called the others.

"Everyone still with us?"

"We're fine," Forte said. "Wild ride, though. Everything still seems to be attached."

"Don't you ever do that to me again!" Blue yelled into her mic. "That scared the pee out of me, Nick!"

"But you're okay otherwise?"

"Yeah, and everything is still strapped down. Good to go."

"Fire up the engines as soon as the wings are extended and regroup on my tailfin light." I blinked it twice and got two positive responses that it was visible.

Tatiana had already flicked on the GPS and called up

our intended destination. The soft green glow of the screen put a strange color on her (and I assume my) face.

"How far?" I asked.

"Just as Sal said, about 100 miles northwest." She turned her head toward me, "Do you think we were seen on anyone's radar?"

"Way below radar and Major Montgomery will keep the C17 that way until he reaches the Philippines. Then he'll pop up on everyone's radar and click on his transponder and suddenly, just another American spy plane in the Asian skies."

The wings clicked into their locking slots, the levers and motors making that happen automatically stopped. I turned the key and pressed the "start" button. The juiced up Rotax 912 ULS engine puts out 100 horsepower in production form. Sal's guys were able to squeeze another 35 out of it boosting its top speed from 120 miles-per-hour to 140 mph, even with the added exhaust sound suppression. Not sure we'd need it, but boys will be boys.

Within a dozen minutes, Blue's Icon pulled up to my starboard wing, Forte's on my left.

"Okay, folks, follow me. Blue take up the rear. Keep everyone in sight but only use your tailfin light. Clear?"

Two acknowledgements.

I wound up the Rotax and picked up a swell heading east, riding it like a surfer, cracking the throttle wide open and lifting off of the ocean's surface in only a few hundred feet.

Anyone who's a pilot knows within minutes if the plane

being flown is symbiotic. The little Icon handled like an agile boat, reacting to every joystick input with a crisp response. The warm night light from the near-full moon gave the ocean the look of a black satin comforter through the panoramic canopy. The 34-foot wingspan and carbon-fiber fuselage softened the ride to a solid firmness without the jarring common in light aircraft.

"How far?"

Tatiana traced a finger over the GPS. "83 miles."

"About 40 minutes," I said aloud for Tat's sake. A landlubber through and through, being in an airplane not much longer than a full-size car and seeing the ocean barely 50 feet below flashing past at over 130 miles per hour can be disconcerting for those with issues about flying.

Not for me. Seascape – rushing under the wings – with the horizonless ocean topped by a dome of black sky shotgunned with white points of light. Off to my right, Alpha Centauri. Above, the pinpoint of light called Mars with Saturn a bit lower and to the Red Planet's right. Directly ahead, the Serpent Head constellation.

The droning of the pumped up Rotax engine faded away. The sky was mesmerizing to anyone to who liked flying at night.

For the others, perhaps with the exception of the Chief, it was tediously mind numbing.

To break up the chances of falling into the same kind of highway hypnotism that happens in a car driving through the desert for any length of time, I'd climb, bank and change speeds forcing both Forte and Blue to do the same.

Use of the CB had to be minimized, thanks to possible voice captures by Russian or U.S. eavesdropping hardware.

"Just ahead," Tatiana said after 35 minutes, leaning closer to the windscreen, hand unconsciously resting on her holstered Colt .45.

I pulled back on the throttle, slowing to less than 40 miles per hour and aiming into the light northeasterly wind.

Nothing but ocean. No bulk of a large oil transport ship. No lights from its conning tower.

"Where is it?" I asked.

"Should be here," Tatiana said, resetting the GPS to a different ratio.

"Hey Nick, what's up?" Forte asked.

"Trying to figure it out, Chief. Looks like a dry hole."

"Could the GPSs all be wrong?"

"Not likely."

Blue clicked on. "Didn't the intel say this is where they're supposed to be?"

"Yup." Thinking it over, "I'm gonna have to break radio silence, gang. We'll circle for a few minutes until Papa Sal or Uncle Artie tells us what's going on."

I flipped on the AV radio and clicked the mic switch three short blips. Checked the fuel gauge. Still three-quarters of a tank. Clicked three more times.

After a minute, "Heading 59.55 at 243." It was Sal's voice, but no sooner were the words spoken, the speaker went dead. He'd shut his radio down.

Tatiana played with the time-distance and nav system.

"Sal is saying the tanker is heading toward Hawaii, Nick. It's 243 miles ahead of us."

Checked the fuel gauge again. "Nothing like my big bearded buddy to stretch the limits. We've got just enough fuel, I'm figuring. Think it'll take us two hours. If the tanker is moving at 20 knots, that will make the distance from here to the eventual location of the tanker about 290 miles. We ain't got that much fuel, I'm guessing."

Forte broke in. "Fly like geese, Nick. You up front. Us in your wing draft. That'll save us some fuel. After half an hour, switch. I'll lead. 'Nother half an hour, Blue leads."

Quick calculation in my head, "Might do it. Worth a try. Let's get a little altitude, too. Should save us a bit of gas."

I took the trio up to 200 feet. Still below most radar systems, but the air was a bit calmer. In triangle formation, Forte and Blue tucked into my back draft, they were able to cut rpms and still maintain speed.

An hour. My fuel gauge had dipped well below half a tank. We'd covered 122 miles. Blue took the lead from Forte who dropped back to a position where his wing tip floated just a few feet off of mine.

The clock swung through its third trip around. Fuel gauge at a hair over empty.

Another click on the earset. Sal's voice. "Heading 62.18 at 32." Click off.

I made the adjustment, pulled back on the throttle.

Blue who was in the lead, "See it, Nick." She swung port and slowed so I could take the lead with Forte immediately behind me.

The tanker perched on low swells, its massive hull dark, foreboding. A white froth trailing behind the ship. I could smell the exhaust. Bitter. Oily.

A forward deck stretching maybe 600 feet in front of a four-story tower of steel, shaped like a T, punctuated with square windows. Light coming from the central windows in the top floor. The pilot house. All but a single bottom-floor window black.

"Got it."

In Indian file, we sank back to 100 feet, then to 50.

From this point, the plan was simple. Land near the tanker. Idle up to the hull. Toss over the magna-dock lines which would attach to the hull and hold the Icons in place. Use the grapple hooks to board the ship. Take out the guards. Free the captives. Go home.

Yeah, right.

Captain Merchenko's radio crackled. "Aboard the Mir. Stop all engines," a harsh voice ordered.

Hands shaking, the officer picked up the microphone, knowing full well in advance the answer to his question. "Who is making such an order?"

"Mir. Stop all engines now! Prepare to be boarded!"

"We are a Russian oil tanker," Merchenko replied as he searched through his pilot house windows for something that would give him a clue as to the location of the commands' source. "You board at your own risk of Russian reprisal." A bluff.

"This is Commander Vladimir Kroski! We are coming aboard *now*!"

In the distance to his port side, Merchenko saw the sudden illumination of powerful spotlights. They played across his forward deck. To starboard, he saw in the reflected beam what appeared to be glints off of the wings of small aircraft.

"What the hell are those?"

I heard the clatter of a helicopter. No doubt about the thump-thump-thump of rotors.

To Blue and Forte, "Land in the wake! Come up on the starboard side ahead of the pilot structure!"

No response. They heard the chopper as well.

I watched as both of the Icons dropped back and fell into the ship's wake. Forte touched down like a duck in a pond.

Blue hit the water, bounced and cut her engine early, tipping the nose into the water and nearly digging her own wet grave. The tail rose to a 30 degree angle. Ocean flooded over the boarding seawings, nose and lower half of the windshield. The small plane dipped its port wingtip into the swell, lifting the craft up on two points – the starboard wing and nose.

I held my breath. Only one of two possible outcomes.

The Icon didn't flip, rather settled back on its hull, the small wake lifting it like a hand of a child playing with a toy airplane in a bathtub then dropping it square and true.

I slammed the throttle to the stops, checking the near empty fuel gauge, pulled back on the stick and banked hard right seeking cover of darkness. With the moon, that would be nearly impossible, but I needed to know the chopper's intentions.

The Rotax growled as I aimed the nose of the Icon into a steep climb.

To my north, a big chopper. Mean as a junk yard dog. Sprouting cannons.

"What is that, Tat?"

"Kamov KA-50. Has nickname. Black Shark." Her eyes strained to see the chopper. "Is attack helicopter used for Special Operations."

"Commandos? I thought the Russian government wasn't involved?"

That would have been a deal breaker. Going up against a private militia was one thing. Dangerous enough. Facing off with Russian Special Ops soldiers? Sorry, pal, for civilians that was near suicide, calling for Seal Team Six.

"Is not involved. These must be hired mercenaries."

"In a Russian chopper?"

"Very confusing."

"Confusion's not a good thing, Tats."

I spun the plane to port, circled higher, above the low-flying Kamov. Out of their view. My little Rotax easily drowned out by the chopper's powerful engine.

The forward three-quarters of the 900-foot oil tanker was flat as a pancake, portions painted as a shuffleboard court; another section as a tennis court. Strange. An assortment of stackable deck chairs were pushed against the pilot house exterior wall along with round lawn tables and what I assumed were deck umbrellas.

"Crap, the only thing missing is a swimming pool," I muttered.

I flew in high and aft of the chopper, banked left and headed toward the stern of the tanker. It was an old and tired ship. Its stacks belching smoke under full power cutting the Pacific with its bow and sending wings of water to both sides. Heading straight.

Dropping the Icon into the wake, cutting power, the hull of the amphibious plane kissed the water and settled gently into the Pacific.

"Retract the wings."

Tatiana twisted a lever and pressed a particular control. The pins holding the wings to the fuselage retracted and the servo motors began the process of tipping and folding the wings toward the tailfin.

I motored close to the tanker's hull. Tatiana reached behind the seat and grabbed the magna-dock, toggling the electromagnet on and tossing it against the near-vertical steel wall. Stuck like glue. She pulled the line in and wrapped it around a cleat on the Icon's Seawing swim-deck just under the doorway.

I pulled out the grapple-mags, loaded them into a pair

of compressed air rifles and handed one to Tatiana. We fired them up toward the deck. Hers went over the gunnel and grabbed onto the deck plate. Mine caught the hull about three feet below the gunnel and clamped to the metal. Contact with the hull turned both of them on and it would take a 10,000 pound winch to pull them off.

I slapped a pair of rope-climbers to the vertical line and stood in the Icon, slipped my size 16s into the stirrups and by lifting one foot then the other was able to ratchet my way up the hull. Tatiana did the same on her rope.

Engine vibrations ran through the hull's steel plates which were covered in a light mossy coating. First chance, I looked down the length of the hull and saw the other two Icons, wings folded, docked next to the tanker, three additional lines snaking up the side. Forte, Yuri and Blue, heads just below the top of the gunnels, standing in their stirrups, waiting for Tatiana and me. Each with an AK47 slung over their shoulder.

I reached the deck, peaked over the edge. No one. Just a vast flat landscape of steel. Throwing a leg over the gunnel, tumbling onto the deck, crouching in a dark shadow.

In the distance across the ship and toward the bow, the clatter of the Black Shark. What was it waiting for? The deck was clear. It could land with plenty of room to spare.

I gave Tatiana's rope a tug. She scrambled over the gunnel and squatted next to me, moving the AK from her shoulder into her hands. Seeing us going over the top, Forte, Yuri and Blue followed suit. When they hit the deck, they half ran half duck-walked toward us covering the 20 yards in less than a minute.

"Any problems?" I whispered.

"You mean beside the attack helicopter that's gonna blow us to hell and gone?" Forte said, voice hushed. "Yuri told us what it is. Not something I want to deal with if we can avoid it."

"I deal," Yuri growled.

Tatiana gave him a curious look. "How?"

"Not to worry. Sister is for loving. Not confiding. I deal."

With that, he hustled back down the deck and hoisted himself over the gunnel.

"Where's he going?" Blue asked.

I knew. Didn't want to say. It was Yuri's play.

CHAPTER NINETEEN

Captain Merchenko could see the helicopter, now 100 yards off the port bow. Its beams of high-intensity light playing on the forward deck.

Holding in the mic switch, "I am repeating that if you land on this ship, I will ignite the explosives meant to scuttle this ship." The bluff gained a firmness that surprised even him. "Your helicopter will be destroyed and you will become food for the sharks."

A silence, then, "You will die as well, Captain."

"True. But that is your order anyway. We have no illusion that you would allow anyone on board this vessel to live."

In the corner of his eye, Merchenko caught the glint of a small aircraft. The light bouncing from the forward deck casting brief flashes of what seemed to be a propeller. Then it disappeared into the darkness.

Geo crashed through the door onto the bridge.

"What's going on?"

"Cat and mouse. Go back and prepare for the unexpected."

Geo stared out of the pilot house window, saw the

helicopter. "Are they coming to kill us, Leonid?"

"Da."

She turned and ran from the compartment. He could hear her feet clatter down the passageway.

"You leave us no alternative, Captain," the voice on the radio said. "We must follow our orders for the good of Mother Russia."

"That is a rationale, commander. And a tired one at that. The Nazis killed millions of our people and said they were only following orders."

"We are soldiers, Merchenko. That is what we do."

I saw the Icon with Yuri at the stick climb into the night sky, heard the Rotax screaming in protest as he pushed the throttle to the max.

"Where is he going?" Tatiana demanded.

"Don't worry about him. He's a tough guy, kid. Let's get on with our own job."

"He is going to die."

"He doesn't want to die any more than we do. Let's go."

I pushed her toward the only entry door I could see on the pilot-house tower. Blue and Forte followed.

It wasn't locked. We slipped in, AKs at the ready, not knowing what we'd find. I pointed for Forte to head along the first-floor hallway while Tatiana and I climbed the metal staircase.

Taking them two at a time, we got to the second level. The walls painted gray, stairs maroon. I pulled open the door on the second floor, pointing for Tatiana to clear any resistance on that deck.

Taking the next flight up toward what I figured was the pilot house, I turned on the first landing and ran headlong into a young dark-haired girl, maybe 20-something, coming down. Her eyes turned into saucers. Her mouth became an oval the size of a small bread plate. She was about to turn and run back up when I yelled, "American! I'm an American. Come to get you off this damn tub."

She skidded to a stop, turned and looked hard at me. "Where are you from?"

"Oregon."

She nodded. "Between Washington and California."

"Last time I looked, yeah. Who are you?"

"Geo. I'm chairman of the U.S. Committee."

"U.S. Committee."

"Yes."

Explanations later. For now, "Glad to meet you Geo. Now where is everyone else? Who's the captain of this floating pile of scrap? How many guards are there and what kind of weapons do they have? I need info fast."

"Captain Merchenko is trying to get us to Hawaii."

That was a stunner. "Really?"

"We are going as fast as Gilligan's Island can go."

"Gilligan's Island?"

"My parents told me about it. That is what we call this

Page
305

boat."

"Is Merchenko alone?"

"Yes. There is only one guard left. Yuri. And the first officer, Mr. Spivak. The Captain shot the other guard."

"Dead?"

"Yes."

"How many Americans are on board?"

"Sixteen."

"That's it? There once were nearly 170."

Her face saddened, "Yes. That's true. Now only 16."

"Lead me to the Captain, then."

We took the last flight of stairs quickly, shoes sending metallic clanks down the stairwell. It smelled of oil-based paint. Dampness.

Geo pushed her way into the pilot house with me on her heels. The Captain, not much older than Geo turned and raised a semi-auto. I flipped my AK47 over my shoulder and raised both hands.

"Here to help, Captain."

Lowering the gun, his eyes wide as a kid at a surprise party, "You are who?"

"Friend. There are three others of us onboard and another who will try to divert that helicopter."

The starch went out of Merchenko. He wavered; his hand gripped the navigation panel.

"American?"

"Red, white and blue."

Through the windows, the helicopter made a sudden

move toward the deck, turning its 30mm nose cannon toward the pilot house.

Pushing Geo and grabbing the Captain's arm, "Quick, get out of here!"

Slamming the pilothouse door closed behind us, the dull thuds of heavy caliber slugs shook the stairwell. Broken glass, hardened steel ammunition ripping through metal plates, battering control panels and exploding munitions turning into death-dealing shrapnel.

We scrambled down the stairs to the second deck, yanked open the door and dove into the companionway.

"Geo, you and the Captain find my people. Get with the other Americans. Where's a secure windowless room on this tub?"

"Deck 3, the Congress Room," she said. "It will only take a few minutes to get the others and assemble there."

To Merchenko, "Captain, we'll get everyone to Hawaii. Promise you that."

He nodded, grabbed Geo's hand, rushed down the hall. I could hear him tell her he would get his Russian crew and bring them.

Turning toward the bow, there were a dozen doors. Some open, others not. I ran to the first and skidded into a room measuring perhaps 10 by 10 feet. A bunk bed, lightly worn carpet, couch with an end table and photos stuck to the wall with black tape. Gorilla tape. I've used miles of the stuff.

The window overlooked the forward deck. The helicopter had taken position just above the bow. Not attempting to land for some reason, but aiming its nose cannon directly at the control rooms on the top deck.

That's when I noticed the lack of government markings. Fuselage numbers were commercial. The chopper was owned by the oil baron. That made the crew mercenaries. That made me feel a whole lot better.

Out of the dark, from directly abow, the Icon flashed over the KA-50, swerved directly toward the cockpit forcing the chopper pilot to maneuver hard down to avoid a collision. Yuri had kicked out the side door window. The AK47's stubby snout resting on the sill. As he circled counterclockwise the muzzle of the AK flashed. It got the attention of the men inside the Black Shark who immediately began returning fire. There were at least two. Twin muzzle flashes from a side door.

Like a bothersome wasp, the Icon again disappeared in the dark. The chopper, looking for the small aircraft, spun on its rotor. At this short a range and at these speeds, radar onboard the chopper was useless. Everything would have to be done visually. And the flat black Icons were tough to see.

Another pass as Yuri popped up over the top of the pilot structure, swooped down to the deck and flashed by my window, AK still blazing toward the copter. There wasn't much gas in the Icon, so Yuri needed as much help as he could get. I smashed out the window with the butt of the AK just as an older guy carrying an old wood-stock Russian carbine came into the room. I guessed it was an SKS 45. Predecessor to the AK-47. Front line rifle a long,

long time ago for the Soviet military.

"I am Yuri." The Russian accent was thin. English clear.

"Drago. Nick to my friends. Hear you're on our side?"

"Yes." He looked at me, hard and inquisitive. "You American military?"

"Nope."

Eyes turned to slits. "CIA?"

I laughed. "To quote a friend, never was nor would I ever be CIA. I'm just a concerned citizen."

Accepting that explanation, Yuri smashed out a second window, poked the carbine into the night air, squinted over the site and put six rounds into the copter. No matter how thick bulletproof glass is, when a slug smashes into the other side of the window, you flinch. The pilot flinched, spun the chopper on its axis in pure survival instinct. Mistake. Turned his flank to us.

My AK on full-auto bucked, dumping a dozen rounds into the open side door.

The Black Shark tipped and I could hear the twin turbo-shaft engines scream as the chopper's nose dipped and under full power scrambled to get out away.

The guard gave a yip in delight.

I toned him down. "We haven't got rid of it yet, Yuri. He's probably just backing away to regroup."

The tension began to drain, the adrenalin evaporate when off of the port bow the Icon sputtered into view. The Rotax engine coughing. Sucking the last fumes of gas from its tank. The landing gear was down and through the windscreen I could see Tatiana's brother frantically working controls to keep the small craft aloft just a bit longer.

The Rotax sputtered, the three-blade prop jerked to a halt. All glider now. Yuri was coming in too steep, the nose aimed at the deck just behind the prow of the tanker.

Whispering, "Nose up, Yuri, nose up. Float like a butterfly."

The guard took a quick glance at me. "Is also Yuri?"

"Common name, I'd guess. Yeah."

We watched as the Icon's nose suddenly lifted, the tripod landing gear hitting hard on the metal deck, flexing under the impact. It slew wildly to the right, its left wing dipping, scraping the deck; planting the small wing-tip sponson into a deck plate. Pivoting the fuselage in a circle that crashed the opposite wing against the gunnel wall, shearing it from the plane.

Two of the landing struts collapsed, the boat-like hull now riding on a single wheel. Skidding across the deck toward the control tower. No sparks, but the carbon fiber hull beginning to shred.

I felt the small craft hit the base of the tower and send a shudder up the wall. Leaning out of the window, the crumpled Icon settled into its own dust. Then Yuri's legs appeared through the fuselage door. Then his butt. Then the rest of him, pushing from the wreckage.

Shaking himself like a dog after a bath, he gave himself a quick check, hands running over his chest, neck, head, legs.

I called down to him. He looked up. Small dribble of blood seeping from his hairline but otherwise a big Russian grin. Two thumbs up.

I pointed toward the deck door and got a quick nod. Yuri ran to it. In the background, the sound of the chopper once again. Louder.

What would be the plan? Come aboard, kill everyone. Stuff them in a hold. Back in the air and put a few missiles into the hull to sink it forever into 18,000 feet of ocean.

"Take my guy to the Congress Room," I ordered the Russian guard.

Scrambling down the stairs three at a time, I flung the AK over my shoulder, hit the metal deck running. Where Forte's mag-dock stuck to the deck, I climbed over the side, grabbed the line and wrapping my arm around it sliding to the bottom. I squeezed into the cockpit, slammed the door closed and punched up the Rotax engine. Gas gauge. Needle a sliver above the empty hash mark.

Disconnecting the line, a hull wake pushed me away from the tanker. Simultaneously cranking the nose of the Icon toward the open sea and yanking the wing lever. The wings seemed to take an eternity, but finally clasped into their slots, locking in place. I put on all the power. The small amphibious plane rode the swells, wings finally getting purchase. Lifting its nose. Breaking free of gravity.

I climbed as quickly as the plane could, maybe pushing it beyond design specs. I unclipped the side window on my side. Circled back to come at the tanker from the stern.

Smoke billowed from the upper control room. No fire, just smoke. The ship was still running under full power. Straight and true toward Hawaii.

At an altitude of 600 feet, it felt like watching a movie. The tanker, white wake. The menacing helicopter, gun in the nose. Low hanging missiles on under-wing hardpoints. Probably laser guided. At this distance, just firing them at the hull would be enough.

The chopper backed off a couple of hundred yards. Decelerated. Hovering at 100 feet.

Sweat filled my eyes. Wiped it with the back of my hand. The joystick damp. Mentally trying to find a way to divert what I knew was going to happen next.

No way to attack from the top. The door gunners had already been warned of the Icon so they were on the lookout for a side assault. That would be suicide.

I kicked out the passenger door leaving a large opening from swim platform to the center of the fuselage roof.

The chopper was battle ready so the bottom would be heavily armored. But choppers gain lift by forcing air downward.

I slowed the Icon to a near stall, came in behind the Black Shark at less than 100 feet. Giving myself enough clearance between the top of my wings and the skid plates on the bottom of the chopper.

In a microsecond, the Icon broke through the downward air blast from the massive rotors. It was like knocking a leg out from under a chair. The Black Shark rocked, its nose lifting at a 25 degree angle. My Icon shoved toward the ocean from the downdraft. The missile tubes erupted over my head. The deadly munitions rocketing toward the tanker. Passing over the gunnels and disappearing into the darkness on the other side of the ship.

Swinging the Icon through a quick wing-tip near-vertical spin, I made a quick calculation, staring at the missile tubes, half were empty. He'd try again.

Resting the AK-47 on the edge of the opening where the door once was, muzzle pointed up, I made a second run at the chopper. This time the pilot had brought the Black Shark to less than 50 feet above the ocean surface. Turned his missile pods toward the tanker.

He wouldn't take careful aim. Just hit the launch button and scram.

The Icon's Rotax sputtered. The fuel needle below the empty hash.

"Come on baby, one more time."

Again from behind, only a handful of feet above the swells, I aimed the plane into the gap between chopper and ocean. Cracked through the downdraft, wiggled the stick to make air turbulence under the chopper. AK straight up into the missile tubes just as the rockets launched. With the nose of the chopper rotating upward, two of the missiles arched over the ship, but one caught the lip of the steel gunnel erupting in a massive explosion.

The down draft sent the Icon into the surface of the Pacific. The hull slamming the water then bouncing me back in the air.

The Black Shark banked hard left and its twin turbos

screeched as it plowed into the night darkness heading east. The commander probably deciding he was done for the day.

The Icon engine sputtered. Rocking the wings to get the last ounces of fuel to slosh around the tank, I climbed above the bow. The Rotax died. I hit the landing gear button.

Lifting the nose, the prow of the tanker slipped under the Icon. Pushing down on the stick, the gear lock light came on just as the two rear wheels touched the deck. The nose settled and kissed the metal plates. I slammed on the brakes, slaloming from left to right to left, giving myself – like a skier – a longer distance to travel, scrubbing off speed.

The Icon came to a halt just shy of the pilot tower.

Forte met me at the pilot tower door.

"Nice landing, Nick. Ever think about getting a bi-wing and going on the barnstorming circuit?"

"Only if you'll be my wing-walker."

He led me up the stairs to the second deck.

"Captain Merchenko is on the bridge seeing if he can still drive the boat."

"Steer the ship. All that time in the recuperation center and you learned nothing."

Forte provided a big smile. "I love my slippers. I learned that."

Long story for later if you haven't already heard it.

He came to a closed door and stood aside. "This is going to blow your mind."

He opened it so I could go first.

The room measured an easy 25-feet-deep by 35-feet-wide. Centered on the wall opposite the door a six by 10 foot American flag painted on the metal plates. A long table complete with red, white and blue bunting – old, worn but still crisp – hanging from its top. A map of the United States drawn and painted to the left of the flag. On the right, a three-by-five foot image of "Uncle Sam." On the short wall to the left, a huge blackboard covered in what were clearly history lessons. Some scrawled in handwriting like that of a five or six year old; others in cursive, by adults. Words on the blackboard included Gettysburg, Boston Tea Party, Constitution, Republic.

Behind the table, standing at what must have been preassigned spots, Geo in the center with two youths flanking her left, two more on her the right. Quick count. Eleven others standing in front of the table, watching me watch them. Ages from maybe six to mid-teens.

Tatiana, Yuri and Yuri stood to one side of the room. Blue was ear-to-ear teeth, her skin stretched in absolute joy.

She looked at me. "Nick, meet the residents of Gilligan's Island." She turned to Geo and said, "Care to introduce yourselves?"

In turn, from oldest to youngest, they spoke their names with pride and a smile. It wasn't until a 9 or 10 year old said "Zachary" that it dawned on me what their parents had done.

Georgette. John. Thomas. James. Jimmy M. John Q. Andrew. Martina. William. Johnny T. Jaime K., Zachary. Millard. Franklin. Jimmy B. Abraham.

In succession, each was named for the first 16 Presidents of the United States.

"Well, I'll be damned."

Geo raised her hand to get the attention of everyone in the room.

"On behalf of this Congress and the American citizens here, I want to thank you for what you and your friends have done." She came around the table, walked to a spot directly in front of me, eyes leveled into mine with the glint of a steely leader. Watch out America, Geo's on the way, was all I could think.

She thrust out her hand which I gladly took. Geo was followed in succession by the others in order of the presidents they were named after.

"You're welcome," was all I could say to each's profession of thanks.

I watched as the Americans hugged each other. Laughter filled the room.

To Blue who was standing next to me, still grinning, I said, "Unbelievable. Now I've seen it all."

"Oh, not yet, my friend," Blue said. "Tell him Tatiana."

"Nicholas, I want you to meet Yuri's and my father," turning to the old guard. His eyes were leaking. "My brother was named for our father."

Forte clapped me on the back. "Didn't think you were going to preside over a family reunion, did ya?"

"Can't be real. This only happens in books." To Yuri the older, "You got beer on this tub?"

CHAPTER TWENTY

As sticky wickets go, this was a fist full of contact cement. How to introduce the surviving Americans into a U.S. culture they only knew second hand. How to explain the international politics that wouldn't allow them to admit where they came from or who they really were. How to continue the charade to keep the peace between the U.S. and Russia, with neither wanting to admit to diabolic transgressions.

How to let the kids know that Ronald Reagan wasn't the President of the United State any longer.

None of those were my concern. Artemus, Sal and now Blue would have to devise answers to those and literally hundreds of other questions. With the questionable help of unnamed bureaus and bureaucrats in D.C.

We were still hundreds of miles from Hawaii giving them at least a week to lay some serious groundwork.

Captain Merchenko, First Officer Spivak and Yuri the Elder were able to jerry rig a new control console, but it would take a pilot ship, tugs and crew to bring the Mir into port.

Sal had maintained radio silence so we had no idea

what was going on back home. Only that a Navy cutter was a constant companion and could be seen on the horizon tracking us.

Sitting in my assigned cabin, Forte and I split a makeshift pizza made from canned tomato paste, some unidentifiable meat, dough from a bygone era and goat cheese curds.

Forte wiped his mouth with a pulpy piece of paper used as a napkin. "This is terrible."

"Not so bad if you don't think of it as pizza."

"And that watery stuff as beer."

"Or the straw mat as a mattress."

"And the shower as a shower."

Both of us fell silent. Mentally recounting the past week.

Then I had to ask. "You going back to Bandon?"

Forte nodded slowly. "If they'll have me."

"Billy's been doing a hell of a good job in your absence. He's been offered the job permanently. Doesn't want it, though."

"He'll be chief one of these days. He's got the makings."

Pursing my lips, "You looking forward to being back on the job?"

"Rabid field mice, bad cop-house coffee and all."

"And what's this thing with Frankie Blue?"

Forte chuckled. "You noticed."

"Hard not to. Late night strolls on the deck under a full

Page
320

moon. Her giving you the hip when you make one of those lame jokes of yours."

"We'll see how it goes, Nicky."

A knock on the door. Forte leaned back in his chair and twisted the knob. Blue walked in, brightened just looking at the Chief.

"Hi."

"Hi back," he said.

Curiosity up, I asked, "How are Yuri, Yuri and Tats doing?"

"Great family reunion. They've been talking constantly. And the kids are all becoming excited about seeing Disneyland. I think we'll be able to pull this whole thing off." Sitting on the end of the bed, "I guess we'll be able to contact Sal in a couple of days. Close enough to Hawaii to be able to break radio silence. That big war ship on the horizon has been keeping us under surveillance."

She looked at the desk top. "That isn't pizza is it?"

Forte and I answered in unison.

"No."

It took five days to get to Hawaii and another day to Portland and a long drive to Lincoln City.

The Russians were being questioned by the State Department – at least they said they were from the State Department – while Sal, Forte, Blue and I headed back to Bandon, sworn to secrecy and signing non-disclosure statements on paper without a masthead or an official government seal. The kids were hustled off to God knows where. A week of debriefing and they'll be longing to return to Gilligan's Island.

Sal was riding shotgun with the Chief and Blue in the back seat.

"Did you really have to paint the Vic white?" I asked for the 10th time.

"Get over it. What's done is done."

"But the side exhaust is gone. The spoiler is gone. At least you left me my wheels."

"Consider it your penance for being a bad little boy. Sack cloth and ashes kinda thing."

A minivan passed us on a curve. "Sal, look at that. I've just been shown the rear end of a damn Dodge Caravan. This just won't do."

"Let me help take your mind off of it all, Nick. Where are you on the D. B. Cooper thing?"

"Christ, I haven't had time to think much about it." Over my shoulder, "Frankie, could you reach in the seat back pocket and pull out the files on Cooper for me?"

A little rustling, then she handed Sal the manila folders. The big man opened the first one with the envelope and letter, carefully inspecting both. Returned them to the folder and opened the second with the clue cards.

Thumbing through them, digesting the information, he returned the 3x5s to the folder, setting it on the seat next to him. He turned to the final folder, my list of facts, and read each of them aloud.

"That's all the facts there are?"

"The rest is nothing but conjecture, Sal."

"Okay, so give me the narrative version of what you think really happened. I'll follow along with the cards and the facts."

Blue leaned forward, arms resting on the seat back to listen.

"We know that D. B. Cooper boarded the flight from Portland to Seattle. We think Cooper was a woman, not a man, based on the clues – Helen Reddy, I Am Woman – for example. We think Cooper was playing a game with the authorities. Asked for parachutes with no intention of using them. She asked for money. She demanded the plane circle Seattle. She let all of the passengers and most of the crew leave the aircraft. She made sure all of the remaining crew was in the cockpit."

I could see the minivan in the distance. Pressed the accelerator closer to the floor.

"But she never asked for warm clothing. Never even hinted at it, even though the cops would have done exactly as she wanted and supplied them."

I re-passed the Dodge minivan on a long uphill straight.

"Hah! Take that!"

"Cooper, Nick," Sal said.

"Okay. The Feds thought she had a partner waiting for her after she jumped. That's clearly not true for a number of reasons. First, she was willing to alter the course literally a hundred miles to the west. She never complained about the 727 flying too fast or ordering the pilot to slow down even though she supposedly was familiar with both the aircraft and its operation.

"Everyone assumes Cooper was an experienced parachutist. But an experienced jumper would know the difference between 150 miles per hour, which she wanted, and 230 miles per hour which the plane was actually traveling.

"But the higher speed didn't seem to concern Cooper."

The minivan pulled closer to my rear bumper and was clearly going to attempt another pass. I pressed the throttle to the floor and even though the sound of the side exhaust was missing, the engine was still able to out-gun the stinking Caravan. I pulled away.

"She opened the rear door at 8 p.m. but supposedly didn't jump for another 20-something minutes. It was minus 7 degrees, Sal. Why wait? She couldn't see the ground, only distant lights. And those not even clearly because of the storm. What was she waiting for? My guess, stalling for time. Knowing the flight crew would watch her through the closed First Class curtain. Play acting the part.

"No one saw her jump. Only felt the plane genuflect. That could be done by simply jumping on the open doorway and tossing out two chutes with some money."

Blue interrupted, "It was all theatre," she said. "From shaving her head to look male to leaving behind clues that led nowhere."

The minivan driver had given up and was falling back.

Blue continued, "Before the plane lands in Reno, the flight attendants and engineer creep back into the passenger area to check if Cooper is still aboard. In the process of checking the plane, one of the flight attendants opens a restroom door, coming face to face with Cooper who aims the gun between her eyes and threatens to kill her if she says a single word about Cooper being on board. That may have been the flight attendant who became a nun and never gave interviews to anyone about the hijacking."

I picked up the story. "The plane finally lands in Reno. It's stormed by all variety of law enforcement, both through the front and rear doors. No one knows who anyone else is because there are at least three different agencies or departments involved and FBI from two cities. Bedlam on board.

"Cooper backs out of the restroom, yells 'Clear' and becomes part of the crowd. Dark suit. White shirt. Dark tie with the proper half-Windsor knot, and perhaps a forged ID badge reading FBI."

Sitting back in my seat, "As the crowd exits the plane, so does Cooper. Walks away."

Sal gave a swoosh sound through his teeth. "Boy, that is a hell of a story, Nick. Where's the money, then?"

"Evidence bag, maybe. Tucked down her pants. It was Reno in November, maybe under a trench coat or overcoat if it was cold. Doesn't matter. Maybe even leave it onboard in the john and come back for it in an hour or so after all the evidence people have left. The fact is, there are a thousand ways to carry off 21 pounds of paper without breaking a sweat."

Sal demanded we stop for a donut.

"I'm weak."

Good timing. We were just entering Reedsport. Hung a left onto Highway 38 and pulled into the best donut shop in nine counties – Sugar Shack. Fresh made. People come from miles around.

Blue, Forte and I all ordered up a variety of cinnamon swirls and sugar twists, but Sal stood in front of the display case, eyes glassy, nose inhaling the aroma from the kitchen bakery, partaking in his ritual of imagining the taste of each kind. Finally, placing an order for a half dozen very specific individual donuts within very specific types.

Back in the Crown Vic, coffee mugs in the cup holders, I picked up Highway 101 South.

Checking my watch, "I have another stop to make before we get home, guys."

No one complained. They were too busy dropping frosting, crumbs, sugar glaze and buttermilk cake chunks in their laps.

Amidst the sound of "ummmm" and "these are good" and "wish I'd gotten another one" I continued my Cooper narrative.

"Clear of Reno, Cooper makes way to parts of the country unknown, a couple hundred thou richer which, at the time, was big-time money."

"Where'd she go, you think?"

"Well, we still have a single clue that hasn't been resolved. 'Song writing rabbit.' Maybe that'll tell us who she is or was."

Sal tilted his seat back getting a growl from Blue. "Hey,

big guy, what is this, coach class on an airliner? You're crushing me, here."

"Oh, sorry," he popped the seat upright. "Was thinking of what I'll do first when I get home. It's been a couple of months." Scrounging around under the passenger seat, Sal pulled out his iPad, clicked it on and waited. Called up WorldLink.com which is the Bandon newspaper's online site.

I watched the headlines come up. At the top of the page,

Krisler Family Admits to Historic Secret

The byline was good buddy Karl.

"Read it out loud, Sallie."

Sal scanned it then began,

"The H. S. Krisler family, long-time benefactors to the growth of Coos Bay-North Bend and other Coos County communities, revealed today that a distant relative was responsible for the deaths of four paddle wheeler crewmen in the late 1800s.

"John Bartholomew Krisler, heir to the lumber company bearing the family name, told *Western World* that his great grandfather had the crew of the Pismo Bay sternwheeler killed and the Coquille River boat sunk to hide the murders."

I couldn't help smiling. Karl had pulled himself off of the horns of the very pointy dilemma. He had obviously talked to the Krisler family and let them make the revelation rather than simply printing the story or spiking it.

The rest of the article listed the members of the crew and Captain Solomon, how the murder was committed, the process Karl used to track down the actual conspirators and events. It also gave high praise to the family's long-time commitment to the region, donations to schools, hospitals and charities.

"Wow," Forte said when Sal was finished. "The boy is gonna get an award for that one."

Blue, of course, had no idea what the history of the story was; the tracking of a ghost paddle wheeler or the major international crime involved. But I'd leave that to Forte to explain in the dead of night as the two sat on a patio somewhere drinking wine.

"And look at this, Nicky." He scrolled down the page, "Mrs. Sworthberg has retired! No more 'Good morning, class' to the poor bumbling kids in home room."

"Where's she going?"

"Doesn't say. Only that she's planning on traveling."

In the rear view mirror, I could see that Forte and Blue were lost by our seemingly inside joke.

I explained, "She would come into the classroom, say Good Morning and it sounded like she was about to decapitate us. Can't explain it, but ever since then neither Sal nor I will say those two words and shun anyone who does."

Forte laughed, "I can attest to that. I nearly got my head chewed off the first time I said good morning to these two."

We passed through Coos Bay, picked up 101 south at the Highway 42 split and soon turned on Beaver Hill toward Charleston.

"Going to Bruce's?" Sal asked.

"You don't think I'm gonna drive the Vicky this way forever, do you?"

"Good point."

Bruce's Street Rods is on Whiskey Run near Seven Devils. Within sight and sound of the ocean, much like Willow Weep.

The gate was open so Bruce was somewhere in the shop. Stopping in front of the large work building, turning off the CV, all of us climbed out, brushed donut crumbs from our respective shirts and pants.

Bruce is a big, gentle guy. Nicknamed "Moose", I've seen him bear hug a small car engine and pick it up.

"Hey, Nick. How's it going?"

He was dusting off his hands. He stopped dead in his tracks, eyes locked on the Crown Vic.

"What the heck happened to that?"

"Don't ask. Sal here had it painted."

Bruce is a paint master. He walked around the Ford shaking his head. "What'd you use, Sal, a foam brush or a roller?"

Bruce looked at me. "You don't want me to fix this mess, do you?"

"Yup."

"Can you leave it for a year or two?" My eyes must have widened. "Just kidding. But it'll have to be stripped bare."

"Gotta do what you gotta do, Bruce."

"Can take it say early next week as soon as I get this Corvette out of here."

Behind him, a glossy white convertible '69 'Vette, red interior, glistening in the subdued light of Bruce's garage. Next to it, his personal black '40 Ford, with Whiskey Runner lettered on the C pillar, a small moonshiner in a straw hat, carrying a jug and runnin' for the hills.

"Will do."

We backed out of the drive and headed to Willow Weep.

Halfway there, Blue nearly screamed, "Oh my God!"

My heart damn near stopped. "What are you yelling about?"

To Sal, she said, "Search Wikipedia for Helen Reddy. Quick." Her voice was gaining volume.

Sal did as asked.

"Now search for 'Harvey.'"

Sal did and the cursor ended up on "Alex Harvey" the writer of Reddy's song "Delta Dawn."

"Do you get it, Nick?"

"You're saying D. B. Cooper is Delta Dawn?"

"Remember the lyrics, Nick. It's about a faded Southern Belle in Tennessee looking for her long-gone dark haired lover."

"You think D. B. Cooper is a woman and is in Memphis."

"Song writing rabbit. Harvey. Alex Harvey. Helen

Reddy. Delta Dawn. Damn right that's what I believe."

Tossed it around in my head, "You may have it, Blue."

Sal butted in, "Yeah, but you still don't know who she is, you guys."

The air went out of me. "What we need are fresh eyes on this." We passed the entrance sign to Bandon Dunes. Turning left, "Chief, as a cop, what would you say to this?"

I tossed the file over my shoulder to Forte. It was the folder with the envelope and letter.

He put aside the envelope and stared hard at the letter.

"Dear Nicholas:

As you may have read, the Federal and Washington State authorities have arrested Clarence G. Oates claiming he is D. B. Cooper, the famous skyjacker. They are wrong. I know this because I am the real D. B. Cooper."

"You may well disbelieve my claim, but that doesn't make it any less true.

"I've enclosed eight cards with individual clues that will prove to you I am who I claim. It is imperative you decipher these clues and insist the authorities release Mr. Oates immediately. He and his family are innocent victims.

"Please hurry, Nicholas, before a serious injustice takes place.

"Warmest regards, D. B. Cooper."

"Okay, the writer is an older woman and knows you."

"Huh?"

"An older woman will use the greeting 'dear' but if it is someone she doesn't know, she would have said "Dear Mr.

Drago." She doesn't. She says Dear Nicholas."

"Okay, we figured it was an older woman. She'd have to be because the skyjacking was 40 years ago. And we figured it was a woman because guys never use another guy's full name. Stuff like that."

"*Correctomundo*, Nicky. And she knows you because she says "Warmest regards." Not 'best regards' or just 'regards,' but *warmest*. Another clue she's someone who is older and knows you well enough to have at least some casual attachment."

He spent the next 10 seconds on the envelope.

"As a cop, I'd confirm the letter's clues with the precise writing on the envelope. Besides, the stamp is upside down."

"What?"

"The writing…"

"No, the stamp is upside down?"

"Yeah. It's one of the geometric designs the Post Office sells. Special edition. Something about the centennial for abstract modern art or some such thing."

Sal's head snapped toward me. "You don't think…"

I began to laugh. Long and loud. Sal joined in.

"Okay, Chief, can you either lift the stamp off of the envelope or read what's behind it from the other side?"

He tore the corner off of the envelope, ripped the seam and held the paper with the stamp against the CV's door glass. Through the paper he could read letters.

"It says…"

Sal and I in unison, "Good morning."

Blue's face scrunched up like an empty bag of Doritos. "Your homeroom teacher was D. B. Cooper? Is that what you're saying?"

"Frankie, if she was or wasn't is up to you now. But she came to Bandon in the middle 1970s. Taught every subject including theater. Never married. Was reclusive in some ways. Now it's up to the Feebies to track her down – I'd suggest looking in Memphis – and ask her."

Sal and I high-fived.

"One other question," Blue said. "Why give you clues? Why not just tell you who she is or was?"

"Easy," Sal answered. "She needed time to get out of town. Knew Nick would solve the clues, but it would take time. Enough time to gather up her belongings and head to someplace else."

Grinning, remembering all the days in Mrs. Sworthberg's home room, "That deserves a beer and pizza."

The colonoscopy took less than half an hour. Cookie lay on the gurney next to me at Bay Area Hospital. She reached across, grabbed my hand. "Now that wasn't so bad."

"Define 'not so bad.'"

She smiled. "Better than what I'm going to ask you to do next."

"Oh, no. Not the old prostate thing."

"Yes, love I've got to keep you healthy."

I pushed my face into the pillow. "Why don't women have a prostate?"

END

Coming in October: Drago #2b – the continuation of the second Drago mystery.

And stay tuned for the rest of "Without a Country – Flight 776."

Did you find the User ID and Password for the Secret Drago #4 page at www.cnwmr.com/DRAGO?

Here's a hint: Four letter word in the last two sentences is the User ID (all lower case). Eight letter word in the last two sentences is the Password (also lower case).

Author's note: For a complete list of what information in this episode of Drago is real, honest facts, go to www.cnwmr.com/DRAGO and click on "Fact Checker."

11747945R00192

Made in the USA
Charleston, SC
18 March 2012